Always! The Wanderer.
Always, the Wanderer.
Always? The Wanderer!
Always.—The Wanderer
#AlwaystheWanderer
Always. The Wanderer?
Always the Wanderer!
Always the Wanderer . . .
Always; the Wanderer,
Always & the Wanderer
Always / the Wanderer /
Always the Wanderer
Always . . . the Wanderer.
Always + the Wanderer =
Always > the Wanderer
Always [the Wanderer]
Always, the Wanderer . . .
Always! The Wanderer!
Always? The Wanderer
Always the Wanderer?
»Always the Wanderer«
¿Always the Wanderer?
Always (the Wanderer)

Always the Wanderer

By George Koors

A Braided Trilogy:

Patrick : February 2012

•

James : September 2011

•

Elizabeth : n.d.

Golden Antelope Press
715 E. McPherson
Kirksville, Missouri 63501
2015

ISBN   978-1-936135-15-8 (1-936135-15-9)

Library of Congress Control Number: 2015954799

Cover art and design by Shaun Gaynor.

Published by:
Golden Antelope Press
715 E. McPherson
Kirksville, Missouri 63501

Available at:
Golden Antelope Press
715 E. McPherson
Kirksville, Missouri, 63501
Phone: (660) 229-2997, (660) 349-9832
Email: ndelmoni@gmail.com

Trifurcating the Imperial Gaze: An Introduction to *Always the Wanderer*

When I began work on *Always the Wanderer* in summer of 2013, I focused on one very important concept: American Imperialism. In that sense, this novel owes its existence to three people. First and foremost, to Dr Hena Ahmad, who introduced me to the great masters of post colonial literature: Homi Bhabha, Edward Said, Tayeb Salih, Assia Djebar, Abdelrahman Munif, among others. Our discussions not only challenged how I viewed the world in a theoretical sense, but also gave me a chance to work through those complex and intertwined ideas that flow throughout the novel. Likewise, Dr Ahmad was (and is) the most scrupulous writer I have ever met and shared with me the kind of exacting attention to detail necessary for a work of art like *Always the Wanderer* to take shape. Second, the work owes its form and experimentation to John Coltrane, whose music has forever molded how I see all art, especially writing. *Giant Steps* and *A Love Supreme*, in particular, have afforded me the confidence to experiment with the written word. Finally, the work itself, indeed none of my fiction, could exist without the idea of "world travel" by Maria Lugones from her seminal work *Pilgrimages/ Peregrinajes: Theorizing Coalition Against Multiple Oppressions*. I am forever indebted to Lugones and her masterful working-through of intersectional feminism. Lugones was able to express ideas in such a manner so as to illuminate my own world in intellectual and emotional ways that I will forever be thankful for and I must credit her work with affording me a chance to develop into the writer and person I am today.

With all of this in mind, *Always the Wanderer* started with the hope that I could navigate and subvert the colonial (or in this case Imperial) narrative of the settler colonizer or explorer. This novel establishes three protagonists who participate, mostly unknowingly, in the contemporary Imperialist political order, a bit of a twist on colonial era narratives such as *Heart of Darkness*. This exercise was selfish at first, a way to work through my own experience as a participant in the Imperialist machine as an English teacher in Saudi Arabia, but it soon developed into something much more important: a larger commentary on how the individual is (or is not) complicit in the maintenance of the Imperial order. I soon found myself with an outline: three unrelated narratives intersecting not in space or time, but in the intellectual, with Imperialism being the central, unstated character.

The form for this, to me, had to be jarring for readers, it had to be didactic and pedagogical in a sense, in large part because I had seen at that time (and still see) individuals give themselves over to a new kind of passive nihilism: "How can I possibly help people struggling in another country?" "How could my actions possibly affect climate change?" "How could I possibly have any say over the politics of my home?" All of these questions showed me an inclination towards nihilism in its most convenient and base form. And so, I elected to not have any of the three main characters meet, and for them to occupy different timelines. This forces the reader to deal with the biggest and most looming hypothetical character: Imperialism. This Imperial character is diverse, it is substantial, and it is pervasive. Out of this thought process, the braided trilogy was created to productively and evocatively split the colonial (or shall we again say Imperial) gaze of the three main characters. Patrick, James, and Elizabeth possess vastly different reasons for maintaining (or not maintaining) their roles in Empire. This juxtaposition of different motivations, when coupled with how I observed readers consuming content on social media sites (at that time in 2013 Twitter and Instagram), led to the decision to blend these narratives together. Once all three sections were written and I set about combining them into the larger narrative, my aim changed from being pedagogical to instead allowing the reader a chance to explore the narrative in their own way, making what connections they find where they make them, giving the reader more autonomy to seek out and attempt to understand the complex interconnections present in the novel. The argument could be made that this work is simply my own Imperial gaze being articulated, and in the depths of my own anxieties, I too have looked to this convenient dismissal. But this is giving over to this passive nihilism, something that, however tempting, I cannot do as an artist. We must engage in the discourse, often when it is uncomfortable for us, and exploring these three characters was as vital a cultural task in 2015 when the book was initially published as it is today.

I often describe *Always the Wanderer* as a fever dream. Over the past ten years, seeing the novel take shape, shift and change into the published work it is now, I have really come to appreciate the urgency that *Always the Wanderer* contains as a piece of art. Over the past decade, as I have seen post colonialism, post Imperialism, and the associated philosophies and social theories continue to become a larger part of popular discourse, I am heartened to see a world where many understand the cultural and environmental urgency all around us to change our societies for the better. But I am likewise disheartened by the fever dream we see around us every day. The new and lazy forms of nihilism that I first really heard from the mouths of fellow teachers and travelers living as expatriates have spread via social media to bolster those disturbing institutions of racism, sexism, homophobia, religious bigotry, and broader hatred in our world. I have an overwhelming sense that no one is safe. And so, I turn once again to art, to literature, music, film, theater, paintings. *Always the Wanderer* occupies a space there, one that challenges readers, confronts them with painful questions about our world; but so too does the novel afford a space for hope, for self-awareness, and to my mind, a space to begin the process of thinking through our world in a hopefully productive manner. Art will not save us from ourselves, but I truly believe that it can help us along the way if we sincerely aim to not perish at our own hand.

GK
July 28, 2023
Washington, DC

Contents

If occasionally we are deceived by a mirage, and if our heads, feverish from the action of heat and thirst, sometimes bubble with ideas devoid of any basis in validity, no harm is done. The specters of night dissolve with the dawn, the fever of day is cooled by the night breeze. Is there any alternative?

- Tayeb Salih, *Season of Migration to the North*

You will find no new land; you will find no other seas.
This city will follow you. You will wander the same
streets and grow old in the same neighborhoods;
your hair will turn white in the same houses.
And you will always arrive in this city. Abandon any hope
of finding another place. No ship, no road can take you there.
For just as you've ruined your life here
in this backwater, you've destroyed it everywhere on earth.
		-C.P. Cavafy, *The City*

• • •

If the bottom were to fall out and everything were to end, this man would not be prepared, instead happy. Patrick seemed shorter than he really was. Meek and unassuming, he stared at the taxis waiting to take him. He had one grey bag. There was little variety in his wardrobe and his possessions were limited. —The Celtic Tiger gives and takes. The evening's redness throbbed in the west. The taxis driven by Pakistanis and Sri Lankans and Eritreans and Indians were dusty but newish. Humming with air conditioning, windows up and tinted darkly the transporters waited. All around him a slight whine of the mundane hinted at his future and Patrick, in lowering his head, noticed that he wore the same black shoes as most of the taxi drivers moving about him. Not a single person wished to meet the new Data Miner for OIL ETC at the airport, a fate that he accepted gladly having nervously sweated through three shirts on the air-ride already. As meek as Patrick was, he remained a few things in his own mind and in presentation to others: horny, and mostly indifferent. He shifted through the bag and a subsequent envelope: the Sheraton. A pyramid removed. A Sri Lankan approached Patrick and guided him into his taxi, taking his bag.

Patrick had grown in Dublin. His mother was as loving as she was devious, and Patrick, whose brief affairs with rebellion had failed, supported her financially, or planned to with this job. Of temperament, he was mild, yet also prone to sudden bursts of joy or anger. Because of this occasional manic streak, he played docile and refused to see any mental health professionals. In the middle of a performance of Christmas hymns in his nineteenth year, he screamed with such sarcastic joy that he stopped attending Catholic mass for worry that others may look at him. He did not believe in God anyways.

He was a typically dirty child. Despite how his mother trained him, his showering was infrequent and ineffective, so much so that his body adjusted its various stenches to account for the infrequency with which soap met it. He had no passion for art or music. He did not have any epistolary affairs. Neither did he typically enjoy sport. However, he did love numbers, and would calculate with relish. Throughout school he casually developed his statistical and data mining abilities. Unfortunately for Patrick, his casual nature resulted in his ultimate dismissal from a doctoral program that he, and his mother, had lusted after. Thinking he could not fail, he did. Shamefaced and hurt, he returned to his flat and phoned his mother with the news that he ought to look for a job. He did not mention his failing, instead scooted around it in a way that his mother understood to be his downfall.

The driver drove around the bay of the city. The streets, clean and painted, flowed by effortlessly. Palms and flowers bordered their scrubbed paths and swept ways. Patrick wanted to ask where the water came from to keep these people alive and the streets scrubbed, but did not. In the hazy light, boats carried families back and forth across water. Cars circled roundabouts and pedestrians walked next to the waves. To Patrick's right the Museum of Islamic Art stood; to his left a winding tower arose, one that he assumed to be of religious significance. In Patrick's ignorance, he took it that the museum had some relevance to the practice of Islam, and that it was likely Christians had some deeper connection with similar institutions in the West. The spire, being so different from the cathedrals that he had known, only briefly captured his gaze: mostly due to his ultimate dismissal of structures containing art and religion for display. At the opposite end of the dusk the Sheraton turned on its lights, which Patrick could not see, and waited patiently for travelers to arrive or re-arrive within its walls.

The Sheraton, a polyhedron with four quadrangular faces peaked to the point of a restaurant right up top. A kind place. Patrick's company, OIL ETC, would put him there while his apartment was arranged. Things, apartments and so on, took time in Doha, as they needed sweeping, as well as a proper man to satisfy a white man's needs. The hotel inspired some, but mostly fit the needs of the many working in Doha with its bar and club. In the bar, they offered more than food. In the club, they offered more than beer. Conferences, and other specialized events, were held at the Sheraton, and for Patrick it would be a place to easily establish himself, if he could see past his assumed shyness, and meet other people, because meeting other people is easy.

Patrick had attempted to overcome that sheepishness when he initially attended university, but found that after he had slept with just one woman that the amount of energy his body needed would be too much. He roughly calculated how many calories he would need to feel spry within large groups, and concluded that he would gain too much weight for its worth. He hoped to find a lady in the street, but freak in the sheets, a kind woman from around coffee shops or libraries. This did not happen. Patrick's often snooping eyes drove women and men away before they had a chance to learn his name, or that he could do standard deviation in his head. He'd sit with his texts and occasionally practice his moves, getting better steadily and at a pace that would eventually fail him.

In a line moving towards Patrick's taxi, the structures towering over the water came to life: piercing blue lights for the oil, that pulsing phallus for the king, the bright lit construction for the Americans, harsh incandescent lamps for the Olympic committee. The driver was silent and drove quickly, but with a smile. Had another human been in that car, she or he or they or (perhaps) it likely would have noticed the Irishman's incapacity for further conversation, after having spoken of money. The flaw rested in the Dubliner's having asked about fare, and after being told that the amount could vary depending on traffic, terminus, and distance, he spent the subsequent minutes ignoring his driver and most of the skyline that welcomed him, accounting for the various possible prices that the ride could result in.

At times Patrick's mother would give him spending money. On the eve of his eighteenth birthday, she tempted him with enough money to acquire several beers and a few shots of liquor from a local pub that he had always dreamt of drinking at. He was unsure of the genuineness of the offer, but spent the next several hours, after calling ahead and writing down drink prices, determining how best to use those monies on his birthday. His mother, who had recently adjusted to a kind of disassociated countenance in Patrick, gave him 2/3 of that total amount. The young man had no issue adjusting for the snag, departed to the bar and consumed only half of his predetermined amount before vomiting in the toilet and being told to go home by the barkeep.

He stumbled through the streets. He had been drunk before, but being so open was a cheap thrill. Although most of the streets were uneven in his neighborhood, his legs were able to hold his mass stable enough to zigzag towards home. At a cross-street, he realized that the sun had not set and that he was intoxicated enough to vomit again, but that he was able to hold it off. He let out a scream of unfiltered joy as he had conquered the challenge that the barkeep had issued; he was able to keep the contents of his stomach in the proper place.

He began to run towards his home, but tripped suddenly, falling into a gutter near his goal. When he arrived home, his mother looked at his scrapes and the indistinctness of his eyes and laughed: she knew already how much it would take for Patrick to reach this point, and had adjusted her gift accordingly. Patrick came to and caught on that his talent for calculation had been passed down from the mother.

Patrick Maguire's mother had an education, but did not make it past senior cycle. She never felt comfortable in the schools she had attended. The looks of male teachers disturbed her and she found her peers unkind. She took odd jobs and would save her money for trips to other cities outside of Dublin. If she were serious, and if she skipped a few days of school, she would be able to afford a ticket to London, train and ferry. She never had money enough for food and shelter, so her trips depended on weather. She would find some way of sleeping, she thought on her first trip. The anti-British sentiment of her father had taken her all the way to London out of disobedience. At the supple age of seventeen, she found herself in the streets of that city and within two hours, she had fallen into bed with a man who had less wooed than manipulated her.

She felt apprehension about the situation, knowing what this much older fellow expected of her. But she had, indeed found a bed to sleep in. From that moment on, she became more accustomed to the ritual: taking the trains and ferries, finding a place with dim lighting and lonely seeming men. She had avoided sex with most of them. There was a method to her batting eyelashes that provoked the men to drink more than they ought to. She encouraged this, observing that, should they be hungover the next day, she could have her way around the city and not worry about too many of their demands. She would use those she liked most to fulfill her own needs.

One man, Lucas, was especially to her liking. His charm was subtle, but with her he was overly caring. They met outside of a bar and he bought them both dinner and drinks. As she explained her love for the city and its people, he admitted to her that it had worn him down. All of the traffic and glamour was becoming too much. The weariness that he presented to her exceeded her awaited level of endearing. She sat by his side as he lovingly explained his problems and shortcomings. The two realized at last call that they had been talking for much longer than they expected. When they went to his flat, she did not make him use a rubber. She wanted his child but not him. His problems were noble to her, and to share in those would bring her joy. She too wanted to let something wear on her, to have something that she loved, but was also a burden. The next day she left the city early, not waking Lucas, and praying that her sin may be realized. She did not return to London for many months.

1

He touched down in Manama. James Williams, no middle name, via Kuwait City near the end of Summer. He was flown out from St. Louis to Washington Dulles and then direct to Kuwait. Flying unsettled him. He needed nicotine as well as the act of smoking, but he accepted the hours of nicotine gum. He lusted after his movement East, and had thought only about motion in that direction since university. In his younger twenties, he was a trim man, but now brooding as he had left partner and friend to prove a point. He would make money and travel to where none of them had dared to before. He had planned on standing out, and when he had finished with all of it he would be so hirable in the States. He expected to be asked questions and consulted. When he walked off the plane in Manama that day he did not know how naïve his assumptions were.

He knew that another teacher was flying on that same flight from Washington, but had no idea who it was. The plane was not near its capacity. Entire rows went unfilled. He remembered a flight attendant giving him a second meal, which he ate more slowly than the first. The empty plane was quiet. Mostly men were traveling East. Some were dressed in military uniforms. No one watched movies in the hiss of the artificial air. The pressure of the cabin seemed to push harder per person than on a more popular flight. He thought of these men being hired to assist kings: a friendly helping hand of the military.

Hard times for some of these kings. Not all could subsidize as Saudi had: Bahrain tore down the Pearl. Later, he would admit having felt tear gas. In a few months he would see the police shoot a tear gas canister at the chest of a young protestor on vacation as he was being driven through town by a taxi. The man, a teenager perhaps, grimaced as he fell to the ground, feeling, no doubt, the pressure of the container having impacted his breathing, perhaps cracking his ribs. He crawled away so that the police would not arrest him: his friends never stopped throwing rocks at the figures in black. It was evening. The event lasted only a few minutes. Soon after James sat in an American chain restaurant in the Juffair district and ordered pasta.

That evening he returned to Saudi. The three hours between Manama and his compound were quiet. His coworkers had not seen any Arab Springing. He did not tell any of them, he let them revel in their time off. Luckily for them, Manama had become much cheaper after the rebellion had started. People left the island and did not return, sold apartments and boats. The thick of it was on streets these people would not visit, but there was some bleed over, as James had learned. At the border, they faced the usual scrutiny and the police let them leave without any troubles. It was then that James composed an email. He did this by hand, wanting to edit it so that typing later would be smooth:

Harvey,

I saw a man assaulted by the police today, just as you told me that I would. It did not happen immediately, but you were right. The other teachers do not care about any of that. Some of them try to find trouble. It all makes me shake to think that people our age, or close, have to fight like that.

He stopped writing. Harvey had no interest in this. They had separated shortly before he had left: Harvey would not handle it well, but was positive about remaining in contact.

The kind of support that James wanted was beyond him. They would meet again, James reassured him. Separation was only a temporary reality, James went on, if we make it so. Even with Harvey's responses to emails thus far, James felt terrible for including him. The growing pains he felt were not for Harvey to understand. He would need to look outward for someone who could be of help.

It was not that James felt hurt by where he was, or that he was scared, but rather it was that he had no time to process. He had noticed many things, in the classroom and outside of it, which he did not comprehend. This moved beyond the language barrier, past even body language: it seemed too much to have dealt with all of the details individually. The immersive sense of James' move to Saudi was for him the most difficult. He would ask for clarity from those outside of this culture that confused him, only to compound his own ignorance. The realization that he had wrongly complicated his own grasp of what surrounded him would arise in the following January, but during the fall he remained aloof. He would not write the email to Harvey, but decided to leave it and to begin the long exercise of examining his own assumptions and biases.

And he was still so unsophisticated on the day of his landing. The 840-minute stretch from Dulles to Kuwait City was the longest he had ever flown. A number of the people on the flight spoke to each other, but not to James. In the last row of the plane, he had walked past most of the other passengers on the way to his seat. He saw in their eyes a kind of waiting. These people were moving for work, not play. There were no vacationers on that flight, he would tell people.

He had tried to research his new home, al-Ahsa, Saudi Arabia, but only knew that it was an oasis. James assumed the city would be ancient, imagined its streets convoluted because of time, having been planned and mapped by generations. The new routes, in his vision, merged with the old, overlapping and confusing. It took centuries to create the jumble that those human beings must navigate. Never having seen a desert before, James blinked out of the plane window. As they flew over Iraq, he stared down at the dryness. His mind wondered what attracted war to arid places.

He learned Arabic slowly in the States. He had no religious connection to the language, he still told his family he was a Christian. Some of the Arab language impressed him. His taste was for its orthography. How the pen moved from right to left beguiled him.

James had reduced where he was headed to an idea. Al-Ahsa's structures were generalized. In his chest, he desired oldness: he wanted it. His own history was of no immediate concern. He hurried the process of his satiation. The Williams family had been in the midwest since the 1890s. As the branches spread to Chicago, Des Moines, and Kansas City, his grandfather settled in north St. Louis city. At the time, Frederick Williams had white neighbors. By the year of James' birth, those white neighbors had long since moved. Frederick mumbled about depreciated real estate prices when James was young. For James and his family, a reality of a new kind of segregation set in. The candidness with which James approached this made him an appealing candidate for the position he won in Saudi: he understood what segregation meant and was not afraid of it. He was not moving to Saudi to find a wife.

The Williams family continued to stretch and grow as James aged. Each member maintained a critical eye focused on all other members of the family. James could feel these judgments around him on holidays and at weddings. The criticisms trained and discouraged James. He constantly felt that whatever his whims were, they would not suffice for his aunts or uncles. It is due to these very people that he found himself on that fourteen hour flight, he later recalled. It was because of those people that he drove himself to those ends. Still, his family was a loving one.

His mother and father did not question him, but encouraged him to express himself how he felt necessary. Even those same aunts and uncles, who subjected all children to their critiques, saw him off kindly with smiles, hugs, and food.

James carried with him pictures of his family and friends. He would need reminders of their existence several times over the coming months. Each picture contained a narrative for James to recreate in his own imagination. There would be emphatic details that James would dwell on: a particular joke, amount of drunkenness, setting, temperature. One photo showed James with his mother, father, and two friends right after he had come out to them. He had come out to his parents in his twentieth year. Two of his friends were stationed outside in case things went baldy. Aside from some initial tension, James' father accepted and hugged his son. James was unaware how his parents truly felt, but grasped that they still loved him and so prompted the photo. In it, James looks relieved, as do his two friends, whereas his parents appear to be exhausted. Their son hardly knew how well they understood him.

In recent years, James engineered important discussions with his parents to have an escape. It was simple: mention significant information before leaving for set plans. It was in this manner that he shared his interview to teach English so far away. His mother gasped at the thought of her son abroad. Maya Williams did not wish to see her son from such a distance, she preferred her view to be limited to hundreds of miles. Even with the nostalgic pangs of love that James felt from his mother, Maya accepted his flight. She became in middle September, before the Autumnal Equinox, fixated upon his return, which she calculated to be between two or three weeks before the Summer Solstice of 2012. By that time, James would be dumbfounded at the world that surrounded him, but still more loving.

Maya's ache for her son magnified with her understanding of his sexuality. She worried about his not being able to marry, about challenges with his having children. With years, she learned to relax. Her worries were not limited to legal concerns. She feared with the reddening of the state of Missouri, whether constructed by media or actual ideological shift, that her son would be unsafe in certain places. Her sense of this was limited, as she was not familiar with much of the state outside of the city and county of St. Louis, which were in truth dangerous for James in a different way. Yet, she trusted the city with her son's safety. Upon researching the Kingdom of Saudi Arabia, learning about Saud and his conquests, the development of a Wahhabist state, and so on, her alarm at her son's well-being mounted to new heights. She read that homosexuality was illegal in the land of Saud. She and her husband made every attempt to dissuade him, offering anything to assist in his transition to working America that they could. Yet, James refused. Just as he boarded his plane at Lambert, Maya wept for her son. He would not die where he was going. Instead, she agonized about his mental and intellectual well-being: it is not healthy to be illegal anywhere on this Earth.

A White Woman's Diaspora

There rang a sultry kind of whisper in her head. In such heat and confusion, Elizabeth had come to live in the small one bedroom apartment within driving distance of a many leveled mall, some grocers, several low price clothing stores, an Afghan bakery, two Turkish restaurants, one Buffia with exceptional egg sandwiches, a car wash, two Mobily stores, a slightly distant McDonald's, a barbershop, more than one large roundabout, two drugists, an apothecary, an Italian restaurant, two upscale coffee shops, a shisha club for men only, a fake Apple store, a travel planner, four gas stations, a Budget Rentacar, six mosques, and a dry cleaner's, not to mention natural desert and beach formations that had been developed and exploited for the use of humans. To say that she lived near these things was a lie that she would distribute once she returned to the United States. The places were out and away, removed by distance from the compound that was her home near what used to be known, at least to Munif, as American Dammam. Elizabeth came from Michigan and especially missed Detroit in the fall. She thought of the city's art museum. In her mind, it belonged to her or she to it for all it had taught her. She minded the absence of public art in her life. Forgetting the mitten, or describing where upon that mitten she had become a woman, she introduced herself to others as a misser-of-arts. Even with Rob's salary, she could be no patron, but she held a kind of solidarity with the artist, the abstraction of the artist, which she asserted nearly every day of her life. On this day, she felt a blur encircle her. This befuddlement did not materialize out of ignorance: her wit and intelligence were unmatched. Elizabeth had, after moments of doubt and clarity, reached a conclusion about her life. For the next hours, she would use the heat and necessity of food to distract her from that, but the scaffolding upon which she had built her decision was strong. The edifice that she so wisely erected in front of herself could not be destroyed, not even by her insights. Elizabeth Erfull could not remove herself from where she was now positioned rationally and emotionally upon one of the most powerful frameworks of existential justification that she would ever recognize. Looking into the sunshine of her window, temporarily blinded and happy about it, she set to distracting herself from what she had done. Elizabeth had no capacity for violence, rather she found no use for it. Her words were, or had been for part of her life, more potent and vicious than the physical acts she read about in newspapers and novels. What puzzled her, added most noticeably to her grogginess, was how deftly she had been fooled.

When she had crossed into Saudi airspace, she laughed so hard her eyes formed tears. Her eyes were sensitive to the brightness of the place: the sand reflecting the hot hot sun. The white of men's robes magnifying the irritation to her eyes. Her husband, dearest Robert, whose last name she refused to take, was on the search for oil. He had proposed the job to her in a very polished, but odd way. Sticky notes, all an unwholesome shade of pink, were attached to each object in their flat that possessed some kind of petroleum byproduct, or as many as the packet of notes allowed for. The annoyance of it was drowned by a promise of early retirement and a cabin somewhere in Northern Michigan or Canada. It had been many years since she had employed the true rigor of her academic skills and she felt good of Rob to have created such a clever design for the pitch to move to the compound. The resentment she felt dulled after some years. She had sacrificed a life of letters for his delusions of globalized living. The mistake of her leaving had been romantic and sporadic. It did not take the light gleaming through her window to register that. Instead, her avoiding that light, which lasted many years, prolonged the realization of her conclusions. The simplicity and clarity of her thinking reminded her of the fire that once burned within her. She had possessed an unceasing desire to learn from books and to interpret that learning on paper. In her movements, from North America, to Southeast Asia, to the Subcontinent, and finally to the Arabia Peninsula, which was the penultimate stop in her life, she learned to neglect her studies. What writing she did, was not theoretical. Occasionally, she wrote for travel websites, reviewing a hotel or activity: what astuteness, four out of five stars on Yelp. The petering-out of her careful and yet pounding scholarship was immediately made easier by her husband and parents, but it was the other expatriates she met that accelerated her laxness of study. Elizabeth had never met such falsely intelligent people in her life.—Have you read *The Help?* and she would roll her eyes. She had sat in so many lectures and thought so little of her peers, aside from her unity with them as a learner, only to find across the world a kind of white person that assumed their own good in a very different, very dangerous way. The people helping or teaching hid so well their colonialisms. They spoke of culture and language. Many claimed to be immersed in the literature of a people or place, going so far as to buy *Girls of Riyadh* to have on a coffee table or shelf. These people, the collectors and creeps, solidified in her a series of deductions that had been long coming: she should embrace and be aware of her own ignorance, racist and colonialist tendencies, and she should get the hell away from all of the people she knew. Elizabeth needed to return to a place, a mental setting, where she could once more learn, and with luck learn from the years and efforts she had just spent.

Her condition was well-maintained. Exercise and sport were available on the compound grounds. Some mornings Elizabeth and some others, wives of other crude men, did yoga. She led these morning motions, however reluctantly. The others felt such gratitude to her for leading them in it as it eased their homesickness and reminded them of the luxuries they would have had in Seattle or Philadelphia. The academy had been pleased with Ms. Erfull, who was quick to remind others that she had not changed her last name in marriage. In teaching her to think, academia prepared her to take to many hobbies adeptly and efficiently. Elizabeth had the ability to sail, write in Arab and Hindu orthographies, edit very well and quickly, do psycho-analytic criticism, operate with an understanding of multiple feminisms, negotiate dense works of post-colonial theory, perform at least three forms of non-bivalent logical proof, make wine, cook sixteen varieties of vegetarian soup, bake four kinds of bread, drive a stick shift, complete small wood working tasks, speak reasonable French, haggle, divide mentally and quickly, run three miles without stopping, drink five scotches in three hours, read speedily, create lesson plans, do some general shopping, and be married to Robert. Most of these things she had no need to do. She taught, not for the money, but to occupy her time while Robert financed their cabin. How he landed such a job she did not know. The compound itself was sprawling and huge. One had to have an American passport to enter. There were restaurants and shops. She did make wine illegally, but only for fun as the Americans living at her compound had a speakeasy sort of bar. They bribed the local police with homemade whiskeys and sold bottles to other Americans. They brewed two different types of beer as well. The bribery that must have been accomplished to secure this scared her.

That dismay was nothing compared to how she felt about the cultural isolationisms that she saw each day. Saudis and Americans living behind tall walls, locking in their privacies as tightly as possible. To deny openness from neighbor to neighbor saddened Elizabeth. She found her job teaching English to Saudi women in order to at least attempt at combatting this.

Rob and most others did not seem to care about this boxing-in-of-things. Their focus on the dryness and rigidness of the land shortened their sights to the chance they had to break down their own cultural awarenesses.—So fuckin' hot, ya gotta turn on yr car too cool it down before ya drive! Such exclamations were common over the steaks those men ate. With time, Elizabeth would come to pity such people and hope for their enlightenment. Yet, there amongst them she could do nothing. She had just opened the blinds and looked out upon the extensive grounds that the Americans had access to. The pool was skillfully placed, so that men and women could swim in shorts and bikinis without even the slightest worry about the Mutawa. She gazed down at them, some of the women she did yoga with each morning, there in their reds, whites, and blues, pieces that they brought with them from vacations to Europe or home. They could even support their alcoholisms and pill addictions within the walls. The local pharmacist was kind with good pills. The whirl that they each must maintain, that their husbands also perpetuated, and their children learned quietly, made her ball her fists and hug herself tightly.—OH, but it is alright, I say, so long as you don't go past the walls. I cannot stand the blackness of the robes. How the women here do it, I don't know. I stay in as much as possible. There is everything we need here. And I cannot believe that they do not have theaters out there. Such words echoed through Elizabeth's head and chest. They had been spoken by another woman at the compound, one who prided herself on only leaving the American fortress to leave the country. Elizabeth was slender and tall.

She did not think of her looks, and refused to wear makeup. Her beauty, although she did not need to speak of it, struck those she saw. She did not need or desire the validation of others, even in her least learned times. Robert respected her immensely although he had proven himself too slow for her. Elizabeth stood in that light, looking at the bodies of the women she hesitantly associated with and picked up her phone: she needed out.

2

At Kuwait the passengers got out of the plane and waited in a terminal. It was less than an hour flight to Manama, Bahrain, but the wait was over an hour. Few spoke. He still could not spot who the other teacher was. He listened to music and chewed nicotine gum. The taste was dull and cut into his gums. He did not know what to make of where he sat in this group of men. He felt young and out-of-place. His position was simple as a teacher: provide English to those who wanted it. James would remember earning danger pay without facing danger, spending it like play money, not having had income like that before

The floor of the terminal greyed between tiles and cool colors. Outside the daylight shone harsh on the tarmac. He took a deep breath: he would have to hide himself from most of these people. The government could kill him in Saudi for his sins. It was not the threat of death that thrilled him about his path. He was excited to see Americans and Europeans out of place, to be in a land run by a different set of billionaires. He would take joy in finding the good people amongst his students and acquaintances, separating the good people from the bad. He wanted to know how to soothe his mother: he suspected that interpersonal relations could be to his aid. He pined momentarily for Harvey. James believed that this experience was formative, and that he needed to exhibit a new kind of strength he had not previously known. He must not fear death as he had assumed he did in the States, or must fear it in a different way. He was unaware of how taboos would be discussed, if at all in the Kingdom.

He developed a pretense in the time he spent preparing to leave for al-Ahsa. He felt that his body language would discourage any discussion of illegal things with students, that his stare would make those things unmentionable. Within a month of his moving there, his first challenge would be teaching lessons on Keith Haring. When he prepared for those lessons, a nervous shaking took ahold of his hands: what would his students say of this art? Would they have any awareness of AIDS? The Saudi government claimed to have 0% AIDS within their borders. Did his students have some connection between homosexuality and AIDS? How could he respond calmly? He stood in front of the class that week and assumed an even tempered countenance. He had trained himself tirelessly the nights before. He had never rehearsed a lesson before. Midway through he realized how manufactured this paranoia was. He had built it up to stand apart and tower over him. He had constructed his own menace. This thought cooled him.

In the Kuwaiti airport, he thought of how he could use the language barrier to his advantage, not understanding what people said to him or not comprehending an accent or linguistic nuance. His students did not make any suggestive comments when presented with Keith Haring. None of his students were anything other than indifferent to the art presented in those chapters. In discussion, they were more interested in music. Their tastes were varied, but hampered by teenaged assumptions that Justin Bieber was more subtle and distinct than he actually was. James listened often to Mohammed El-Bakkar in the States. He first heard Port Said in a restaurant and had asked the waitress for the name of the song. Some of his students had heard of El-Bakkar. They prompted him if he knew of Mohammed Abdu and he did not

At moments such as those, James felt a connection with his pupils. Some were older, nearing his age, and some twinge of their youth was still in him. The lessons were simple and he often left time to focus on what the class needed most that week, practice in one area or another. He could not express to his parents how this bond had formed. Yet, Maya worried even more for her son at this point. He could not share with his students much of his actual self, which limited their attachment to each other. The classroom ought to have a fundamental openness, thought Maya, as she watched her son on a digital screen. She believed him to be stifled by it all, but happy to be where he was. It concerned her to think about how much he could withhold. The three spoke often, as father, mother, and son. Maya noticed that James called on them more often now that he had left for Saudi than before. He loved to explain his daily life and any noteworthy adventures he had undertaken.

James chewed on another piece of nicotine gum. It would be a small comfort to him how cheap the cigarettes were in Saudi. In the wake of the Arab Spring, the King had subsidized many things in order to keep his people in line. James was unsure of the extent of these subsidies, but sarcastically thanked the King each time he bought cigarettes.—Smoke 'em while ya got 'em, Abdullah. Some of the passengers departed for Kuwait, while still others joined. The throng of people awaited the preparedness of the plane. James could see the waves of heat on the tarmac. He imagined how oppressive the heat must be in this country. As a part of his research into the region, in preparation for leaving, he read into the first Iraq war. Over 1,000 Kuwaitis died in that storm. He remembered photographs of people dead on the hot ground, oil fields burning. All of it saturated his view. James stood from his seat and neared the window, recreating the war for his own eyes: a city destroyed, people battered.—All for what? He spoke this out loud and a man near by perked up,—Excuse me?—Nothing, James replied.— Just thinking out loud.

James sat once more and realized now how close he was to his destination. For the first time, he was curious about why he was being picked up in Manama as opposed to Kuwait City. The trip to Kuwait City would not require crossing any bridges as the trip to Manama did. He expected there to be some reasonable account for this, especially considering the drama at the Bahraini Pearl earlier that year. Khalifa had done well at dispersing the protestors. James thought about how difficult it must be for his parents to stand by as he traveled through such contentious places. James had never been in a fight before. He was not overly political either. He felt neutral towards many things, and subsequently did not concern himself with certain humanitarian issues. He did not support violence or conflict, but understood that it was a part of the human experience. His questioning of any war was rhetorical.—What ends does each side hope to achieve? Years later, he would remember his indifference bitterly.

After returning to the States, he grew to resent that sense of amorality he had in his younger 20s. He would be roused to join political movements or protests, worked in schools and as a community organizer, and found himself seeking coalition with those around him that he knew to be experiencing hard times. He would offer support to nonreligious or religious causes. To those around he would appear as a kind heart, but still others saw him differently as he approached middle age: they said his actions were a penance for deeds they did not know and did not care to know. In those years, a certain pain could be seen in James' eyes, even in his walk. Not a physical agony, but a deeper, more emotional discomfort. Even then he spoke fondly of his travels, and of that year in the Middle East. Whatever sadness he knew, he continued in spite of it.

They were escorted back on the plane and soon landed in Manama. He exited through customs. The officials were all older men and did not bother him. Few of these Bahraini airport men smiled: it was near evening and they looked worn. No windows allowed natural light into the customs stations. All over posters advertising Formula 1 racing exclaimed the wonders of the island. He didn't have a phone, he had no idea which of these people was his colleague and not in the Navy and he had no idea who was picking him up. The need for an actual cigarette became apparent: he jittered. The airport was small. Even with the crossing of a border, there was little tedium at customs. He made his way through all of the necessary steps with relative ease and began looking for his baggage.

As he stood at the carousel, a balding man about 20 years older than him walked up and asked if he was headed to al-Hufuf or al-Ahsa,—Whichever they really call it . . . The man did not seem to know the difference. Gary Obdachlos bumbled and confused himself: he fidgeted noticeably. He had no idea why he was here: he did not seem to be a teacher. His khakis didn't fit him well and he wore a red sweatshirt. They gathered their bags in silence. James collected Gary's bags because he seemed too intimidated by the Navy men surrounding the carousel to interrupt their circle.

The Riches of Robert

Robert had suggested that they take jobs in Saudi seven days and sixteen hours after speaking to an American contractor about business development. After some time on the western coast of Canada, central Thailand, and semi-northern India, the couple had subverted their own standards and married, whereby Robert quit his job as a community involvement administrator at a university in New Delhi for his new position in Saudi. The lives they lived together, Rob investing his time in expansion projects wherever he could, was limited to the time that Robert devoted to avoiding his work. The philosophy that he assumed seemed simple enough, put in the work and see the time earned on the other side of retirement. However, he did not have a 401k or any relevant investments devoted to his future,—We can think about kids after I have $500,000 saved. His misguided ideals centered around amassing large amounts of funds, which after having been transferred to the United States sat in abstraction in one bank or another gaining no interest or added value. It occurred to Elizabeth that his thinking was fallacious, but that his heart and head were aimed in the correct direction. She believed, for a time, that they would return to the States and move the money. She had, even with her academic awareness and ambitions, always wanted to move money, if only once. She had gotten the idea from her father, who would speak of his childless co-workers fondly as they were able to push and pull their money in new and different directions. They had avoided the urban plight of Detroit with ease and sat in their suburbs thinking of lake houses and retirements. Elizabeth's father placed what money he could into her college fund and awaited the realization of her own privilege. That life would at times be hard for her he saw as inevitable, but it saddened him. As Elizabeth dialed the number on her phone, in that beautiful and brilliant sunlight on that day, he sat in his home amidst an unforeseen retirement. The emotions he felt could not and would not be expressed except with subtlety. Each week, without fail, either he or Elizabeth would arrange for some talk over the internet. Rob he did not care about, but he needed the audio and visual reassurance of his daughter's being alive. Elizabeth called Abdelrahman, her driver, to pick her up for shopping, and she thought of William F. Erfull and his money-making. His abilities as an engineer held him in employment for much longer than most in the Motor City. She admired his mathematical talents and his eye for design. Just so, he encouraged her to analyze in ways that he could not and did not have the talent to,—I'll never get how you know that conclusion is correct if there isn't some concrete method to reaching it.

The money proved well placed in Robert's pockets and the compound seemed new so the couple adjusted easily to Saudi after their uneventful marriage. The two visited Elizabeth's family and were married in a courthouse. Many years earlier they had made the true commitment. Both had boarded a vessel and were hurled through the thin air only to land in Bangkok to teach and do business. Fresh from study, the pair discussed this move in a forest before selling their possessions and buying tickets. That year they spent together teaching and planning. A kind of silence developed between them. It showed weakness to the other expatriates to be so pensive and not to account for what one missed, so Elizabeth and Robert moved carefully among their coworkers and each other. Unaccustomed to a life abroad, they made the mistake of not reinventing themselves. Even though all people do this poorly, making grand and revealing mistakes in their refurbished narratives, it is a process of growth that befits the expatriates in Thailand and many other countries. Lacking such inventiveness removed the zest of their new lives. Robert shifted his attention to discerning how to earn a salary that he could feel happy about. Rob was a simple human, one who only needed a screen and a representation of mythical currency to make brighter his day. Soon after moving to the bustle of Bangkok, he became distracted away from his partner. Their sex remained, but it was monthly at best. They did not leave each other because of the ease of remaining. And so, the stasis of their lives settled in amongst them and became more than their guest, but child. It was for this reason that after Canada, Thailand, and India that they attempted marriage. It would be so supposedly difficult to divorce once inside of Saudi that they would noiselessly and fairly submit to the formalization of their heterosexual union. They felt no cliché in coming together, nor did either find any inspiration in the paperwork or ceremony. The being that was their relationship remained the same with all of its dependencies and blindness.

The heat of the sun reached Elizabeth's arms and face as she arranged a time with Abdelrahman and looked disdainfully at the lying breasts of a woman by the pool. Her head, filled with ideas, emotions, syntheses, and compositions, screamed at her. It had been years now with Robert. This was their second year in the mini America. There were, of course, many years before this, the second year. Each day she changed between calling him Rob and Robert. She could not find the exact tone with which to approach him or feel comfortable. His was not an easy name. Robert was formal and high-nosed. She felt country-clubbish, more so than by simply living in that compound, by calling him that, but it was also sincere and kind. Rob seemed boyish, simple, but more down to earth or middlebrow. Bob was out of the question, as the man was not nearly silly enough to be known by that name. Bobby could be a wonderful pet name, but she felt it too childlike. Rob never noticed her varying between Rob and Robert. He did not listen well for detail, but grasped the general matters at hand with little effort. This ability to be ignorant, but only slightly so, made him invaluable in the business world. The more time Robert spent abroad, the more people he convinced of his competence, even though he possessed so little.—That's business! As each year he began to earn more, Elizabeth wondered if she would ever continue formal work at a university. It was not beyond the couple to do this, but, as Elizabeth learned, Robert had a set amount he desired from Saudi. He would not leave until he had 110,050 US American Dollars in an account to his name. Why did Robert pick this specific number? He told Elizabeth that he dreamed it, but he always lied about things. Kids were not in their future.

Robert was not a smart man, nor was he dumb. He was the middle. He did not feel intimidated, as he ought to have been, by Elizabeth's intellect, yet he was also not inspired by her prowess. He could not pick a team to back in any sporting event. He did not crave any exotic sexual act. Rob was low risk. That phrasing comforted Elizabeth as much as it had confused her. This low risk man had taken off to foreign lands. What she had been coming to understand in front of that window was that Robert had seen her ability and took her as a low risk method through which to explore the world. Because Elizabeth could learn languages and customs so easily, he would only have to be a bystander and wait for her to explain it all to him for free. What he presumed Elizabeth would earn was a way to have money in old age, which he assumed academics universally did not have.—Why would there be so many old profs if they all had money? No one can actually enjoy the mess that is a university year after year. His craving for travel was only aroused by Elizabeth's talent in the languages. He did not care for the study of Arab culture, tradition, Islam, or anything relating to his location on the Earth. Robert was the not the first to receive a college education in his family, but he was the first to attend university and not want to. He studied out of obligation and looked around each day for a technique that would allow him to have a long, uncomplicated relationship with a woman. He did not, nor would he ever, come to be aware that he had so cleverly tricked Elizabeth into spending those many years with him. In her thirties, she shook upon her feet while waiting in that sun. She did not move herself and only kept looking at the other women. They now owned something that she did not: the ignorance that bewitched and enthralled them. She learned that the holding-on-to-of-that-mindset allowed them to feel such pleasures in their bikinis and with their liquor. She thought that it might be calculated for them to have been brought to such a position in life. What willful acts they undertook, she had not been allowed. Elizabeth found herself surrounded by people she had pretended to like and had been introduced to at the whim of someone she no longer trusted.

Inside of their bedroom they covered the walls with the mementos of their previous travels. Books in different types, textiles in a variety of colors and origins, baskets filled with small trinkets from markets she could not remember, idols, paintings, maps, flags. She turned away from the outsideness and saw the clutter for what it was, a mask. They oriented their bed to lie east-west, as Robert preferred it. This preference lay in a superstition that he would become infertile should he sleep positioned north-south or south-north. Sexual fright ran in his family, one reason why they so seldom fucked. His father and mother only made love on Mondays, Wednesdays, and Fridays, and his brother did not make love during the full moon. Why his family, those pesky and strange, but stable, Schiefs, felt these attitudes was never explained to Elizabeth. She wrote often of his unease with the world. It struck her that his childhood life, and the lives of his family members, was so normal and without drama that they invented these strange discomforts and necessities to spice things up. Within the first months of their time together in the compound, Robert developed a kind of unspoken competitiveness with those around him and saw his time at the company as not only his career, but also his life's work. He was a dusty man, whose smile seemed disingenuous, but his words came from his mouth in a soft and pleasing manner.

Elizabeth met him at a bar in the early aughts, one that played French hip-hop and Portishead; she walked in the room, scented and tall. Without realizing it she fell into his group of misguided students, men and women traveling through classes trying to find a new job or source of money without having to be responsible. Robert was motivated in a way that brought him face to face with Elizabeth and allowed him to get jobs. He had studied business. Elizabeth was actually educated. The underpinnings of their relationship were that he was the most interesting of his group of people. There was an ease to the manner of his speaking and how his shoulders drooped. His friends from college, who mostly made more money than he ever would, envied how he inched his way into Elizabeth's life. She was not a person of many friends. Her determination at university was noticed by most, and with skill Robert convinced her, on a cold and wet day in that forest, to move away. He held her hand and they both wore grey sweaters. Looking at each other with the potential that people in their twenties feel, they decided to move, to go in, and Elizabeth postponed her relationship with the higher levels of the academy.

The car moved into an area that suggested business. The towers stood tall on the left and yet their lights and stature did not impress the person being driven. Patrick took to this skyline as a person who had seen it all would to any magnificent set of buildings, with disinterest. The driver, who noted his fare's silence with relief as he had been asked three times already that day if he liked it here, looked forward to finishing his shift and hoped there'd be warm rice in his small quarters when he arrived "home." He had it good. He shared his room with only two others, each person working a different shift for the company, so that at its maximum the apartment only held two sleeping taxi men. The money that he sent to his family was enough for them to survive. He had seriously contemplated drowning himself after six different white women on the same day were fascinated by his country of origin. One had stayed in Sri Lanka at a resort that his cousin worked at. She, in her worldliness, told him all about his local customs. He laughed at her in a pitying voice. At her destination, she refused to leave the cab, wondering if he had been to India for a silent meditation. He was unsure how she had moved between topics so fluidly, so he responded with her fare, and a smile. Patrick's silence was a welcome relief. He knew the only thing they had in common was a need for quiet on this ride. Those he picked up at the airport were always the saddest.

He had flown back to Sri Lanka once for a vacation. He recalled his initial flight to Doha, all of the men subdued and quiet. Looking at pictures of their wives and children, thinking about when they'd return, expressing their relief that their families would live. That flight had been full of pensive men. One actually cried, taking his head into his hands, quietly noting that his employers would take his passport and not allow him to return unless they saw it fit. He had sacrificed a month's wages to return one time.

When he departed Doha for those brief three weeks with his wife, the flight was the exact opposite. Joy spread across the men's faces when they boarded. Several ordered beers, Kingfishers probably, and laughed. They joked and were merry with each other. He found that there was not so much animosity toward the Arabs, or the place, but toward the situation. A discontent with one population being able to use another in such a simple and caustic manner. His job, driving this taxi, was not hard work; he could do manual labor. But the conditions of his contract were strict and his housing was inadequate. What he sent home was necessary for his wife and young son, and what he kept nourished him. Patrick did not ask the name of this Sri Lankan, nor did he inquire about his life. They caught eyes in the rearview mirror.

As they approached the Sheraton, the buildings grew taller. People meandered about and women walked among the crowds. The veiling customs in Qatar were more relaxed than those in its neighbor Saudi. Here, white women could dress as they wished, and even show some leg. Although it was best to be conservative, Doha was prepared for many different cases. Patrick, who had done no research about his destination, aside from applying for the job, was momentarily taken aback by this. In a sense he was relieved as they approached the hotel. The drive's overhang had warm lights and an Indian man or maybe another Sri Lankan opened his door. Under the glow of the carport, Patrick noticed that the doormen and bellboys all looked frantic, and one could say, even slightly hungry as they collected his single bag and walked him through the sliding glass.

—We have bars and restaurants for your entertainment, spoke the concierge. She was small. She had that sense of servitude which Patrick thought attractive of people in the hotel industry. She was Russian or something like it. Patrick looked around. Sharp angles rose upward. Down, the floor was Arabian or maybe Persian with blues and reds mixed together in triangles. The lights were dull everywhere. The fake plastic green of small palms counterbalanced the warmth of the perhaps genuine sandstone. He received his keycard and muttered his thanks. His bag was transferred to another human who led him to an elevator. The man with the bag looked intently at the Irishman, but did not fully meet his eyes, there was no need to.

His elevator-mates were a couple who had recently been to a bar and a bellboy, who did not smell of vodka, and whom he had not had the confidence to dismiss even though he only possessed one bag. The man and the woman whispered to each other about their time in Singapore and wondered what adventures awaited them in the days in Doha. The bellboy did not say a word, and his eyes hinted at his knowing that the bag he carried would not provide much of a tip.

Patrick had only dated one woman in his life, a country girl he had met at university named Laura. She never introduced Patrick to her family. Her voice seemed fake, in a sense he wondered if the Irish country maid bit was a kind of farce. Instead of complicating their relationship with his suspicions, Patrick merely listened.

Her father was a drunk, a sob story she brought out at the bars. She found great joy in the irony of explaining how much he'd drink before hitting her while holding a good, strong Irish beer in her hand. Occasionally, she broke out into bursting song. Laura had a reasonably well trained voice, but her choice

of song often made no sense. She had even broken into song
at a Bloomsday celebration with Patrick, assuming that Joyce
had had some idea of the "folk" song she belted out, when only
later she learned that it was Bob Dylan. A hard rain fell on them
shortly after.

When it came to love-making, Laura and Patrick learned
at a similar pace. He was eager, secretly, to reach a point of
explored kinks and perversions. She, because of her terrible,
yet idyllic, childhood, wanted to subvert her idea of her own
love life. This went so far that she told Patrick to do things to
her that would make her father angry. Neither was as devoted
a Catholic as they put on to their families. Becoming disen-
chanted with the church was old hat. Rather, they remained
apathetic, partaking in masses on the important days, while
at home experimenting with different sexual and philosophical
ideas. The crux to all of this talk was that each got off just
in discussing it. There was no need to really act anything out.
Insofar as Patrick would desire to dominate Laura, to demand
things from her, her being open to that notion was enough to
make him ejaculate on his own, and enough for things to begin.

Simply enough, Laura and Patrick ended their relationship.
She would be moving to London for a job and she knew, although they had never traveled together, that he would not
take well to a city like that. In a sense, he was relieved to see
her go. The months they had spent together suggested that she
could control his schedule indefinitely. His mother had enough
of a grip on him that he wasn't sure if he could have handled the
permanence of another woman in his life. At times, he missed
Laura with a great intensity. He was often able to see past this
emotionality with masturbation or even simply going to a bar
to look at other women. He seldom set out to pick up a woman
in whatever capacity, and instead took to thinking very deeply
about what kind of person each potential mate might be. Laura
had attracted him with her deftness. She spoke frankly about

their need to pretend to be Catholics, to put on airs, to be deviant at home. Still, that was only over a period of months. She only met his mother twice.

He considered if he should try and rekindle things with a person like Laura, or if he should date another person and how similar the two would be. Laura, with her accent and laugh, was a beautiful woman. She was short with full legs and arms. She had a firmness about her stomach that made Patrick jealous. Further, her hair was a combination of blondes, light browns, reds, and yellows in such a way that he found entertainment in playing it. He worried that he had passed up a chance with her. There certainly could have been more resolution to what they had had, but Patrick's inaction meant that as he stood in that elevator in Doha they had not spoken in nearly four years. He shook his head to see if he could force the idea of emailing or calling her out of his mind. Certainly by this point she had had many other partners and was likely married with child. Whereas lowly Patrick had slept with a few women he had met at clubs in Dublin and a prostitute he stumbled past once, hungover, unsure of where to go.

3

Gary's voice dragged in a kind of hoppy way and he carried bags that seemed cheap-ish. James did not tell him this. He had forgotten his sunglasses and would laugh in the middle of sentences out of nervousness. The Manama airport was small and clean. Somewhere past the young-ish Filipina woman with her hair covered, smiling, and selling creamed corn would be a van to take them away, to shelter them from the heat and to carry them to their compound.

They moved to a coffee shop at the entrance to the airport and no one greeted them. The chain sat empty and the baristas wiped counters in their restlessness. He told Gary to wait. He needed a cigarette badly and he could tell from the look of the sun beating on the pavement, that it was very hot outside. He mentioned to Gary that he'd like a smoke and that he would find a pay phone while outside. As he smoked he could not see a phone. He did not see a van either. James had not been left like this before. He did not have money for a hotel room and he knew that Gary would not have the cash either. Over 7,000 miles and he could not find a ride. James took out a cigarette and lit it in the shade of the entrance. He preferred smoking when it was cold outside, but appreciated a cigarette in almost any temperature after such a long amount of travel. His first cigarette had been from a pack he found abandoned on the road as a teenager. The cigarettes did not appear to be wet or dirty.

When he was a child, he hated smoking. His mother smoked for much of his youth and in the 90s he was made fun of for having the smell of smoke on his clothing. As he matured into a teenager and discovered the cigarettes on the ground, James decided to experiment.

Lighting the first cigarette was a joy and a mystery. The taste of the smoke seemed to resonate through James' entire being. The high the nicotine produced approached subtly, at first, only then to overwhelm him. He sat on the ground in a wooded area of Forest Park he could never remember. It was summer and the light shown through the leaves of the trees with a particular luminescence that pleased him. The high itself was brief and never to be had again in that beautiful a form. Still, James loved the act of smoking. Even after he quit, many years later, he would be happy that he had begun his addiction so calmly and delightfully.

Palms stood strong in the distance. He could taste the salt of the sea in the air around him. He had no idea what to do if they were stranded—This will be history soon, but still a nightmare from which I will have to awaken. Some administrator had given him a phone number to call in case he was delayed or no one appeared. But the number had the Saudi country code. He wasn't sure that it would work in Bahrain. The organization of it all saddened him. The people who were tasked with picking him up had no notion of the nervousness that Gary surely felt, or even that James himself knew. Men in bright white thobes stood by taxis and eyed him. He did not want to talk to them. His clothes clung to him hotly. Outside of the airport he could see some of the city. Its buildings seemed in fashion, (at least before the Spring) well designed. He wondered to himself if it was really possible for a King to demand such things as buildings or highways. He didn't finish his cigarette.

He returned to Gary and they had an exasperated laugh about being abandoned. He wondered if they should ask for help, or if they should grab a meal and wait: he wanted something with bread. Gary's demeanor was surprisingly unaffected by the absence of the ride.—Ha. Hahahaha. He stood by the luggage and looked around with that airport gaze that James noticed people get. He spoke little after he failed to find a phone. Someone swept around the cell phone kiosk next to the coffee shop. After the Navy men cleared out the entrance was quiet and cold. The air-conditioning worked its hardest to keep the cool within the building, but as the entrance hall emptied, there were fewer humans generating heat, and so the temperature dropped, however minutely. James possessed a sensitivity to heat and cool. He felt that his body was more aware of his surroundings than he often was.

At university, he had friends who called him Brother James. His sensitivities were so noticeable that his dorm mates thought them to be biblically inspired,—Brother James feels the cold! Alas, a tragedy approaches. However isolated these jokes were, James did occasionally attend church. Further, his serious demeanor, Christian seeming as it may have been, caused the nickname to spread from friend to friend. When Harvey and James began seeing one another, Harvey had fretted at the idea of James' Christianity. Although it was overblown, and James was not an ardent believer, Harvey could not understand the humor of it all. He did not share the same circles as James and grew uneasy after many people referred to his new partner as Brother James. Harvey did not know the people very well, and James felt there was an element of race involved in Harvey's confusions: whatever white assumptions he had of someone being referred to as Brother X, Brother Y, or Brother Z contained a seriousness that he was not open about with James.

In order to put Harvey at ease, James planned a simple meal and laid it out for him. The seriousness of the conversation was a great strain on each: the miscommunication had hurt them both. That night they did not share a bed, but stood awake separately, each wondering to what extent the other had been completely serious and honest. James' frustrations grew much more complicated than he had expected. Harvey felt a guilt he could not understand or describe. With time, the two ignored the discussion they had had. James pretended not to worry about Harvey's assumptions, while Harvey put on that he comprehended more about James than he truly did.

The Gambler

On the other side of Elizabeth's apartment building, a family from Boston had taken residence. A mother, father, and their older and younger sons resided in the modified two bedroom. She and Robert invited them for homemade wine one evening, but as the father and husband had escaped to Saudi to ignore his debt, gambling, drinking and cocaine problems, they declined the invitation.—Really Elizabeth, come by any time, but we cannot have Father drinking that wine of yours so you'll have to come to us. You need to know your way around here, all of these people have a special way about them: how to get laid, how to get fucked up. It is healthier for us here because Father is removed from the badness, but we can still get ours and even with kids, Mother winked. Elizabeth, who had to handle this at the request of Robert, responded,—Many thanks.—Well any time that you want to come join the ladies and me, we call our group the Sisters in Saudi; stupid isn't it? We get together Mondays, Wednesdays, Fridays. Elizabeth scheduled her classes for MWF the next morning.—We get up to any kind of fun. I have to keep myself in good shape for Father, not stumbly or slurry that is, but that doesn't stop the rest of the sisters.

Mother, Polish, had attended Boston University at the expense of Father during her first pregnancy. Her goal in doing so was to attain some sense of pedagogy and English language teaching so that she could return to her home, Gdansk, and afford a life in a house slightly outside of the city with Father. Father, who had been around, encouraged her. His thinking: she is twenty years younger so upon his successful retirement, they could move between his beloved Boston and her grand Gdansk. There could be no stopping the pair, both being occasional Catholics who listened to the Bishop on Christmas and Easter. What sins they committed would be absolved with Father's sometime-donations to the church and Mother's confessions. Mother was explicit with the priests. It did not matter who listened to the sins, so long as they were heard. Mother told of the places they had sex for pleasure. OH how Father enjoyed seeing her nude, spread before him as if on display. Her lack of shame arose from her loins, she giggled at the idea of the holy father imagining her. She confessed to having vainly shaven her pubic hair, to having cursed at Father for coming too soon—Three minutes, Father, really! Their lives were wonderful. The Bostonian Father had inherited from his father, the Bostonian Grandfather, a large sum of money and a detailed Rolodex. Using these in unison, Father had found work after returning from his first trip to Poland, and found a wife during his second trip. What joys the housing market presented Father in those single days. Flipping and selling were simple, easy tasks. Brimming with capitalistic vigor, Father returned to Poland to revisit his youth. The Soviet fall allowed Father to teach, coordinate community programs, and hike the chilled forests of northern Poland. The utilitarian grey of Soviet-inspired architecture still remained when he returned and impregnated Mother. Neither knew, but this was the middle point of Father's first downward spiral. His money depleted rapidly, and soon with his bride in arm, the new year of 2008 did sing *auld lang syne* to most of Father's money. Mother was able to finish her studies and have her degree printed, before Father was forced to scramble for jobs. His applications were widespread, the older son was already eating and playing, and the younger was on his merry way to join the world. After some hectic months, with money slipping frantically away with expensive "when will I have the chance again" champagnes and cocaines, he found a job and jaded sobriety in Saudi Arabia. With everything sold, the young family, with an old, Viagra-enabled Father, settled into the compound. Loans and debts began to ease as the four adjusted to the sands. Father's retirement had failed, and so too had Mother's dream of movement between Boston and Gdansk.

Elizabeth and Robert sat alone together. In their compounded relationship, they engaged one another while sitting on opposite couches in their living room, often finishing the wine that would take Elizabeth two months to make. They each shook their heads at the family that shared their southern wall. Elizabeth thought of the image of women that the young boys must have. She worried that they would not engage any young girls their own age. There weren't many children living in the compound. Their socialization presented the biggest challenge. Robert spoke of the nightmare that such parenting must be. Robert, who would never be a father, considered Mother's position as the only woman that interacted with her children on a regular basis, the compound school had no female teachers oddly. The dynamics of that family affected the children with obvious gusto. Father, whose resentment at failure in America showed in his eyes and hands, created for his sons a myth of the States. They had visited since moving to Saudi, but nights were spent listening to Father emphatically remembering baseball or pie. In the minds of his young sons, the entire nation halted for great players of sport. These strong men could do no wrong, their sins were so often forgiven without question. Mother wanted to participate in this world building, but she spent her time constructing positive images of women. She worried that there would be some askewness in her sons. This would develop into a deep misogyny, she felt. In response to this, she showed them films with strong female leads, and had them read novels with female protagonists. Separated as the compound was from the society beyond its walls, Mother was cognizant that what her sons saw would leave an imprint upon them, the black veil becoming more than some bit of culture, but actually a symbol of womanhood. This childish judgment, no matter how she fought it, she could not defeat. Her sons were raised by Father in a land of structured sexism.

Elizabeth recalled sharing a taxi with the Bostonian Father. He spoke longingly of horses and of the science of betting on horses,—You've got to use your cash recklessly. Apparently, winning and losing played no part in the horse-race-bet. Instead, the Bostonian Father insisted on rating jockeys and horses based on a system that he had learned from a Kentuckian while in the Peace Corps in Poland shortly after the fall of the Union. His wrinkles reminded her of other angry fathers and those loud men at stores that never remembered what size pants they wore. As Elizabeth held herself above gambling, the Bostonian Father did not share any details about the Kentuckian system, and as well did not pay his share for the taxi.

Father did not speak of his children or his wife when he was not in their company. His capacity to ignore them and envision his hands as being younger and softer drove him to speak about gambling with any who would listen.—Have you ever lost $5,000? Father questioned what kinds of illegal gambling must take place in Saudi. Games of luck were outlawed in the land. Father learned to gamble from Grandfather. As a child, Father watched Grandfather and his friends play cards. Their games were loud and smoky. All of the men had their superstitions and fidgets. They were not friends with Grandfather, except in that they would bet him money. Some had worked with him, one had been in the war with him, another he had met at a bar. Grandfather assembled these people weekly to sit under the dull light of his basement to play cards, eat, and drink. He insisted that Father watch the proceedings and felt that it was a part of his growing up to smell stale cigars and pretzels. The games were simple, but how the men reacted was spectacular. Unemotional as Father was as a younger man, he wanted badly to feel the manic highs and lows of these betting men. None of the men were wealthy, so their risk equated to not being able to feed self and family. Father did not know the hyperbole that went into these facets of the game. His own density and lack of aptitude for sarcasm made him feel that all was wagered in Grandfather's basement. The red-in-the-face reactions, the guttural-then-palatal-then-fricative ejaculations, the fist-balling-then-fingers-spreading-movement demonstrated to Father that all of these people could feel extremes. With each day he grew older, Father wanted those extremes more extremely. As he experimented with different means, he found he needed a greater variety. Ups and downs were both welcome, so he bought pills and cocaine, gambled safe bets and dangerous wagers. The truth of Father's addictions was that he was addicted to feeling. But he had felt so much by the time his sons were born, no grand emotions were provoked within him. A calm came over him on the days of his sons' births. Even though he had lost most of his money, he had been thrilled to do so. Now with children, he could no longer afford the recklessness he had fallen in love with. Even finding that he had fertilized an egg within Mother by accident had rushed an increased amount of adrenaline through his brain.

As their taxi moved, Elizabeth and Father did not speak much after his race-horse-mumbles. She had never been to a horse race. Once she had visited Kentucky. She and two friends had driven from Michigan. They camped. On the third day, they visited a breeder and heard about the training and sexing. Elizabeth thought to mention this to Father, but felt that he would be disappointed by her lack of interest in it and memory about it. So it was with Elizabeth. Each day, or nearly, she would be presented with a chance to continue a conversation's thread or interaction's momentum, but most commonly she failed to. She felt that taking the responsibility for an exchange meant guiding it caringly, as a result she ignored most things she did not care about. Elizabeth had spoken to Abdelrahman about running some errands. Soon he would pick her up and drive her. He no longer drove Father. After some incidents of argument with the man, Abdelrahman left Father's calls to ring. Although the man had no need for the money he received from driving, he did enjoy the motion of it. Abdelrahman's father had been a slave in Saudi until the 1950s. To that end, Abdelrahman's personal successes afforded him a perspective that he no longer needed to be accosted by Americans or anyone really.—That fool and his gambling can take another car. The idiot and his idol: money is not a kind mistress to that man. Across the city, he prepared to visit with Elizabeth. He turned on his car and A/C to let it cool the leather before departing.

4

James had a predilection for sin. This fondness came from an intense paranoia as a child. His grandparents instilled in him a fear of perdition that he could not hide. They took him to church more often than his parents did. They did not chide him for not wanting to kneel with the congregation as they did, but after the mass was over both Frederick and Mary made casual comments about the Lord and the ways He worked on sinners,—You know, James, He does mysterious and wonderful and powerful things to good and bad alike. James began to worry that he would sin his way to Hell and that this would shape his life. With a fixation only a child could muster, James spent his early teen years contemplating his downfall. He thought of it so much, and eventually so fondly, that he did not realize that his fear prevented him from engaging in the sins he thought would consume his life: James was a good person.

It entered his mind as all thoughts did and remained there unnoticed for some time. The television had allowed his feelings for men to first be known. He wished in later years that he could remember the exact show, but in reality knew it was the sexualness of it all that he had noticed. At first, when he recognized his thoughts and feelings, the worry that had absorbed him took hold. This, surely, was a sin that he could not measure. He stared into the television screen, his mouth hanging open, hoping for some kind of solution. He thought that the sin itself was embedded within him, and that he would have to possess a guilt that he could not bear for many years to come. It was with this depression that he encountered his cousin, Walter. Walter was older and immensely critical. He had come to take James to a movie.

James felt sick with his own anxiety. Walter sensed James' sadness. James tried to minimize his feelings for the comfort of the interaction: he did not want to see a movie, but could not say no. What surprised James happened quickly. Walter spoke,—You know, our grandparents may feed you thoughts that scare you. Your mother told me that you have been acting strange lately after going to church with them. You are not alone. They try to put that fear in all of us. But you just have to know that we love no matter what in this family. We have been through too much to dismiss one another for reasons that are out of our own control. Just try and be loving and you'll be fine. Try not to buy into those phony sins.

James took a deep breath and thanked his cousin. It was this attempted eloquence that made him realize the power of a concept like sin. He stopped attending church with his grandparents. Slowly, he worked through his fear of hell fire and became, for at least many years, terribly indifferent to fundamental ideas about good and bad. As he came to accept his own person, he too accepted the world around him, but did not share in any idealisms. He knew that all humans sinned and were flawed. He did still love his family and friends, but to hope for a better world, he thought, was inane. The worry he felt for himself faded, and as he grew older he came to understand that others, as well, did not care what sins they committed, nor did they understand what to sin really meant.

The police would beat people up in his neighborhood, they said, for information. Violence like this inculcated a fear in him, and others he knew. The casual nature with which the officers beat and harassed was remarkable. St. Louis, the brooding, cursing city it was, sat on races and classes so that they did not move. It was not that James hated white people. He wanted, only once, to talk openly about race or class or money with a white person he did not know to see what they would say. It was the lack of dialogue that irked him. It was how so many did not comprehend the pains of their neighbors that shook him. The silence had erased the glossiness of his vision.

And so, an indifferent James began to think about sin in a new way: how it affected those that believed in it. He liked sin. Not that he enjoyed sins, but he was fond of the dilemma. Eventually, James would come out and feel the relief that he had wanted all of those years earlier. Politically, he was not usually inspired to join any cause or movement because he thought there would be no traction for actual change. When Obama became president, he felt the staggering affects of disbelief. But he felt, fundamentally, that there had been no changes on the other levels of society: still the poor were poor, still men were beaten and shot in the streets by police, still women found substantial challenges all around. Hope did not change James' outlook.

He looked at Gary. Where was he to prove all of this? His indifference extended onto those men and women fighting for something he did not understand in streets that he hoped not to visit while here. He had been told not to travel to Bahrain. He wondered quietly to himself what kinds of trouble the people on this peninsula got themselves into. He had watched executions on the internet. He heard rumor that each town had a special square dedicated to those events. Within two months a fellow teacher would work away at the armor of James' indifference with his own idiosyncrasies.

James, who at that time could not be moved to support a cause good or bad, sat to a late lunch with Todd at a Pakistani restaurant near the *suq*. They had worked a half day and were preparing for the weekend. Aside from the casual chatter about students and compound life, Todd nudged James in a peculiar way.—Have you seen any of the videos? James had and was not keen to watch them again, let alone in such a public setting. Todd explained, —In a week, we have vacation. I am going to Riyadh. I am going for two things …

It was at this point that James noticed a strangeness about Todd's eyes and a quirk to how he carried his weight: James guessed him to be overweight by 30-40 pounds. Todd cleared his throat and leaned in,—There is a square in Riyadh where they do the executions. They inject whoever it is with a bunch of pain killers, they knock 'em out. Then they take them out to this square and an executioner pulls up in his car, he drives the thing around with the hood on or whatever, and then the guy does it: he decapitates the prisoner. Quick like that. I read on the internet that there is no warning; I am taking the week to case it out. OH, I have got to see it.

James withheld his disgust.—Hmm. Not my thing, I'd say, but good luck with that. Todd had activated in him a reaction, an emotional charge that he had been feeling more and more in recent weeks. Not wanting to satisfy Todd with his feelings James nodded and said no more. The morality of it did not shock James, but it was Todd's insistence that he see it which bothered him. There was some element of Todd's needing to be scarred by it, to have seen the life taken. The two men continued their meal. Todd never mentioned the second reason for his vacationing in Riyadh. In Manama, James and Gary sat together, each reading. The plainness of the airport, how sterile it was, was comfortable for the two. It was as though their locations had not changed at all, only that they were waiting just as they had been for hours and hours.

James thought about how different his experience would be from Gary's. It occurred to him that he would tell his stories differently, his impressions would come across separately and to varying people. From each of the two men, words would spread, however contrasting, allowing people who once knew nothing to grab ahold of something, to be able to judge others, form opinions and ideas, expand, or even reduce, a view of the world, and this is where it would all start: a Starbucks.

On the fifth floor, Patrick walked into his room, thoughts of Laura's thighs trailing green behind him. He turned to the Indian bell boy.—Have you got beer?—Of course, sir. On the lower floors and the top, as the concierge mentioned, sir. Patrick handed the young man some money that his mother had exchanged for him before departing and the boy left with another thank-you-sir. Shyam had also arrived in Doha to support a mother. He looked to the 6 rials skeptically. New Delhi, his home, where he wanted to sit with his mother, was a place of calm retreat for this high-spirited man.

A park, Rajiv Chowk Park in Connaught Place, near his family's apartment, in the center of the city, had a dirt path and at the very end a theatre troupe would do outdoor meditations and rehearsals. Shyam always watched contently, as any person would, the people moving in fluid unison according to some unhearable rhythm. The producer and director would each watch with frowns. Once Shyam had determined the show schedules, and from that how often they would appear in the park, so that he could always watch them. His family could not afford to go to the theatre, his mother a maid and his father an auto driver, but the young Hindustani would be able to at least see some of the craft.

His school did have some theatre activities. He volunteered constantly. Whenever he had any money he would head to the cinema and watch for as long as he could go without eating. Now in Doha, there was a cinema at the mall that showed American and European films. They were not to his taste, as he swelled with emotion and national pride at the many songs and romances of an Indian film. Even still with this job, he could rarely visit any cinema. He sent much of his money home, saving for marriage and a better life in Delhi. Fondly looking at Patrick, the frown the Irishman had reminded him of the director yelling at his actors.—English people wouldn't watch you, he'd scream at them,—but to mock you. We are free of that now so show it on your faces. Shyam felt sick thinking of that man's aggressive attitude. He never hesitated to deride those around him and without fail some member would offend this director, this artist, so severely so as to inspire a deeply rooted and uncomfortable belittling.

On a warm afternoon in January years earlier, the director had lost his cool so early that he could not speak. He stopped the warm ups and stared at the group. Using his finger, he guided the people away from their usual position at the end of the earthen path. Employing the same finger, he pointed at an artificial rock, made of concrete, or so thought Shyam who could not see it directly, and calmly demanded the actor nearest to him read it. That actor whispered it and the entire troupe looked downward in shame and the director, while the producer shook his head, whispered something at the troupe. Shyam couldn't rightly hear what was being said, but knew that after the rehearsal he would have to go look.

His life in Doha was simple. Each day he put on his uniform and worked the Sheraton. He had acquired a license recently to purchase alcohol. He told long term Sheraton guests, those who paid him in cash and tipped, that he'd deliver them what he could get from the store. Most often people asked for whiskey and/or Budweiser, no Kingfisher for these people. This Patrick had the look of a man who needed a Kingfisher, and of a man who would be staying in the Sheraton for at least a week. He did not offer this secondary service, but instead thought of the rock that the director had shown his actors. Two hours after the head shaking, Shyam went and looked for the piece. It was subtle, the markings in the rock were worn and covered in dirt. The fake rock itself was off to the right slightly, and had clearly been moved to be out of the way. Shyam had to sink to his knees to read what the thing said. He knelt down, and frowned: It's a white man's world.

Shyam left Patrick's room and made his way down to the lobby to await more guests. Typically, with his coy smile, he would successfully wait on white women. His life leading up to his move to Doha was hectic. He tried his hand at various jobs. He lost sight of his interest in live theatre and no longer went to the park to see rehearsals. He needed money to marry, to support his mother, to live his life. His last resort would be to move West. A man in his neighborhood had found the hotel job for him and made the offer. When all was sorted, Shyam sat on a flight excited, but naïve, about his trajectory. He looked at the men around him, also flying from Delhi to Doha. He prayed thankfully that he would not be doing manual labor. Sadly, he did not know when he would be returning home. His ideal would be five years, but he could not know. The fabricated nature of the hotel's furnishing and design had none of the character that years of wear and use could work on a place meant for sleeping and living. He pined for something more real, with some sense of reality beyond clean smell.

But alas, Shyam was dutiful in his position. He respected his bosses and he dealt kindly with hotel guests. He never snipped at anyone, even the sullen Patrick who did not realize that it was his world, or at least claimed to be his. Patrick had the look of a man who had no understanding of what privilege is, and as Shyam observed the sadness on his face, no awareness that he had access to that privilege. Some people should be made to look at poverty, and to taste it, in order to better comprehend their own lives. But Shyam stopped his philosophizing and took the bags of another guest,—Can I help you carry that?

• • •

The Irishman beheld his surroundings and found them sufficient. A bed, a bath, and a television. Patrick had rarely ever enjoyed staying in hotels. Once, in mighty Belfast, he had stayed in a hostel with his friend John and they had gotten so roaring drunk that Patrick deliriously assaulted John on the second evening of their stay. John's glasses flew to the ground and so ended the golden age of their friendship, as well as Patrick's stay in the hostel. Patrick reflected for a brief moment on this and noted to himself that since John, he'd had very few friends. He also wondered why he had been friendly with John at all. They had met in school. Having nothing in common in terms of studies was the foundation of their relations: Patrick couldn't stand the idea of competition with his peers so he avoided anyone involved in numbers. John worked with literature and read books that Patrick had no interest in, thus making it safe for the two to be friends.

The assault was prompted by a comment about Bertrand Russell. John, whose Christianity was offended by Russell, had noticed a series of his essays in Patrick's bag. It was a simple turn of his eyes that Patrick noticed. They moved about their day simply and normally, finally purchasing beers. The more each consumed, the more bothered John became at Patrick's reading choice, and so much more did Patrick become upset at John's shifty eyes. In tandem, both looked unsettled, even angry by turns, with John asking first what was wrong. Patrick immediately determined that he ought to deny any emotions he could have. John then asked more directly about the book,— Why do you read that pervy maths-man?

They were sitting in the bedroom that they shared at the hostel. At the mention of Russell, Patrick exploded. His emotions escalated so suddenly, his face flushed so deeply red so instantly, that John was taken aback. He moved slightly away from Patrick towards the wall, and Patrick, standing and panting, simply pointed at John's face. John had seen Patrick lose his temper like this before, each time nearly coming to violence. Neither of the men could speak and the assault became inevitable. Patrick moved forward and struck John, engaging in his only realized instance of physical abuse, up to that point in his life, on another human.

John was knocked back by the smack, regained his posture and left the room. He informed the hostel attendants of what had happened, requesting a new room away from Patrick.—We will have him leave, thank you for informing us. Ought we call the authorities? The conflict itself was more of a realization that these two people were not compatible as friends or partners in any way. It was clear that each was looking for reasons to be skeptical of the other. The trip to Belfast had been planned months before, as Patrick had never been and had made a promise to go to the city. John wanted to get out of Dublin often and arranged the trip when it would best fit his schedule.

In the meantime, the two became increasingly tense, as is often the case between people. By the moment that John arrived at the desk, his cheek had swollen and in the harsh artificial light of the lobby it was determined that Patrick would be asked to leave the hostel immediately.

Accordingly, Patrick slept in the train station that evening, using his coat as a blanket and departing on the first train in the morning. When the staff had asked him to leave he calmly packed his things and left the building.

Now back to Doha! Without unpacking, Patrick moved to the bottom floor. The glass elevator went dark for a moment and lit up again facing The Irish Harp.—Dammit.

—Never far from home, he whispered. Patrick could hear the chattering expatriates from outside the bar. He entered. The words of the drinkers vibrated through the dark woods of the place and it was as if Patrick could almost feel their socializing being articulated on his goose-pimpled skin. The many corners and nooks sucked patrons in, making them invisible to Patrick. The Filipino bartenders served him promptly.— Guinness and whiskey. —Bangers and mash. 9 o'clock. Men and women in nice-ish clothes filed in. There developed in his mind a kind of warbling. It finally occurred to him how far away from his home he was. The dim lighting and hard woods of the Irish Harp challenged him to be happy. It was plain that he would frequent this bar.

To his right there was an American wearing a baseball cap and a red t-shirt. Eavesdropping, Patrick learned that this person worked for the Bin Laden Group. This American laughed.– –Seriously, they pay me quite well, he intoned to his eating partner. To Patrick, this post 9/11 American presented a pleasing kind of irony. Because graduate school and the Celtic Tiger had both wronged Patrick so hardily, it made him happy to hear about people having to compromise something in order to make their living. This young man, also so far away from home, seemed to agree with Patrick in taking pleasure in this set of circumstances. It was as if, to Patrick, the American had some badge of honor for having to work for the family, whose son so dramatically changed his country.

Despite the kind of vibrating emptiness that grew in Patrick, he listened with pleasure and pity to this American businessman. A second whiskey grew warm inside of his belly.—Too much? He asked no one in particular. He waited for the combination of food and liquor to take ahold of his mood, hopefully improving his countenance.

The smokey atmosphere was cut by the beginnings of karaoke. Americans singing, spreading their voice: flat,—THEY tried to make ME goooo to reHAB and I SAID no no noooo. At tables men and women drank.—Everything is imported, joked one of the bartenders, including all of the people here.—The golf club here they say is great, but all of that water. . .Where does it come from?—SSSome of them WAnt to BEE AAbussed.— They are building for the World Cup already. I wonder how all that was arranged.—*Nix ist so wirklich als nix, ja?—Doch.* Patrick finished his potatoes in the crowd of voices. As more people arrived, he found it difficult to continue listening to his American. This inspired a further kind of isolation in him, focusing on his remaining food and drink. He began on the sausage and ate as quickly as he could. The grease from the meat dropped onto his shirt and he dabbed it with a napkin, while chewing slowly because he could sense his own homesickness building. His beer was gone and so was his sausage soon enough. Feeling himself full enough that he could not get drunker he paid.—Enough, OK.

It had taken years for Patrick to learn to control his consumption of alcohol. He greatly enjoyed the bite of hard liquors. His mother would chide him about drink, saying that it was unnatural for a son of hers to be able to drink so. She was a teetotaler. Her drunkenness came from a source unknown to Patrick. What is it that moves her, he often wondered. She had no hobbies, but reading cheap novels. She did not smoke or drink. He wasn't sure if she visited with men. He had a feeling that he would need to visit with a woman soon. Often, he thought of his own sexual needs when contemplating his mother, because aside from Laura and her he was not familiar with any other women. He knew that this was unhealthy, so he tried to focus on the many voices that surrounded him. As he paid, he noticed that small groups of people were gathered all around him and he made note to see if he could find such a group to accompany him.

There were no Arabs or Qataris in the bar. From what he noticed, there were only western people and the various bartenders and waiters. His nostalgia for his own home calmed slightly when he realized that he had coalition of homesickness with most around him. There was a presence in the bar that suggested that the place was an escape from actual surroundings. It did not have windows to the hot, Arabian outside. It had no Qatari memorabilia. Nothing resembling local culture. No representatives of that culture. Here, the white people were served kindly and amongst themselves. Separate but equal, or so thought Patrick.—Clever segregation like the Americans do. Probably set up by an American, given the fluidness of it. He had no experience with race relations. He knew vaguely of the troubles in America and France. His upbringing made him sensitive to the Catholic-Protestant divide, but even to that he was seemingly ignorant. He wondered how long it would be until he met a Qatari.

Patrick removed himself and within the hour was asleep with his shoes on. As he slept taxis carried men all over the city: to the *suq*, the Intercontinental, the W, and other well established venues. At some of these places, these very men (and occasionally their retinues) engaged in conversation with bartenders or working women. Generally, they spent money and enjoyed the commodities they got in return. Beer, whiskey, and women were good enough prizes anywhere. Understanding that their night could not go until dawn, many of these men would depart, before bar time, at around 10:35PM and move on to their apartments for a nightcap or a visit from a special friend.

Two of these very men returned to the Sheraton from the Belgian beer bar at the Intercon. They shared flights of beers and smoked cigars together. They had had, at some point in the evening, a mild argument about taxes, each showing his homeland proudly on his sleeve. Finding that neither could drive home to the Sheraton, they hailed a taxi. However tempting it was to drunk drive in a foreign country, it remained a terrible idea. While stepping out of the taxi and into the lobby, one turned to the other and said this,—I have her come on Fridays. There's something about it. I know I pay her to fuck me and I know that she makes a good living off of it and that she fucks other men in addition to me. But, I'll be honest, there's something about it that works away the loneliness. Just a short visit to stop the loneliness. The other stood in agreement. He too knew the pull of that loneliness. Seeing family on the screen of a computer, being left to emails with friends, increased nostalgia for sporting events and holidays. They walked into the hotel together, not mentioning anything after the admission. He was newer here, and much more shy than his counterpart. Something about the honesty bothered him and made him happy. He was glad to know that someone else felt similar pangs, not because of where he was, but because he was so far away from what he really knew. For its worth, both men loved Doha. As a city, it spoke to them softly and kindly. They were beginning to understand its nuances and deeper characteristics. But even so, they were not sure how much longer it would take them to feel at home.

Doha is a seemingly balanced city. Alcohol is sold in hotels and by licensed dealers. Other parts of the city remain dry. Its *suq* has been remodeled to be open to tourists and hungry people. Once that same *suq* was in danger of being demolished, only to be saved by a generous patron. The museum is wonderful. Around the bay there is an open and clean walking path. There are many opportunities for sport. Shopping is possible not only at the *suq*, but at the more contemporary market, the mall, which also possesses a cinema. It is a city balanced on the oil wealth of a king, the infrastructure of a former colony, the ideals of a religion, the awareness of capitalism, and the backs of workers from the subcontinent. Pleasant as it may be for most white people and Arabs, the hot sun still has its way with manual laborers. The two men, one of whom visited with a woman weekly, and another who never would out of fear, as well as the perverse satisfaction he got out of merely being in the same bar as some working women, were wise to the pits and valleys of Doha.

They managed calm responses to what they observed, a city stuck in between its location, its wealth, and its histories. As small of a city as Doha geographically was, they both appreciated that it remained off of the beaten path. Dubai was the focus of many people's attention with its looming phallus. Doha's towers were shorter, but more elegant. Its resorts were less successful, but more endearing. But some kind of contradiction met them at all of the positives. Some deeply embedded hesitation moved them. They spoke no Arabic. They had little knowledge of the long history of that city, let alone the peninsula. Their monies were stored peacefully in digital areas, awaiting conversion into pounds and dollars.

Above them, Patrick slept. The three would not meet, but perhaps in passing. As the two rode upwards in the same elevator that Patrick had by now three times ridden, the second turned to the first and asked,—How much does she cost?

5

After about 40 minutes, two men came towards them. One was tall, balding and wearing shorts and small glasses, the other was heavyset and equally tall, wearing a hat. They were Canadians and they sauntered with gaping grins towards James and Gary. They introduced themselves as Scott and Jim Younger. They were here to take the two new lecturers back to al-Ahsa to teach the next day.—You all are probably looking for us, Jim laughed. Initially, neither Gary nor James noticed the men as they drifted towards their table; the two had seen pictures of Gary and James, not the other way around. When they approached the table, James smelled on them the stench of liquor, days old, and there was an element of sadness that settled within as he took in the staleness of the two men. However, they were kind on the surface and Gary and James were relieved to have been found.

Jim stood in a manner that brought out the drunk in his eyes. The broad shoulders that rested atop his torso suggested that he would be formidable in physical confrontation. Still, there was a noticeable shyness behind Jim's height and weight. Being the clearly younger of the Younger brothers, Jim took first to the younger of the arrived teachers: James. Jim assumed that James shared some sense of adventure he could identify with, as Jim had found the job in Saudi, and had prompted his brother to join him. Jim asked James where he had been, where he had lived throughout this world. James responded,—I have never been outside of the United States before. Was I supposed to have taken a detour? To this Jim, Scott, and Gary all responded with curiosity. How had this person decided to travel to Saudi then, of all places to first use a passport? Jim looked at the blackness of James' skin.—Are you a Muslim?

With this, James responded apathetically, and changed the topic.—What makes you ask? How long will it take to al-Ahsa? Scott appeared much older than Jim for only being a few years his senior. At James' question, he assumed his role as the elder brother.—It will be only three or so hours, depending upon traffic at the border. James was grateful to have a ride to his new apartment and to be able to remove himself from airports. Yet, he was unsettled by the eyes of Jim. He did not have any aversion to drinking or drunkenness, but from their introductions it seemed they did not have much in common. James spoke quietly of this contradiction,—A thirst for booze, but living in a dry land. The airport's sterile quality magnified the stupor that Jim and Scott must have been in. Gary, in his nervousness, did not seem to notice, or if he did he made no comment. James thought for a moment that it would be more agreeable to be in this situation with someone who was assertive, power in numbers. What reaction would the Saudi border guards have to drunken Canadians entering their country?

They gathered the bags and continued their small talk. Jim took to James' youngness and spoke of Tupac, but James had always preferred B.I.G.

As they left the airport, Jim stopped for a snack at a stand and got the phone number of the Filipina woman handing out magic creamed corn. He did it because he could; to him in his state he felt that she owed him her number. She smiled at him as she scribbled a number down, and looked deep into his eyes as she handed over a number that she did not know or care about.—Of course, you should call me next time you are in Manama. She, selling corn in an airport far from her family and fiancé, felt a distinct satisfaction at lying to him. She hated men like this one, too tall and wide for her liking.—So you live in Saudi? Whoa! She looked at his height and width as justifications of his arrogance, as his being willing to act irrationally. As she wrote the number, a number that she always invented on the spot, she made a coy smile at him: next time. She knew that this would increase his hope: in a week or two, he would call the fictitious phone number and be momentarily disappointed.

Her mother had trained her before she left home to be wary of men, regardless of where the men were from. She felt a healthy skepticism towards Saudis, a doubt of Bahrainis, a dismissiveness towards Americans, a mocking suspicion of Brits, a sarcasm towards Canadians. Each day, she climbed out of her bed and went to the airport. There, she prepared the magic creamed corn. She sold it to many people. With each day, she expected some harassment, and most days her predictions were correct. She grew so accustomed to this hassle that she could often anticipate which men would approach her. She did not guess; she foresaw. Her depression at being so far from home was reduced by her being prepared for sexual harassment. She remembered when she first handed out a false number. She felt a thrill at having lied to the man. That thrill, minimal as it was, represented to her a small power.

Some miles and hours away, Jim would feel stifled by gender segregation, but he did not care if he met this woman again. Scott smiled at Jim's silliness and engaged Gary as best he could.—You won't need that sweatshirt in this heat. They loaded the bags in the van and James smoked again in the sun. They had illegally parked and James took a picture of Scott holding Gary's luggage as he finished a cigarette. The Bahraini air was fresh and salty. In the distance, James saw the city in its shininess. There was a manicured quality to Manama, even though its people revolted. James thought in that moment that the shiniest cities would be some of the best for protest and revolt.

On Using Oil Money

Robert was paid each month without having to pay any taxes to Saudis or Americans. His earnings were transferred separately to different banks in the United States, one in Rob's name, one in his father's name, and yet a third in Elizabeth's, whereby Robert attempted to avoid any notice of his tax-free income by the IRS. This money, none of which was invested, was paid to him in full in Saudi riyals to his Riyadh bank account on the fifth of each Gregorian calendar month. On the sixth of each month, Robert would visit the bank and withdraw 2,800 riyals, amounting to slightly less than one fifth of his monthly earnings, for expenses locally. With cash in hand, he would return home and log into his online account and would begin the transfer process, with the remaining four-fifths of his money being divided, at whim, between the three accounts. Robert believed that irregularity would be an advantage in tricking the US government. After having transferred his capital to the States, or at least having begun the process, which required business hours of both the sending and receiving banks and so took some time, he would give Elizabeth 1,000 riyals and keep the remainder in a jar in the kitchen. All of this was more than Elizabeth knew of. She did not know exact details of his wages and did not have the patience to sit with him while he debated which account had been kind enough to merit the largest amount of wired money each month. Most tedious of all, he would construct a budget after having dissolved his monetary holdings each month with the Bank of Riyadh. He accounted for vacations, relevant holidays and birthdays, planned spontaneity and so forth. As the months passed and Elizabeth and Robert renewed their visas, each of the three accounts swelled happily. Occasionally, Robert felt that the couple needed to spend some money on more than Kindle books and food. In this case, on the sixth of the month he withdrew 6,000 riyals of which he gave Elizabeth 4,000 and declared that they ought to spend oil money. The mechanisms within Robert's head that led to this conclusion had no consistency. This could happen two months consecutively or not for six months. Elizabeth did not anticipate this well and became greatly flustered at Robert's sudden materialism. Rob encouraged her to obtain objects that he thought she desired, technologies and fads she did not need.— Wouldn't an iPad be nice? Or perhaps not. What about a nice camera? Gadgets cluttered their apartment after these spending sprees. Robert would choose restaurants to eat at and have Abdelrahman on call during evenings when he wanted to visit somewhere with Elizabeth. She did not find any joy in this frittering away of riyals. Even with the increased spending, the coffers still grew on their monthly cycles.

Robert could also drive and had bribed his way into a Saudi license without telling Elizabeth. She gladly left the compound to walk through *suqs* and malls and see the people. She never covered her face, except when role playing with Robert. It turned her off to see Robert's picture on that piece of plastic. His name in Arabic was not elegant. He quickly bought a used car, which fell apart within a week. Elizabeth noted the greed in Robert's eyes, how it was miserly and how it desired material objects, but cheaply.

In their living room, while she read, he would feel the notes with his fingers. Sexually he rubbed the faces of kings. He arranged the notes into piles in front of him on a table and took pictures of the money. Even the grocery money rubbed him the right way. He counted the bills that Elizabeth used at the store. She had come to refuse most of his rides and hired Abdelrahman to take her away to gather foodstuff. Beforehand, Robert would pedantically count the 400 riyals out for her, as if it were an allowance or a gift, and the corners of his mouth would rise erotically, his baldness becoming more apparent. When he finished tallying the bills he winked at his wife,—The sum in whole, your baksheesh! This emphatic and pathetic wink repeated itself over and over in Elizabeth's mind as she prepared to be taken to the store by Abdelrahman. Her conclusion still could not be avoided. Within the hour she would attempt to hide her progress with the spending of money, but she knew it was of no use. The buying of things offended her deeply. All she felt drove her from the apartment for some need of clarity. She hoped the Arabic chatterings of the grocery store would suffice to distract her from what she knew to be true: she had married an idiot, who was greedy, unintelligent, and manipulative.— Robert was such an ass.

It must be stated that she had known this for some time, for years in fact. The undeniability of this conclusion had simmered steadily and reached a rolling boil that afternoon. Settling seemed easy enough for Elizabeth. She could tolerate Robert's lack of nuance, as well as his quirky sexual direction and his eccentric and limited greed, but she could no longer handle the culture that allowed him to act so. The foundations of the compound rested on travel for wealth, a colonial and capitalistic attitude that with each passing hour and minute unnerved her at her very core. No longer did she wish to be complicit in the actions that would afford that cabin. She had allowed Robert to fool her into all of these travels and adventures. She had thought there would be something more to it than her initial judgments. She assumed early in her relationship with the man that she was being too critical and that he would grow to learn and love with her by his side. This optimism lasted for quite a long time, through their twenties and into their thirties. Elizabeth introduced Robert to many books and ideas that he had not known before and for the most part he seemed receptive. They did a silent retreat together in India. Elizabeth had dreamed of such a trip, something that would spiritually enliven her relationship with Robert. To that too he took well. He spoke fondly of it to his family and friends. But in truth, Elizabeth's initial judgments were correct, more accurate and precise than she could have imaged in her young age. Her failure was in not believing in herself, for she had not developed the confidence she needed at the time to tell Robert to fuck himself and go bother someone else. Certainly, she loved him and had feelings for him, but they had grown apart. This growing was silent and slow. There would never be a need for difficult or convoluted divorce proceedings. When Elizabeth left Robert and returned to the States, she separated from him with ease, even with his being abroad.—Easier than expected. All that stopped were their discussions, sexual encounters, and his transfers of oil money into her account. Before any of that, both felt a loneliness within themselves that they refused to speak of. Neither was ignorant of the other's feelings; rather they each insisted in their own way of keeping mum about it. Elizabeth would read or double check her grading. Robert brought work home with him; he would procrastinate all day at work in order to have more to do at home in front of his wife. In this way, they sat across from one another on different couches in the living room of their apartment.

The loneliness that Elizabeth felt drove her from their home to spend the money that she earned from her teaching. Her driver, the taxi man who was offended at the Bostonian colleague's being a prick, confided in Elizabeth that she ought to spend time for herself, trying to understand what she may never understand,—another culture. He sensed that she was dissatisfied with her life among the displaced Americans. Abdelrahman encouraged her to think of how she would write about those American oil people. He wanted to know how they would look to her on paper and how they would fit in with the surrounding Arab communities.

Abdelrahman was well-read, nearly as well as Elizabeth, and they recommended books to one another each time they met for a drive. Each year, during the hottest months of the year, Abdelrahman would travel with his wife to Beirut or Alexandria. He loved being near the water, as he was in Dammam, but more importantly he could buy banned books. That is to say, the Jordanian and Egyptian governments banned different books than the Saudi king did. This meant that each year he would smuggle many books back to his home—I use brown paper bags to make covers for the books our last night in the hotel. The border police never open the books, they do not feel the pages with their fingers. Some books damned the Sauds. Others were sexual in nature. Still, others, his most beloved, were written by women.

Abdelrahman accepted where he was on the earth. He felt a deep-seated anger towards the culture of authority that surrounded him and had enslaved his father and grandfather. Abdelrahman had studied much and his affluence allowed for travel and a beautiful house of his own despite the enormous hurdles he faced. He saw in Elizabeth a similar resilience, but worried that she had become too downtrodden by her circumstances. To counter this, he recommended to her happy or playful books. He asked his wife how to console her. Bringing the two women together for coffee, Abdelrahman out of some rare kindness tried to befriend Elizabeth.—Where I fail, Asilah compensates. That is why this partnership works, or that is what she tells me. This did not go unnoticed. Elizabeth had a generosity and capacity for giving. She sought to include Abdelrahman or his wife in the occasional outbursts of 4,000 riyals, even though they had no legitimate need. However philanthropic each attempted to be, Elizabeth could not find a way to spend her money responsibly, and Abdelrahman could not find a way to reassure his friend.

Dammam allowed for people to spend money with ease. There were high-end grocers with fresh meats and sea foods. Along the Corniche there were restaurants, a Jarir bookstore, a marina. How the Corniche was engineered for walking families impressed both Abdelrahman and Elizabeth: al-Khobar was pleasant. But there were no trips for them to this place. The artificial beach and the Hungry Bunny were of no significance to the two in their discussions and trips. The rides and fun that could be had there meant nothing to Elizabeth and Abdelrahman. Elizabeth would never learn how to properly spend her oil money. She never thought of treating it as a play thing to be thrown around. Abdelrahman thought well of her for this.— Her heart is not corrupted by simple greed, he told Asilah.

• • •

Patrick opened his curtains and watched the light break over the bay.—If only I'd been slightly better at math, or at least more dedicated. On a small radio next to his bed he listened to the prayers.—OH, the hypnotizing throb of a man somewhere singing to his Lord. The bay was quiet. Across the bay from the Sheraton was that museum. Patrick didn't care much for art. Pei. Abidin. Raad.—Perhaps that'll sink someday. He didn't breakfast and spent his time looking at his own roundish face in the mirror. His pock marks had faded, but still he lacked a certain confidence about his own visage. The call to prayer became background, only a factor of the environment as he changed clothes.

Squat as Patrick seemed, he was not hunched. He exited the hotel and climbed into another taxi and rolled towards a building downtown, just out of sight of the bay.—Take what you can to get by, Patrick said to the driver with a genuine smile as he paid.—All tigers die. The office stood at a medium height amongst the many buildings. Cars carried people to offices and shops and hotels. He went up and found his work: a floor of people doing things for a group of Arabs they'd never meet, and didn't care to. They had a desk for him and a computer filled with numbers. There was a rattling kind of noise produced by the people of these cubicles and offices. It was as if they were in a cage or kennel, with the door open, simply going about the calmest and easiest way to get fed. His desk didn't face a window and very few of his coworkers spoke to him. The cubby had walls that were composed of tac board, the grey wavy kind. He would have put up pictures had he thought ahead to bring any. His mother did not give him any kind of sentimental things to clutter his new life with. He looked at a small pink packet he'd been given by a balding man.—Welcome, welcome. The money's good, in a Texan accent.

Musts:
-IDs
-Cellphone & SIM
-Visa
-Bank Membership
Shoulds:
-City Guide
-Driver's License or Driver
"You're safe in Doha! OIL welcomes you to your new home."

—Manageable. Patrick hadn't gone past London until yesterday, but he could do it. Thirtysomething and he could do it. He organized what he had, pencils, a TI-89 calculator, the pink sheet, neatly and casually upon his desk. He delved deeper into the packet, learning his various usernames and passwords. The work was straightforward. Data mining and processing. He'd use simple statistical functions, software already available from the company, to assess which investments were valuable long term and which were not. The computer did most of the work, but the humans who owned the corporation still distrusted technology enough to require humans to check the work. Such was Patrick's job.

He logged onto his machine and began to come to terms with the tasks at hand. He had forgotten to ask that man if there was a restaurant or cafeteria in the building. He had not packed a lunch, or even thought of nourishment. Slowly, he came to terms with his calculations. He figured that he could develop his lunch habits alone. He would watch to see when people left for lunch, as well as where they headed. If there was mention of places close by or taxis or any other markers of movement or stasis. It all suddenly became doable.—Now to wait to get hungry, he said.

He dozed off in his chair. The cooling purr of the air-conditioning made him sleepier, but the cold worked on his skin. He jerked awake and walked to a water cooler. He hadn't eaten since the Harp. He sat back down and checked over the accounts in his charge and without much effort understood that a lot of money came in and much also went out. He gazed out the window and looked to his watch. 11 o'clock. The bald Texan, whose name had been Terry or Jerry, had remembered to inform him that his lunch hour was flexible on days when Ali was not busy and stopped by his desk with a small frown to let him know,—Most people go to the nearby mall to eat, or take taxis elsewhere. It was at Patrick's discretion where to go, but he was welcome to join Terry or Jerry that day if he chose. Patrick refused.—No, I think I'll go it alone today thanks. And as Patrick had never met a man by that name he departed before noon. The late morning sun pounded on his head. His shirt clung to him desperately. Patrick stood hungrily in the shadow of the office building. He flagged a taxi and an Indian led him away from the offices.—I'm new here, where should I eat? prodded Patrick. He was careful not to think of the tip.— The mall or *suq waqif*, Boss.—What's a *suq*?—A market, Boss. Good.—That sounds authentic.—Very good, Boss.

They drove back around the crescent bay. The water shone bright in the sun. They eventually left the tall buildings for the dustier side of the city. Lower to the ground, there were Arabic marquees and people shuffled about. On the taxi's radio prayers, similar to those that had been backgrounded earlier in Patrick's day, became foregrounded. Patrick knew little of any religion, aside from some verses of Job which he remembered his mother enjoying, but he found the call soothing. His frontal auditory experience was interrupted by the Indian who had noticed Patrick's producing a slight drone in tandem with the verse,—From Mecca! I have it on the radio. All day they go around and one day maybe I can too, Boss. Even you!

Here the businesses seemed to be owned by real people. The painted streets became slightly more worn. About walked fewer white people than the other side of the bay. At some point the Indian man, who being from Bangalore preferred a slightly wetter heat, had made a left turn followed quickly by a right turn. At a roundabout with a boat perched in the middle, Patrick was let out.

The old-looking vessel sat immobile in the sand. No sense of movement could be observed in that ship and it had clearly never seen the water. Patrick disliked boats. He had an aversion to the risk of drowning. So Patrick liked the look of this particular craft more than most. The roundabout was filled with taxis and people. None of the humans moving about seemed to notice that ship. Patrick wondered if they were all used to the sight of it.—Who would build a monument to water on sand? Happy I am that I rode an airplane to this place. Could do it by boat. Sink the hopes that would. I'm already sunk. Good to be paid though. I guess I could stand a boat that couldn't sink like this one. But that defeats the fundamental role of the thing. It cannot ever move, but remains immortal. It'll never die, but never be useful. Good thing all of us have to die: we could be of some use then. I guess if God existed and he or she or it or whatever was unable to extinguish they could not do anything but sit there. Sitting in the sand like a child. Maybe this example we should follow. All of us sit around being careful. No. No. Useless damn thing. Could have fed a family with the money used for this symbol.

Patrick walked into the sun and looked down at the bricks laid out ahead of him. Clean tables watched over by Egyptian and Lebanese men. The structures looked old, but in a new way. They had been rebuilt and remodeled. Once owned by a family now owned by a single man, they had beams and walls replaced, innards taken out and redone. They were shells. Somewhere inside each casing were the old, the antiquated hidden from sunblinded eyes. He stopped at a restaurant that seemed halfway down the bazaar. A dozen black umbrellas shielded patrons from the star of the East. On both sides of the *suq* people strolled or sat. Further down he heard children moving towards him.

He sat at one of the black tables in a wicker chair. All around him men and women ate and spoke. A man,—I'll take the lamb! What a bar at the Intercon, eh? Another man,—The key is to haggle all of it, that is simply how it works. A woman,—Could you not smoke that thing here, there are children. Goodness, think of your own lungs. Those children from American wombs navigated the mass of peoples. Plates of salad and breads and meats laid about, picked over by careful eaters. Cigars and water pipes that smelled of berries and double apples smoked lethargically in the heat. Half empty glasses with black straws sweated relentlessly in the mess of food. People moved past the tabled families: couples and young men sought food or coffee or smoke. *Suq Waqif* offered these humans the nourishment they needed. Some kids had schmags on their heads. They had bought them from an Arab man, the only Qatari they'd meet. The cool paths that wound through the buildings moved away from Patrick. He did not want to explore the innards of the place should he become lost. He stared about the various restaurants along the main open air line of the market.

Somewhere in the distance the prayers were called. Recitation moved Patrick in some way. Its natural qualities struck him. His elbows and knees grew slightly weakened. Swelling through the alleys and nooks of the *suq*, no one stopped to pray.

This did not surprise Patrick. In most places, God is not dead, just irrelevant. Most smart people worship money.

The man who recited the verses had spent much of his life learning how to do so, and thereafter refining his style. He modeled much of his style on Sheikh Maher al-Muaiqly. His main objective was, like the Sheikh, to one day recite at Mecca. He knew it to be a lofty goal. His father insisted that reciting near *suq waqif* was respectable, especially for his family. Yet, he could recite for more attentive believers. He knew that most of the *suq* didn't stop to observe prayer. His mild offense to this caused in him feelings of quiet jealously as he called out. He hoped that someone from Saudi would hear him, be inspired by him, and use their *wasta* to get him closer to his goal. In Saudi, all things stopped for prayer. In Doha, some things did. Staying in the hotels across the bay, one had to turn on the radio to hear.

He often knew his mind would be clouded as he recited. This built into his personal style a kind of tension that attracted to him some younger Qatari followers. It was that they could sense the more modern anxieties in his voice that drew them to him. But still, he remained dissatisfied. Naturally, he only needed to pray. While the act developed in him a certain pressure, he also alleviated his nerves in the act of reciting for the *suq*. Somewhere outside of his place of prayer, Patrick wondered who the man was and what he felt. No interest in beauty stirred in Patrick, only a calm and casual sense of observation that those who listened with faith to the recitation would have found condescending.

And yet, the inflating and deflating nature of the prayers continued. Patrick would not know any of the movements those praying men and women did. The man who had sat Patrick at a table under a dark umbrella did want to pray, but he could not. The money stood at odds with his religiousness. Patrick ordered and took in the sounds around him. The chatter of those eating mixed with the prayers into a chorus of voices that moved slowly through the air.

The Egyptians brought Patrick his mutton and a bottle of Perrier. The young Saudis who meandered past in expensive sunglasses chuckled at their own rebellion, ignoring any wishes of the person who was reciting. British women behind him spoke of nuance and character—Retains the best of the old and pairs it with the high end of the new. At the restaurant directly across from Patrick, a Russian ordered more tobacco and his mistress another coffee. The smell of the meat enhanced the call and seemed to make it louder in Patrick's ears. Without tasting the lamb, he ate his potatoes and enjoyed the severity of the call mixing with the smell. His patience for the meat could only last so long.

The richness of the mutton hushed those prayers. This call rang differently than Mecca's in the taxi, but Patrick did not pretend to be able to notice the difference. Patrick's eyes moved about again over the market. At a distance he noticed men selling wares, antiques perhaps and trinkets to the foreigners. Gold and sandalwood and linen. There was no need in the Irishman's life for souvenirs. Such sentimental objects only crowded what little space he had. There would be no time in the future when he would need anything more than his memories of this place and this meal. His mother needed no other proof of his continued existence than an occasional phone call. All through the market there would be things he could have sent to her, once he had been paid, but would not. She did not care for such trinkets, as she had no one to show them off to. Patrick and his mother each had their own reasons for not being nostalgic, very separate reasons.

Patrick's mother did not have many friends, like Patrick, but those women she did occasionally socialize with were adept at monopolizing conversation in such a way that they never knew much at all about Patrick. This had been the case for so many years, for so many lunches and dinners, that she simply gave up the idea of presenting her son as a topic of interest to anyone. She began then to throw away what art projects and school assignments the young Patrick had completed,—No human, including the boy himself, could possibly have any need for them. She saved space around the house. She, after some time, started moving through her own childhood possessions, giving away old toys and disposing of art projects and so on. Patrick, who did not realize that he gave homework and so on to his proud mother only to have her throw them away, observed her removing any traces of her past. She did not keep many photos. All that she retained were essential items to the house and her memories. She kept what money she could, but Patrick learned from her at an unusually early age that children are expensive.

Patrick's own sentimentality was now only a function of his homesickness. He missed the smell of Dublin. It had a much less dusty quality than Doha. For his own purposes, he learned to smother his own emotions as a young man. This caused an occasional outburst, but mostly kept him quiet. What point would there be of remembering fondly those bad times he had had. And so, over the years, there arose in him a kind of nonchalance. His passions were deadened and he felt a kind of tingling in his chest whenever a normal person would get emotional.

Despite his sensibilities being so similar to his mother's, their separate lackings inspired discontent in each. Both understood that the other had some deficiency and they would do their best to point that out and exploit it. It was a kind of game they played with one another, knowing that whatever temporary injuries they caused could supposedly be covered up. They knew that there would be occasional snaps, when one or the other would get angry, and those were the unspoken points to this game.

Now that Patrick lived so far away, the nature of this back and forth would have to change. He was not sure how, but in some way they would modify how they bothered one another to translate better for the distance. Patrick noted to himself that he would have to keep an open eye for those things that would bother her most deeply. It would take some experimenting, but he believed he had the upper hand.—She may have my money, but she doesn't have me. When he finished he paid quickly. The prayer had subsided, understanding that it had been overlooked. For some time he walked among the various restaurants. Here, he knew, he could consume the foods he would lust after. He moved back to where the taxi had left him, sampling the aromas of the many places to eat. In the middle of the roundabout the boat still floated in sand.—Perhaps it would age to death. Patrick meant to ask someone about that boat, but wouldn't remember. Taxis crowded one side of the circle and argued loudly over fares.

To his left across the street, Patrick saw a small food hutch, a buffia, surrounded by dozens of men, Indians, Pakistanis, Iranians, Ghanaians, all eating quickly, not savoring their meat or falafel. He chose another driver. With a quick Accra accent he departed.

—Diversity. Man come together. Sit in one place and hear a dozen or two languages. Progress. Developing the undevelopable. Move through those people. Understand the movement. Nijinsky in the desert, as she would call it. Upset the norm and pay the tax of Enlightenment. How many airports are there in Pakistan? The waters of a forgotten bay used for wealth and wealth. Infrastructure. Order. Far be it that a meat so delicious, a lamb, bring us together. Far be it from me to disagree. Where were the religious anyways? There's progress. Father, Son, and the Holy Market Capital. The Americans pretend not to talk about politics or religion, so why should anyone? Send your men to share in the wealth. Pigs in cages. Gilded, beautiful cages. Stop for a moment for the light. Women can roam here. Safe and sound in Doha. Cute as buttons. Tasty as mutton. Perhaps a bomb will ruin all of this. Or football. Or that museum. Develop the unruinable. Man come together. Stasis.

Thinking of HyperPandas

On this day she walked through the Mall of Dhahran after tipping and shaking hands with Abdelrahman. She walked past the Café Liwan, the multiple sun-glass boutiques, past the escalators and apparel stores and straight toward Hyper-Panda grocery. She had scrawled a list, hoping that a series of planned meals would further postpone her leaving Robert.— Wheat bread, flat bread, red and yellow onions, lentils, white rice, vegetable broth, hot peppers, green peppers, carrots, ten pounds of potatoes, coffee, black tea, sugar, cumin, cucumber, pasta, spaghetti and elbow, ginger, tomatoes, assorted nuts, peanuts, almonds and cashews, chocolate, vinegar, dry yeast, flour, concentrated grape juice, olive oil, paprika chips, aluminum foil, wax paper, bagels, thyme, green olives, garlic, butter, hot sauce, eggs, tofu, cabbage, black beans, tomato paste, curry powder, and napkins, she spoke it all aloud. The list was written on the backside of a student's homework, a short essay about the importance of self-expression.

Elizabeth seldom felt so domestic, or at least did her best to deny any such feelings. The black of her robes held in the heat of the day. She had opened Robert's jar and replaced all of the money with a note: Be back soon. Elizabeth had no desire to cook. She slowed her pace in the direction of the grocer and took out her list. Stopping she looked at her student's handwriting. Teaching had been an idealism for Elizabeth. She thought

she would gain something from it that she did not. More so
Robert still felt this way. Conceptually it added to his presence
in and around the compound and office. Elizabeth, who loved
her students dearly, had grown to see the teaching in another
light, one she did not teach Robert about.

As she arrived, the call for prayer went out and the gates
closed behind her. Patrons continued to shop or stopped to
pray. As they played the prayers over the loud speakers, Elizabeth noticed that Panda was especially empty at the time
(3:08PM, Sunday, Asr). She acquired a cart and placed her
empty bags on the child's seat. She flipped back to the list
and looked around to find a suitable starting point. In front of
her was a small counter that sold technologies: iPhone, Galaxy,
various tablets, some headphones, small speakers, some Playsta-
tions, various games, and under-the-counter movies. She had
no general interest in any of those items, nor were any on her
list. The store, although clean, possessed a certain kind of grime
that had built itself on the sand and dust tracked in by customers. The florescent tube lighting produced a grayish light,
and left artificial shadows on shelves and counters. Her mind
seemed dulled. She worked too much or too little she thought
and shopping did not stimulate or excite or expand. Her reason for being in that HyperPanda at that moment was not to
ensure sustenance, but it was also not to find the pleasure of
using money. To her right she gazed towards the appliances
section. Two island sets of shelving moved away from her as
she moved in their direction. She had not had toast in months:
not since a very hungover breakfast in a hotel in New Delhi.

Whirlwinds never did work for Elizabeth. She fumbled back
those sixteen months. The sweat of her palm seeped into the paper of the list. She envisioned that room, sparse as it was, with
its tables and chairs. The night before Robert had suggested a
sushi buffet, which served all-you-can-drink drinks.—I cannot
think of a better time to go, Rob exclaimed. When Elizabeth

awoke, she could not tell if she was hungover from the mai tais or the dragon rolls; did they drink more after? The food and drinks were delivered on a conveyor belt that moved between the various tables. It must have been in Friendship Colony or somewhere. Elizabeth could not think.—Where was that place? I always talked to the auto-drivers; I should remember. Their lives were more exciting in those days. Elizabeth did not enjoy drunkenness, and neither did Robert, but the expatriates they went around with were entertaining to watch in their stupors. Kingfishers and duty-free, they would drink themselves silly in the evenings. When they arose from their poisonings, they went off to help at an AIDS clinic or orphanage. Some had paying jobs. Robert and Elizabeth were in Delhi for a job that Robert had found doing community planning and outreach. The vague department he worked at coordinated events in different neighborhoods throughout the city to benefit the poor and Robert planned logistics. Elizabeth consulted the many from the United States and Great Britain and found a volunteer position reading books to young children. She discovered on her first day that the entire library of books was in German and that the administrators did not care. And so, she played with the children until lunch, wherein she scrambled to a bookstore to find any children's books in English she could. What books she found she brought with her to the school. That afternoon she returned to their apartment and typed from memory as many stories as best she could. Once Robert got home, she made him go with her to buy a printer so that she could make more books. In total, she typed 13 stories and a partial collections of Grimm's tales.—Why did I do that when I could have simply interneted? When the administrators discovered these handmade literatures, they asked Elizabeth to leave.—We did not approve of these acquisitions. The Admins were from Washington, D.C. and they were as cultured as they were heartless.

When Elizabeth last ate toast, she spoke to Robert.—I would like to see about PhDs eventually. Damn I feel sick, but no better time. Rob, listen, I know that you are attached to life abroad, but I would like to find a compromise. I have so many ideas for research that I just cannot see through out here. It is not the people or the place, but that I need a university. Rob shrugged at her.—Yeah, but how boring will it be to go back? It's so different out here . . . So different out there, he waved his hand aimlessly. Elizabeth did not continue pressing.—In time, Elizabeth, I want to go back too. But you see, I am just beginning. Soon we will have more of an idea.

The toast and eggs were brought to their table. Elizabeth looked outside to the tree and back down to her mango lassi. The notion of breakfast had been a mistake. Soon the mixture of lassi, egg, toast, and juice inside of her stomach began to rise up. She vomited and looked at her partially digested food and bile in the restaurant bathroom. She found herself so repulsed by the sight of this. She convinced herself that it was the previous night's fish that had done this to her. She could not believe that she still ate meat. She forced a guilt upon herself that remained in the back of her mind for years, and she decided not to eat meat ever again. She was in her very late twenties and had simply matured past it, or so she would tell Robert. But in reality, she puked in the bathroom of a New Delhi restaurant and hated herself because of where she was and was not. When she returned to the table she did not finish her toast or lassi. She and Robert sat across from one another. Usually at that time, they sat next to one another, but Elizabeth could not handle physical contact with her sickness. She was thankful that no one had joined them for this meal. In silence, Rob reached for her toast and ate it with jelly.

Elizabeth was still standing in front of the technologies facing the appliances. She set the list in her cart. It already had signs of being handled by clammy hands. She stared blankly.

The expatriates she knew here were no different from those she had known in New Delhi, except for their wealth, of course. Here the Americans were limited outside of the walls of their compounds, but inside they lived the same idiot abroad way that they did elsewhere. The cultural isolationism that forced these people into compounds was somewhat kind to Americans; it prevented them from getting too many looks. The physical barrier did nothing to change or alter their exceptionalist views of themselves. They still degraded and condescended to the people around them. They did not establish community with locals. In New Delhi, the expats ate in restaurants with the affluent youth of the city. They met Indians who ached to be European or American, and with them acted out a subtle separation of culture.

In both India and Saudi, Elizabeth knew Americans that engaged in slum tours. These people gathered on a Saturday morning to go view poor people in the collapsing housing absent of sanitation. Some treated these events like a kind of art,—To have seen a slum in India is akin to a fine gallery in Western Europe, but a slum in Saudi is something exotic and rare, a true privilege. Slowly the vans would go down the oppressed streets of beggars and homeless children. Dickensian or Orwellian or Kafkaesque they captured pictures of these victimized people, who had no money for food or shelter or fun. Being told not to give to any person on those streets, the white people refused to get out of their vans in those newly remembered neighborhoods. The people who were gawked at and objectified, turned into cultural objects, were unable to drive these vehicles of tourists from their homes. The police, if present at all, mocked and belittled them. Many of the people noticed this and decried the actions of the police, condemned their barbarisms.

Elizabeth had never been on such a tour. She openly criticized those who did, which meant that whenever Robert had the chance to see a poor place he did so, but secretly. The bullshit of that privilege and entitlement made Elizabeth red in the face; she cursed when the people laughed and reminisced about such things. —Stand and hold hands with your privilege, fuckers. To believe that over the centuries, humans had developed a taste for different kinds of poor people . . . That there was a sophistication to various forms of poverty. The authenticity and hardship of these low-income areas were discussed in order to assess which area was worse. They would ask,—Were the schools substandard as well?—Were the sewers up-to-date?—Were there religious institutions in the area?—How clean were the streets?—Did you see their clothing?—Did any of the children laugh? The abstract division of one set of humans from another, thought Elizabeth, was the most fundamentally hateful decision that any creature could have ever reached. That division acted as the foundation that supported the slums and ghettos. That division allowed for a simple creation of monetary objects, things that gutted and destroyed barter systems, and were invented by the same people who possessed them. Some of the earliest printed coins came from India.

Elizabeth's hands hurt, she was gripping the handle of the cart with such intensity. She released her hold and rubbed her hands. Still people prayed. It had only been a few minutes. Her cart still sat empty. She decided to view the appliances first, after all she had taken all of the cash in the house. She would have no use for Saudi riyals in the States so why not leave Robert a parting gift.

• • •

Patrick walked into the office building and went up. One o'clock. Patrick was testing his bounds with lamb meat lunches without realizing it. Amongst the desks was a Canadian man dressed in baggy pants and an ill-fitting shirt. He laughed stupidly. —Patrick! Managers said names with that cadence. His name was Malcolm and he was one of Patrick's bosses. Malcolm was an alcoholic.—Pat, I'm an alcoholic. He had his teeth knocked out at the bottom of the bottle.—Hit the bottom, but I'm sure I'll tell ya about that later . . . The replacements were quite believable.—Aren't they nice? He smelled of smoke and droned on about American patents.—You smoke, Pat? His laugh, though dumb, was genuine and unique in such a low level way that made him appear affectionate. He offered quick winks to some of the men about the office. He knew things. Prostitutes handed out by Mamasan, as he called her,— MamahahahaSAN! He'd almost been arrested for soliciting in Canada, but he was a Mason or whatever and that helped.

—It's a pleasure to meet you, Patrick spoke softly,—I'm the replacement as you know. Damn that PhD. Patrick slumped over to his desk, full of meat and potatoes.—You'll have a great time here, Malcolm called,—Great time. Patrick set about his numbers again and wondered if he'd be here long enough to have a good time.

Malcolm took to Patrick well. He pestered him enough, distracting him easily away from his accounts at times, to speak more with the meek man who hid his height. A kind of friendship developed between them as they finally reviewed the accounts that Patrick had charge of. This was the only kind of training he would receive and this relationship was something that neither had experienced before. Malcolm was much older than Patrick, and yet Patrick still had a deeply rooted fear of physical violence coming from this man. In that respect, it was difficult to tell Malcolm no.

Malcolm had a manic sense about him that Patrick couldn't understand. No alcohol. He'd given that up with his ideas about committed relationships and his home in Canada. Malcolm's appetite was grand. His understanding of the geography of the city was enormous and he knew where to find good cuts of meat, women, cheap rental cars, good clothes and middle-priced dates. The Irishman captivated Malcolm, whose supposed heritage thrust him into demonstrating a kind of solidarity with Patrick.—Fuck the Queen, eh? Patrick had few things to be proud of other than his hatred for the monarchy. As he and Malcolm sat considering the accounts at the end of the day, Patrick thought deeply about what had brought this Canadian here. The obvious answer would be the alcohol. But Patrick was concerned with what was underneath that. He lost himself for a moment as he stared at Malcolm. They decided to leave work together, as Malcolm would show Patrick through the mall.

He would show all there was. And he smoked everywhere. Along the corridors of the very clean modern *suq*, he would light a cigarette casually and if a guard or anyone else approached him, he would mock them as he finished and put the butt out.— My bad, my bad. He explained to Patrick that when he quit drinking he had to have something, some kind of dependency to continue. —Destroys my lungs, but life is death anyways. Sure, nicotine and tar and all that can kill, but I'd be dead already if it weren't for it all. I wasn't alive when I was drunk; I was a zombie. So like a lot of American Christians, I am reborn. Malcolm was convinced that his physical body would have died had he kept up his drinking, but he put it all so casually for Patrick that it almost seemed contrived. As if Malcolm was forsaking the consumption of alcohol to fit in with people who all had some malfunction.—To be a part of the group, one needs something, really anything, wrong with them. Abnormal is the new normal, or so I feel. The mall presented itself as a paradigm of order and constancy. Against it, Malcolm set himself up as a misfit, an oddball fit for Patrick's consumption.

Patrick was relieved that this Malcolm fellow had been doing all of this. It meant that someone was trying to socialize with Patrick and that he did not need to put any effort at finding human contact. It seemed that most of the people who worked for OIL ETC were from Canada or the UK. There were no other Irishmen, at least according to Malcolm. The company itself acted as a liaison between firms and governments. When an oil company had to report to a government, OIL ETC was brought in to mediate and make sure that everyone remained at least a millionaire. Patrick had only known of his own position. He had not spent the time googling the company to know anything more than his job description. Malcolm loved the idea of it.—Keeping the rich and powerful in place, lubricating it all.

Malcolm claimed he was rich. He didn't speak like he was rich, but that was ok. He seemed to be becoming Patrick's friend. Malcolm told Patrick stories about himself, regardless of who listened. Malcolm sensed that Patrick could be a friend and a passive friend could do Malcolm good. As they navigated the mall, neither found anything worth purchase. Patrick was still tight on money, awaiting an advance from the company, and Malcolm had no need for any of what he saw. He did spend a long time considering scents at a department store. In the end he decided that he did not need to mask his own musk any more than he already did. Malcolm and Patrick got into a taxi and Malcolm instructed the Indian driver how to get to a place to smoke and related a story to Patrick:

—I left Canada a long time back. I know you're running. I don't know if it's to or from but no one knows that. The violence and the alcohol got me. Clichés and cigarettes for me now. I remember one time. I was at a bar and a bunch of oil guys had just come south from the fields. I am sure they had just been paid and were ready to have their way in the town. I always drank whiskey with whatever and I don't remember what I had it with that night. There was some bullshit on the TV and we bet on it. It was a rerun of a gameshow, *Family Feud* or something. These dudes had so much money and a lot of them had it in cash, you know, the stop by the bank and take it all out sorta thing; afraid of the government. The last thing I remember was a guy in flannel telling me to bet on the TV.

—The next morning I woke up to a cop staring down at me and not a single one of my front teeth in my mouth. Here Malcolm took out his front teeth and looked to his right at Patrick with a grin before re-inserting his incisors, canines, and premolars. The cop told me this, Malcolm? We found you last night on the sidewalk just past Joan's Bar. Do you have any memory of being there? He knew I didn't. We don't know who exactly knocked your teeth out, but Joan herself told us what you'd been up to. She said you were betting money you didn't have on some TV show with some men from up north. She said you lost and that you stormed out and got into your car after drinking more than anyone else in the bar and she sent those men you owed money to after you. She says they stopped you from driving off and might've roughed you up a bit, but it looks like the liquid diet you'll be having is more than just a bit. Anyway, Joan won't tell us who the men were, which is her right. I knew what happened. I didn't need to be there, at this Malcolm pointed to his head,—To know that. I told them to fuck themselves. I told them their goddamned mother's should've smothered 'em. I told 'em all kinds of shit. Because that is my violence. I bet I got at least three hits in on those bastards before they had me on the ground, their boots on my teeth. But my violence worked. The words, Patrick, those are what's at stake here. They threw me down to the bottom, but I'm better for the false teeth. What they gave me was the truth of my own brutality. I can assemble severe words in any state and they proved my own effectiveness, my talent.

—What happened then was they tried to remove my force from my mouth and they did, albeit temporarily. But in stopping short of ripping out my tongue, they allowed me to maintain my voice. So I looked at that cop and told him I'd quit drinking and I did. I told him I did not care who kicked my teeth in and that whoever it was should be happy they did such a good job at it. I left the taste for liquor behind and moved on, paying more conscious attention to my speaking abilities. That's why I can get a job selling things to people I don't know or care about. You know, I don't need Canada or booze to win. I can convince anyone of everything, just as I convinced those oil fucks that their mothers were all whores and they were just lowly brutes. So I've focused my energies onto gaining from my talent. My violence has mutated into persuasion. Every day I am presented with a new group of humans to persuade. It may be some businessman from Africa, a call-girl from China, you, what does it matter? I have risen above the rudiments of language and begun my own pursuit of power. The politicians have it mixed up, you see. Those who go unseen and live their lives with the utmost knowledge of their own power over others are able to extract the most positive results. The problem with my alcohol was the fact that it made me visible and reckless. It made my emotions and urges known and when I exerted any kind of power over others, it was done out of belligerent violence, not subtle and overwhelming power. I'd love to meet those oil men again and thank them. I needed my teeth kicked in to realize what my mouth was really capable of.

—Now, you crunch numbers, give them to me, and I calm everyone down. In the end all is well. If we get bored, we could fuck with them all. Perhaps, if I ever want to leave I can remove calculation from the interaction and stir it all.

At their destination, the two men entered an old building with an open courtyard that was filled with men and palm trees. The two sat on the ground.—Patrick, I do not want to confuse you. I rarely understand another human's will outside of when I have manipulated it. I relate this to you because I know that your silence acts as your voice and that terrifies me. Needless to say, I can find you what you want here. For liquor stores you're on your own, but do not hesitate to request a woman or whatever else. The Irishman nodded and looked around, letting the noises of the place wash away Malcolm's presence.—It is good to have a violent man befriend you. In this city, Patrick was unsure of his own bearings, and to him it was advantageous to have someone who could be confident for him. Malcolm was not the kind of friend he would have forever. Their knowing one another depended entirely on location. Never would they interact in Dublin, London, or Toronto. Confined here, they could use each other. Elsewhere, their friendship would be of no use.

To Patrick the place where these men smoked seemed pleasant enough. All around men smoked and talked and watched sports, and Indians shuffled about with fresh coals. The walls of the building were dyed brown and all of the men sat on rugs with various pillows in short walled cubicles. Some drank tea or soda, while all smoked and talked. The talk could not stop— Hamed! Hamed! Moya! Malcolm smoked and talked as well. Patrick mostly ignored him still and Malcolm didn't mind. He was almost sure that here he would be able to meet Qataris.

It seemed that Malcolm took him to find these people in order to prove his knowledge of their country. The content of the speech did not matter to Patrick now, instead it was the confidence. To be able to show off a geographical understanding. The awareness of such a former transformation, from one form of violence to another and its use as a talent, a kind of ever-present strategy, made Patrick interested in understanding himself more. Malcolm lacked a filter, and his understanding of that allowed him to develop his own kind of self-censorship, a powerful tool when surrounded by money.

Here were Arabs. Patrick gazed at them. Crisp white linens everywhere around him. Smoke. Patrick heard another call. It pulsated. Malcolm stopped talking. The air began to fill with calls. One at first. Then three more. The sun was casting shadows around the palms. All of the men sat on the ground. Patrick crossed his legs and sweated. The call continued. Both of the white men observed the prayers as something they could not understand but must listen to.—That need, Patrick said quietly to himself.—The up and down of money grabbing. Bloodshed in the numbers. Allow one's self to derive potency from those numbers and show how people need the abstractions to persist. A diet of calories, water, server farms and magnetic strips. Update the wiki to let the people know. A change in the software to allow the people to starve for what I care. Trickles of media and bad news let the people know that they are alive. The worse the news, the more alive they all feel. The numbers, our gods. The numbers are not persuasive or violent. The numbers are strength. A fervent kind of strength that people fear at night and love by day.

The two expatriates smoked the last of their tobacco. Malcolm and Patrick had reached an agreement.

6

In the van, the two Canadians had an open bottle of wine and a liter of Pepsi that was half filled with rum. Scott and Jim drank as Scott drove through the shiny, well-cleaned streets. Manama was rich and polished. Slick palms and low green bushes rose out of the medians in the roads. The traffic slowed their movement away from the airport. The group crossed a bridge into the city center. Hotels and office buildings towered over the highways in the fading sun: windows clean, doors swinging. Cars on the highway buzzed, windows up. James could not see the drivers. The traffic got worse. On their left a sedan drove pass and Scott laughed,—A woman! Look, Jim, a woman driver. Jim leaned violently across Scott who was driving.— Well, damn. The two were stinky with their surprise. They both seemed satisfied with the rarity of it all. It looked and sounded as if Jim and Scott noted each woman driver so as to mock the Saudis: they were brothers from Canada; surely their mother drove a car. It was obvious to James that these men should mock the people that surrounded them. The criticism had a certain amount of nuance to it, but was so simple that James believed them to have no others. Certainly, neither Scott not Jim would have any deeply rooted arguments against Saudi humanitarian violations or transgressions. It would be too complicated for these two to create an in-depth argument against the government that ruled where they lived and worked.

They sat in the van with the air conditioning cooling them and finished the wine and rum.—Drink it, gents, Jim said,—While we have it. James got slightly drunk. Gary sat next to him and only laughed and said he'd have preferred weed, but the rum was fine.—Something about the calmness, you know, and Jim nodded.—You're right about that, but the rolling and the packing, I just do not have the hand-eye coordination. Gary's white hair made him look older than he really was. The alcohol relaxed him. The jumpy quality of his voice receded and he seemed more normal. Jim leaned back and on learning that James and Gary had never taught before was surprised they had gotten the job. Jim talked to them about it: teaching incoming university students, being a part of their adjustment to university life.—You two have been young, right? Jim's haughtiness shone in these moments.

For weeks to come, Gary and James would find each other in the hallways and checkup. This was limited once James and Gary found their own allies amongst their colleagues, but for the first month or so it was pleasant. James tried his best to be modest with Gary, whose vocabulary and cadence were simple. James, who was able to talk about literature, music, and philosophy, soon fascinated many of his fellow teachers. So fresh he was with them, using his wit and vitality to establish what his age could not. Gary took on with a different crowd. There never developed any animosity, very much so because of their having reached this country and compound in unison. On occasion, they would meet and laugh about what they had gone through on that day, so many weeks or months past. There was a component of sadness to these talks, which they ignored with the interaction's brevity.

With the pleasantries aside, Scott wanted to know if they'd like a proper drink before crossing the border.—Let's show them something, Scott's voice was harsh,—Give them something to remember. He looked to Jim at his side and James and Gary behind him in the traffic. Scott's idea was that visiting a public house would allow them to avoid the rest of the traffic in front of them.—Wait it out, patience is a virtue and all that. Of course. James hadn't realized that there would be bars in Manama. He'd heard rumors from some of the teachers he had spoken to that he would be interested in visiting the town. Gary said,—Yeah, why shouldn't we? Scott laughed loudly at this. Jim's carefree sensibility was exacerbated and he screamed,—Diggers! They changed their route and headed deeper into the city where they were to find this Digger's. The traffic opened up as they made their way. As they left the wider highways, the narrowness of the city impressed James. The polishedness of what he had seen faded as they slowly moved inward.

The haze of the rum affected James. He looked out of his window. He wanted to take pictures of what surrounded him, so that he would be able to show his mother and father where he had landed. For the rest of the ride in the van he was proud of how far he had come. He did not notice the desperation implied in having to move so far away to find work.

He rested in the back of the vehicle and laughed at his progress. James had done it. When those around him thought it ridiculous to go, he had proven that he could do it. Regardless of where he was headed, of what he would spend the next years trying to comprehend, he had at least made it in terms of geography. He had moved himself far enough away from his own comforts that he thought he had succeeded in reaching some new level of maturity. In truth, it would take him some time to realize a new sense of mature well-being. He was not ready for immersion in another culture. But at that time, at that moment in flux, that was of no concern to him.

A Toast

The toasters, on a middle-height shelf around her navel were black, silver, dull white, red, and grey. She felt one hesitantly, her hand reaching away from the flowing black of her coverings. —What world have I traveled to? She posited the question without reluctance, quietly, as if speaking to someone of importance. In that touch she noticed behind her a woman of amiable quality, looking at her with questioning eyes.—Certainly, I have moved or been moved from my world. Can you say to what extent I can claim this as a friendly world? In her youth, Elizabeth had dreamed of moving to Greece. In the Mediterranean, she would meet a well-traveled and multilingual man, and fall deeply in love with him. But her dream, one that she wrote of constantly in journals and on napkins at fast-food restaurants, had no pleasant ending. She wanted the mother of this man to forbid marriage, as Elizabeth was not a Greek Orthodox Christian. In a fury, the love affair would be broken without the man's knowledge and Elizabeth would move calmly back to Michigan. She knew that she had no claim to that Greek fantasy, and nor did she have a claim to where she currently stood.

The woman behind her was a reassuring illusion. The eyes of this ghost spoke to her of a need to question, to parse and re-parse her world and to commit with confidence to her conclusions. There was no woman looking at toasters besides Elizabeth. —Still, she reiterated,—Is this a friendly world? What can I say constitutes a friendly world? Being at ease? Feeling safe? Is that all? Friendliness implies more than unmolested existence. It asserts a sense of common interest. In that way this world is unfriendly, for its lack of public art and insistence on gender segregation. But am I then belittling it for what lies on the surface? I have felt commonality with my students. There must, of course, be people in this place who love art and cherish expression. I must then find a balance between what the king decrees from on high and what the people truly feel. Yet, with the separation between cultures here it is legitimately difficult to judge; without explicitly asking the people in this store, without interrupting their prayers for my own intellectual needs, how am I to tell? Abdelrahman would know? Or, at least he would be so kind as to . . . Perhaps I ought to generate a prompt for my students about what they define friendliness as.

At the university, Elizabeth's English students impressed upon her the importance of her own understanding of herself. They shed their *abayas* and *hijabs*, their outer layers, on the women's campus and wore European and American clothes to their classes. She sensed a kind of openness in her students that she did not see in them on the streets or in family sections of restaurants.—But what is it to live in a place and not fully understand one's position in that geography? Can a friendliness develop with my part-time involvement in community? How could I possibly act as an advocate for rights outside of the classroom? Should I return home and spread the word of women who are so oppressed and maltreated? I see their faces three days a week, elated at the supposed freedom of my classroom, but how can freedom be boxed in by windowless walls? Even with that enthusiasm, some of them are hesitant or silent in class. They are not all *Girls of Riyadh*, nor do they all wish to be. Could I be an advocate when the people I most commonly associate with want nothing to do with my students or their families? Saudi does not welcome humanitarian groups or developers. If I am then unwelcome as a proponent of women's rights, what risk is it appropriate that I take while within the borders of this kingdom to speak about what I feel needs to happen? Ought I risk my own health and well-being for these people? Should I appeal to those in the States? The internet would allow me to subvert, to reach out: hell, even al-Sanea saw that and her book is fairly fluffy. And doesn't she live in Chicago? Munif had his citizenship taken away from him for political reasons. Al-Hamad's heart is in the right place, but he has some learning to do about sexism . . . I am digressing. What use would it be to anonymously call Americans to action; they already have such negative and generalizing views of Arabs. It would be attempting to kickstart a dead horse. I could take the risk of asking a student.

Elizabeth shared her aspirations for further study with her students one semester. She described different programs and their requirements, ignoring the lesson plan for that day. Afterword, she felt superficial to have done so. She had a feeling that her students would be positive towards her in most situations, so long as there were not any adverse potential outcomes to a discussion or activity. As shallow as it initially seemed, Elizabeth more and more launched into personal stories, allowing them a deeper glimpse into her life. Because she had a new group each semester, she was able to refine each story so as to elicit the most excitement and wonder from her attentive and gladly respectful students. Listening to stories in English was valuable practice after all, and she began to work these times into her syllabus in the second semester of part-time teaching.

The populations of her classes responded kindly to her, but still Elizabeth could not understand the deeper semantics of her orientation. The dust of the display accumulated darkly on her finger, and she remembered her reluctance towards Robert and the marriage. They had stood in a courthouse in Detroit during the spring and their witness was a friend of Elizabeth's, —You need a witness and don't know who to ask? Elizabeth blushed, embarrassed. —Listen, it won't last long and we will pick up some drinks afterward. Robert wants this job and says that being married is an actual factor and we have lived together for years now . . . Jacky, who could be persuaded by Elizabeth with little effort, agreed to witness the nuptials. None of the three had met the judge before. —Do you take Robert, she intoned lazily.—Do you take Elizabeth? And so on it went, Jacky all the while humming the tune of *I Can Change* in her head and staring mostly down at her shoes.

The entire event lasted less than an hour and prompted Elizabeth to create a certain, less than willful, fantasy to tell her students. Their families gathered on a lawn with suits and dresses. Some kind of religious figure presided. Fathers cried and mothers wept. Elizabeth pledged to her class that the event was beautiful and well-planned. Everyone involved had worn their formal attire so well and the food tasted fresh and satisfying. The dancing, the part of the story that elicited the most laughs and smiles, was fun and well-timed. Hardly a single person stood still, and those who did only needed a break from the fantastic band that took requests and played all of the songs Elizabeth could imagine wanting to hear on a comfortable Michigan lawn in late spring. Then she would forget the most important part of the story, intentionally of course.

Here she built an assignment into the narrative. She began to recount the toast. Her mother and father gave it together and a single tear ran down her father's cheek.—So proud and happy for the future. He gloated to his friends about her and her mother awoke each day happy with the work they had done as parents. Elizabeth went so far as to brainstorm actual lines from this speech, the bits that would stick with her for the rest of her days,—I knew Elizabeth was in love with Robert when, and so on, nothing subtle. When she noticed that she had deeply affected the class, she split them into pairs and had them write toasts for each other's weddings. She knew that their weddings in Saudi, those that had already happened or those that would in the future, would not have champagne or bands playing covers of ABBA, but the idea was romantic and teachable. Her tale would cease, and so would her imagined narcissism and nostalgia. With relish her students would discuss what their weddings had been like or what they dreamed they would be and soon the class buzzed with pencils meeting papers. The day of this activity was amongst the most exciting and happy days each semester, even if it fit into heteronormative gender stereotypes.

But the high of her success in the lesson dissolved quickly and she remembered visiting a bar after the courthouse. It would be easier to get proper visas to Saudi if they were married. Life in general would be simpler for a married couple than it would for two people having to pretend. Elizabeth had written a small speech about the good times and bad that she wanted to share with Robert, but in Robert's rush the judge skipped past any opportunity to share written vows. Robert did not hurry the ceremony maliciously; he had no idea of Elizabeth's efforts. She had meant it to be a secret and did not speak up when she ought to have. At first she regretted not sharing her promises and assurances with Rob, but then she realized that they would be over his head. She had wasted the time she spent justifying her relationship. The vocabulary she had used to describe this to Robert was not shared; he would not be able to enter the discourse. He would be baffled at the conciseness of her assertions. Most likely, Robert would accept her words immediately and without contest and she would leave. After Elizabeth had spent so much time creating an alternate version of their relationship, that Robert would never hear, she could end it all so simply, likely with less than five sentences. The ghost behind her remained and placed an invisible hand on her shoulder, a mental symbol of solidarity and encouragement.—Make your own friendly world; you know how.

7

Digger's was no joke. Australian themed and small, Digger's sat on the bottom floor of a hotel run by some Indian businessmen. When the brothers from Mumbai opened it, their father worked with men from Bahrain. The business suffered from its lack of ambiance. The two men moped around town. An Australian, with whom the brothers often discussed politics and who worked in media relations for the king, suggested that they bring entertainment into the place.

—Walking through the entrance you can feel the stickiness on the bottom of your shoes, the tan Aussie mentioned this to the brothers.—It deserves something that fit the dimness and dinginess. Inside, there was an empty stage at one end and a bar running two-thirds of the way down the length of the establishment. The two brothers sought after entertainment. They sent after musicians and women, all the while avoiding showing the establishment to their parents, whose natural reaction to the business was familial pride, a pride that would be easily withdrawn should their sons play around too much.

Jim got four Guinnesses and they sat at a table near the empty stage under intensely artificial lighting. No windows allowed natural evening light through the walls of Digger's. The particle board and plywood had been painted black on nearly every surface. Behind the bar, some neon lighting cast further artificial shades around the place. The bartenders took care of the late afternoon patrons. James sensed there would be a different feel to a place such as this at night. It looked sober in its fluorescence. There was a kind of mumble to the bar at that time. In the air, it was suggested that all of these people were recovering from the previous night by preparing for the upcoming evening. The hair of the dogs that bit all of these people was distributed in a reverence for money and what it could buy. Towards the stage, the tables had ashtrays that went partially cleaned. James smoked and drank his beer as Gary listened to Jim's stories.—I drive a motorcycle over there, he meant Saudi, of course, and we will teach you how to drive one too. It is the fastest way around al-Ahasa. Gary looked skeptical.—Isn't it dangerous? Jim laughed,—That's what I love about it. Scott occupied himself with a woman across the room. However bare Digger's was, it had an egalitarian nature to it. All were equal in Digger's so long as they spent money. Those who spent were separate from those who were treated as objects and bought and sold. James and Gary were ignorant of this, but both felt as if they were in a market that was empty, after everything had been haggled over and sold.

It was brighter than he would have liked it to be. Inside, there were a few men, Indians, Americans, and presumably some Arabs, and many Chinese women. The women approached and sat by them with Scott, who described the country:

—It's a great place for a weekend away. Not a dry country, so you can get good stuff. No moonshine here. We spend a lot of weekends here. They have cinemas and bars. Digger's is great. They have a great band. A good Filipino cover band. They'll play any song you like. You'll be back here at some point. It's good to stop off for a drink before going back to the desert.

As he spoke he fondled the woman he had brought with him to the table. She sat on Scott's lap. Scott had a kid in America, Jessica. She played basketball for her school and was eight years old. During the summer she visited her father. He told her about the desert and the camels. At school, when her father lived so far away, she gloated that he was an explorer and adventurer. She assumed that, because he lived so far away, he must be more talented or capable than the other parents she knew. A few years earlier, all had been different. One day her mother had packed their things and they moved: her father could not afford the house anymore so they went. Scott sold that house. He had become unemployed and his drinking had pushed Jessica's mother to her limit. She had no patience for the father of her daughter. For months she had longingly looked at apartment listings while at work. Her job afforded her enough to live with her daughter comfortably and so she moved away from Scott and closer to work and school. Scott, in his kindness, remained accepting of all of this. He visited with Jessica often, but within months had been offered a job to teach in Saudi with his brother: he had forged a resumé out of desperation and the company, at Jim's suggestion, did not check references. He had fooled his way into money by way of family connections, but distance would be the sacrifice.

Scott had a daughter whom he'd never tell of Tina or Xiaoqing as she was really named.

Xiaoqing boarded a plane two years earlier not yet fully aware of where she was going. The Bahraini government knew her as a masseuse, the kind that Navy men would visit periodically and some businessmen as well. Xiaoqing, with the help of her madam (a retired prostitute who had stayed in Manama to manage the business), developed a system known as boyfriending, which she enacted with skill upon Scott.

She knew that Scott's passion for drink would drive him crazy late in the evening, so after one late night session, she got his phone number and began to send him a series of messages. The system was slow, but sudden. She'd want to see him earlier in the day. When boyfriending, Xiaoqing would make a man lust after her so heartily that lunches and presents would be bonuses to the payment she already received for her massages. In this way, she supplemented her lonely income. Madam told her that her life was limited by the place she found herself in, and so she would need to do something for herself.—Live so that you do not dread waking up in the morning. Xiaoqing sulked when she arrived in Manama. Her removal from her home was a blur to her. The city rose around her in its smallness. She had not had a chance to say goodbye to her family. Madam knew she needed some help to make her life livable and so had taught her the system.

Xiaoqing was talented at the nuance of it. She had learned to balance and could have multiple boyfriends simultaneously. In tandem with Scott were an ARAMCO oilman from Georgia, a member of the American consulate in Manama, and as of the previous 3 am, Jim. This play, unwittingly developed by Xiaoqing in a situation involving two architects from Virginia and their wives, saw Jim being convinced that the beautiful Xiaoqing had fallen for him, so much so that she would even consider leaving her profession for his sake, but that she knew it to be impossible. This, considering his ego, flattered and thrilled Jim, and insofar as he was Scott's biological brother, and he did not assume a playful or condescending tone with the man behind whose back Xiaoqing moved. It was a wink that capitalized upon Jim's ignorance and illuminated Scott's.

For the coming weeks, Xiaoqing would not live happily, but she would eat better and have some new clothes. Her nostalgia and longing for home had been lifted from her shoulders: she became interested in simple pleasures and deadened to much of her reality. Her resigned nature was seen as coolness by Jim and coyness by Scott. Madam laughed at her success with the two Canadians, but warned her of violence,—Do not get too near the line, lest you step over it. There was a devil in Scott and Madam believed that Xiaoqing would awaken it with her tricks.—You must exercise caution.

Scott, who couldn't resist rum or beer even in those hot sands, would arrive earlier Wednesday afternoon to begin drinking in the city. By occasionally contacting Scott throughout the week and saying that she missed him (despite the fact that she found him brutish and unintelligent), Xiaoqing had made him want to see her first.—Sober, she told him. Scott absent of liquor meant that he'd be quieter and more reserved. The reason was that he never had many thoughtful things to say and therefore did not have the courage to say anything from the list of never ending illogical things that he did have to say, for example,—Good 'ns those chink types, or—Where is the classic rock 80s Crüe loud stereo?, or—My kid knows me and I know it, or finally—Fackin' cocksuckers know who plays hockey 'round here. To make up for his lack of verbiage, Scott would buy food or gifts, mostly women's clothes and candles, and hand them over to Xiaoqing and say,—Tiny Tina happy! Xiaoqing was then able to share those trinkets with newly arrived masseuses, Madam, or enjoy them herself in the small room she called home across town. It was the sharing that fundamentally calmed her. Her sadness moved away, along with her homesickness, because she could work a smile onto the face of even the most sleep-deprived and upset of her colleagues.

The basis of her tolerance for Scott rested on his money. As her customers viewed her body, she associated them with the objects they could provide. Deep within her she had only two goals: to return to her home before her mother died and not to kill herself before then. The gifts she received did well at improving her wellness, although she did not believe that she could be whole once more. Scott's personality reminded her of the two men that tricked her those many months earlier. The quickness of their actions resulted in her kidnapping and enslavement. She wanted to know why Madam stayed so long in

Manama, but did not ask out of fear. The drugs that she had been injected with lifted their effects as she boarded a plane. Upon landing, Xiaoqing knew for certain the trajectory of her future. She felt thankful only for Madam's system, which could be used to provide a certain amount of happiness through simple materialism. Xiaoqing understood the most that could be had by herself and the others, and that it was not much at all. Her job was not only to serve these men, but to be a sad person of the Earth, who also served the people who were sad about such existences as hers, even though they never did a single thing in their lives to help. The truth of it was that as much as these people loved to write and be sad about the mistreated peoples of the world, so much did they also enjoy exploiting them. Not only for their philanthropic causes, which padded their bank accounts, but also for their own mental reassurance that they were awake to the cruelty of the world.

Scott and Xiaoqing had met on those afternoons during his time off and had fucked for the past three weeks. Today, she had received a message from him after he was supposed to have left and she appeared at Digger's knowing there would be no sex, but drinks and maybe food. She noticed that Jim was drunk, and that there were two new men with them. The first, a white man with whiter hair, would be too easy for her to manipulate; she would have to remember his face. The second was kind, but had a look of passive anger or sternness to him. His skin was a deep brown and his short hair was well kept and natural, but had suffered from travel and lack of sleep. This one did not look at any of the women with lust or interest; she felt a curiosity in his eyes, and knew that he suffered to see all of this. Xiaoqing laughed at him and sat on Scott's lap.

Patrick woke up. Midnight. The blinds had been opened and the bay flickered with sleepy life. The palms blended into the darkness. He rose. His feet were fat, and not long. He had slept in his clothes and when looking in the mirror could not notice a degradation in his appearance. He took the elevator down and left the Sheraton. He disliked the closed and temporary feeling of hotel rooms at night. The service staff of the hotel looked pleasant for the time, not being bothered by people sober to the fact of their location. Further down, the Irish bar would be half full with patrons. The bartenders thought of the men and women that surrounded them with a kind of disdainful admiration.

One barkeep called himself Brian. So many people in the Harp called him that that he seldom remembered he had another name. Brian seemed fine with him.—Easier for them to pronounce. He had chosen it at school, long before he would have even thought of selling liquor to white people. The idea of taking American names thrilled all of the children there. They grew more excited, the more possible names were presented. The teacher, whose brother had gone to America, spoke fondly of the name Johnny,—That's what he called himself there at the factory. She gave the students some time to decide how they would be called, to select their new selves.

She wondered if any of her pupils comprehended the symbolism of it, to pick their own name. Likely not. They simply saw it as fun, as play. One of the students asked her what her English name was.—Jenny, she replied with a smile. She had seen movies with Jennys in them. For some reason she imagined herself as a blonde Jenny. She did not especially want to leave her home for America as her brother had, or as her cousin who was a maid in Arabia.

Many of the students started sharing their names. Brian remembered that there were three other Brians.—I am Brian the number one! Another laughed,—I am Brian the first! The simplicity of the name resonated with them: it was easy to remember and to say.

In the Harp, he wondered where the other Brians were now. He wondered if it was possible that any of them had gotten more use out of the name than he had. Regulars knew him only by that.—Brian! A shot and a beer please. They had no idea what his father might call him. Never could they guess at how his mother might refer to him when relatives asked after him. It all seemed too easy for him to brand himself for these people. Some who had had enough to drink would ask where he was from. Even fewer asked if he was married, had any kids back home. He could not remember if any had asked his real name. Perhaps, they thought that all over the world people were assuming English and American names, finally conforming to the needs of the rich. But it was all a ploy.

All of the people who worked at the Harp went by an English or American name. They referred to each other by those names exclusively. Brian did not even know the real names of any other staff member.—Hey, Will!—How're you, Amber?—What's up, Denis?!—Why would one of these white people ask, if I do not even? He looked around the bar. The half-full dark room was slowly winding down for the evening. There would be more people, more tips, in the bar come weekend shifts. He marveled at how these people needed to sit in the dark after a day of working. Was the sun too strong for their soft skins? The Harp was a straightforward place to be. He visited an internet café upon arrival and took some notes on the wiki page about Ireland. Those notes were entirely irrelevant to his work. Instead, he needed to learn about beers and whiskeys, as well as the food that they served. It all came to him quickly and without worry.—Lamb with potatoes if the guest is very hungry, burger with fries for the picky patron, soup and salad special for the light eaters, chips and beer cheese dips as starter, Harp for people who do not enjoy heavy beers, Jim Beam for the unsophisticated American whiskey drinker. It all sounded simple in how it satisfied what they, all of these people who had their English names since birth, needed from life. Rarely was there a patron who ordered a variety of drinks or dishes. Once he had seen someone a few times, he had a general idea of what they wanted. Their predictability made him like them more, but still he was nothing more than indifferent to all of them. The worst thing was when they would talk to him about their problems. He had no idea about most of the things they were upset about.

Their relationships were fickle and superficial. Their thoughts about their peers were immature and underdeveloped. The way they navigated the world was naïve. What Brian was certain of was that there was no reason for these people to make any more money than he did. Their gripes were no heftier than anyone else's. Their debts were simple enough. He hoped that one day soon he would have enough to return home and not think about the salty heat of Doha. It would be a relief to leave behind all of these people who come to this bar. He remained impressed that these white people would think that he was a friend because he served them beer that had been shipped from as far as they had come. At the end of each shift, Brian would look at a world map he had brought with him and trace the distance between where he was and where he wanted to be.

His feelings for home were not strengthened by the people he met in Doha. He was only slightly nostalgic. It was simply that, with his body and mind, he wanted to escape them, to get away from them, for they bothered him on a much more fundamental level than he had ever known. He would need time to process how he had interacted with them. He would need space to consider what lessons they had taught him. He would need time and space.

Leaving the hotel and part way down the drive Patrick stopped. There weren't cars about. A silence had entered the air of Doha. The buildings shone dull in the night. He continued. Through the hedge to his left he could see the lights. He followed the hedge to its end and found a park.—Empty. He walked to the water. There again was the museum across from him.—Morning Star of someone. Patrick strolled along the curve of the bay. In painted boats, men slept. Across the bay he could see dozens of vessels and lights strung alongside red and blue and green panels. He stopped. The streets were quiet. He yawned. Patrick looked to a stone bench and sat. He recalled again that boat in sand. How much longer that boat would last than these here, but how much better these functioned. He thought:

—Alone. Sit and wonder where we all went. America. Arabia. Across the waters. Lots of energy for these lights and airplanes and taxis. Getting somewhere. What should a taxi driver say to a rich man? What to make out of the empty suggestion of public space? Where are the families? Emptiness like sparseness. Tours to nothing. Could there be people at the market at this hour? Poached eggs at tobacco moonlight. So late an hour and no degenerates. The darkness lulls to sleep the workers. If not for them, then who? Have these men no place to sleep but the boats? Could there be some moment, when the boat becomes unsecured from its moor and they float away? Surely, it must be an attraction to take all of the families and couples out onto the water. Who first had the thought to ship these men here and have them pilot these boats? The sickness they must get over when sleeping with all that rocking. It must be cash they make, but do they bank? There is no market for these men. Sailors confined: no seven seas. Because they've nowhere else to explore they take the small and make it large with monies. If I were to wake one of them would they take me about? If I could handle it, but no not likely.

The bay of Doha was calm. Somewhere, the city relaxed away the heat of daylight. Behind his back, the lights of the towers, the places of commerce, projected themselves on to the water, producing reflections for the lonesome Irishman. Occasionally, he heard a car drive past. A man stirred in one of the boats, but his own legs would not move. His focus drifted, and he was not able to draw into his mind any concrete ideas or figures. Even numbers failed him sometimes at night. The here and now of it settled him more solidly onto the stone bench. There was no matter in which he would make decisions at this time of night. There would be the complexity of reaching conclusions in life without the rigorous presence of his mother. She was not overbearing, but decisive. He would need to call her soon, to make his way to a bank and see about a cell phone. She would not factor the even-tempered nature of this body of water into her daily life as Patrick would. There may be, in some metaphysical way, a deeper respect for spaces that Patrick feared than for those he cherished. With his mother, he found an overlap: although fear and comfort were obverse, they were related for the man.

Being unsure, he did not wish to compare the presence of his mother, that is, sharing a location with her, to his fear of drowning, but he did so. It calmed him mentally to flirt with rude ideas, but he practiced to keep them inside of himself. His outbursts, although most often controlled, resembled a violence that he knew in others, that, for example, which Malcolm had confided in him. Malcolm's being in Doha with Patrick consoled him slightly. The ebb of his homesickness at times switched directions and knowing of such a person eased him. Once Patrick had gotten terribly sick while his mother was traveling and he realized how few people he knew in Dublin. Laura, having no desire to speak to him, would not care for him. He sat alone in bed wondering how he might ensure that his next bout of sickness would be aided by someone aside from his mother.

He could look into hiring some kind of help: a cleaning woman or someone similar. Then he would at least share a room with another human, or more importantly, have the option of not doing so. Patrick's concern was such that he could deny. He wanted badly to be able to turn down or reject, but more often than not he found himself not having the means. On the stone bench, he thought that perhaps Malcolm wished for that as well. He craved to deny people his violence, but still to exert himself upon them. There would be no time for his provocation when he would be able to glean from them what he yearned for. Malcolm was smarter for it. Patrick did not know how he would adjust his person to be better suited to having such a friend.

Patrick had always contemplated moving abroad in order to reinvent himself. Yet, here with a solid chance of, at least, experimenting with creating himself anew, he had spent his first day so concerned with food and prayers that he did not remember to alter his life's balance. Whatever truth or Truth Malcolm presented to him, he would have no chance of verifying its basis in reality. Patrick was no inventor, but he could alter subtly the facets of his life he chose to. Those he did not mention to Malcolm or any taxi driver here; those that really mattered to him, but he did not mention, would cease to be part of his history: because he was generating his own history afresh in the presence of people who had not known him and who lived far removed from the physical realities he had once known.

He would not be able to do it. The thought of it happening without his realizing it frightened him. He meant no disrespect to Malcolm or any of the people he'd meet here, but for some reason he was glad they would perceive his false self. Another thought gave him a start and rooted him more deeply to the stone bench: he would portray his being disingenuous so often and for so long that he would change into that tarnished self. The end of it all was that this may have been the progression of his life thus far, and he had only now recognized it. But in the end it didn't matter to him. He released himself from the stone bench and ambled back to his hotel.

The Sheraton had, in its lit angles, an openness about it that fit those who slept there. Its many conference rooms, in addition to its pools, were well maintained and clean. The more resounding characteristics of the openness were framed by the elevator, which in rising to the top, a restaurant, carried people up and down and about their business. The approach to the hotel always had drivers and cabs in waiting. Guests lived easily in the Sheraton. The fortunate presence of soft sheets inside of the building made this temporary place of residence a home indeed to the many outsiders who bedded there. As a space, the softer angles of the concourse moved together to distract a traveler away from the shifting shapes and sizes of the desert, while retaining the colors of such a place. There would be, at any time, many people inside who did not belong to the Sheraton. Most of these people met at a restaurant or bar within the premises, and so the hotel opened itself to those people warmly.

Unlike a more distant resort, which had removed the presence of alcohol, and thereby the presence of many patrons, the Sheraton stood tall and strong as a balance between the Qatari and all things that came here to give money. Really, the place was a mediator, carefully joining together those who had and those who wanted. The deliberation could come together, proceed calmly, and in the end the building that faced the bay would be better for it. It, like many hotels, had proudly housed "famous" people. Newly, artists came to the city. The building was not sure if he had slept there, but at least he had eaten atop: Takashi Murakami. None of the colors and sounds of the place would appeal to his sense of Superflat. Yet, even in the face of someone so minded as Murakami, the building could remain confidently upon its foundations.

Some things troubled the building, however. Some people did not want to be within it. These people hoped to never return: to forget it. It was hard for it to decide why they were affronted, as it had only simple ideas of emotion and could mostly feel only good or bad. Most affected indifference towards the hotel, which was appreciated. Indifference to it meant a simpler life. Occupied with their own issues and goals, those humans could use the spaces within to accomplish what they needed to. If that accomplishing were to stop, then the building would cease to have a purpose, there would be no need for the people to be inside. It, being able to welcome as many people as it could, would have prided itself on doing its job well, had it known pride. The building often asked itself if its conceptual range would develop: if there would be a time that it would know more than good, bad, and indifferent. There could be a sense of value within it. It comprehended death, on a rudimentary level. But simple thoughts aside, the place was happy to absorb all of the sounds, sights, touches, and smells it had. The gurgling tooth brushers. The light-stepping pee-ers. The thumping stumble of a drunk. The soft drag of an over-full eater. The rushed tapping of the shoes of a worker. The relieved hands of a worker who is now off. What it could feel of love, it felt for these. That sensation of a love-like thing was only temporary, as the building did not remember faces well. And some humans were ignored: the building was finite.

Patrick walked into his room and stripped. Belly out, toes free. He forewent a visit to the Harp, he could not be sure it was even open at this hour.—At least I can handle my liquor. Nerves of being alone. Show up somewhere to look at the women. Can't buy them. Liberation. That sense of calmness that permeates. Sitting in the silence. Glass conducting the waters of the bay, as she would say. Hill and Morin producing the bars, are those their names? Can't remember. Wouldn't expect that in the land of the Holy. Jealous because it doesn't seem to be someone-you-know's Holy. I wouldn't drink when alone, but I wonder if I could be with someone here. Too much. Too little, perhaps. Sit and wonder where we all went but nowhere. The pressures of sleep preside over the courts of judgement, although tinted with darkish light. I'd wonder where all the taxi boys sleep. Possible that they share a room somewhere? All of them sleeping on mattresses and rugs covering the floor of a single room to save money: kids back home have to be fed before the mother has to go away. The resistance that one feels, the tension that is built into a seat belt. Do you think that the nuns and priests and brothers wear that pressure? At least their pilgrimage has pasta. Wherein do I fit in the cartoons: denial that is one's favorite state: and too far ahead go those copyrights. I'd think that it's lonely at the perch of the empire, but only Vickie'd know 'bout that. To what extent do those taxis have fun, considering that they owe such amounts to their companies at the end of an evening or beginning of a day? Easier to buy a taxi than a lady at this point, and cheaper too. But those cabbies cannot go after the same women I can? Is there a different class of working woman for them? Best ask the Canuck. Not out of any wish to have a different person to consume, but I am just sure there is some sort of system there. Where do they all apply for those jobs? Do those boat men and the taxi men share some kind of solidarity? Rivalry based on pretense of transport mode? It could not be that they compete: different types they all are. Do any of them, the boaters, drivers, or working women, do they ever visit the museum? What junk museums and churches are: ornately blinded with beauty the masses writhe. Perhaps. Their weekends must be sporadic, all of them. I do not feel that those people, although treated poorly, could do much to change that. But there are more of us than them. So few Qataris. As if they saw their city rise up and needed to fill it with imports. In reality, if all of the foreigners wanted to upset it all they could. Power in numbers. But there is probably no organization. Corporations are good at dispersing peoples. Although the working women probably don't have a union, they ought to. Probably shipped around on ships in those containers being fucked by the crew without knowing they were whores in the first place. Is it condescending to feel pity for them? I heard that there is some art opened recently at that museum. Or soon. Long way to express one's self, but that is one of the stupid points I imagine. A man shouting "deal with this deal with that make it all" while interns dream of one day being on top of it all. What would you tell a parent if you got a job across the world working for an artist: hullo, I am good enough to go be an underling, see you in some months! I am that, too. Damn that PhD. Never could have finished the thing even if I tried. All the exams and such are not for my level of involvement. I know that I am good at numbers, so why can't I just be good at them already? What a complicated mess I made of that all. I could not seem to calm myself down enough to see it through. That was the real issue. My own emotions did not want me to ascend with my peers the final step. Well fuck their proofs as is. Seems like I've landed in a fine spot. Even if the sheets on this bed are a bit starchy, still soft. Never mind that. The place breathes well. Not like those hostels back home. That's another man's business: judge the temporary homes of people. Write it online. Inspire fights between couples over which would be best for their little bastards while staying on the islands, wherever those islands are. Surely, there is no exam for that person. No way to say concretely, you are good or you are bad. It is only the judge that makes people think that they are good at judging: persuasion is the true talent there. Perhaps, Malcolm ought to consider a career change. He's too brash for all that. But the internet upsets the judge sometimes. The internet outsources to the people. Makes the judge red in the face to think that people can yelp their neighborhoods into proper gentrification. Did Americans invent gentrification? Seems like a thing they'd cook up and gladly hand out to the rest of the world: it's cherry flavored!

His eyes closed. His mind continued as he eased into sleep. He had worked himself into such a mental fury that all of his energy had been used and rest would be a requirement. There in the room, his belongings slowly scattering themselves about the place. There could be no stopping his clothes from taking their rightful place on the floor and the few books from remaining unread upon the desk. His laptop was opened, sitting on a chair. Otherwise, he had nothing. He would not even buy things to make the place look nicer: it was only temporary. Once the company had determined where to put him, he would have a nicely furnished apartment. The apartment would have a bigger desk, one that could fit the three books and the opened laptop. A closet or armoire would house his clothes and his refrigerator could hold some sandwich meats and Patrick had no idea how meats ever got to him. He only cared for their taste, not their production quality. Murakami slept and Patrick did too.

Classroom Unease

Elizabeth continued staring at the toasters and looked at her hand as she fondled the grey.—Do my students travel into another world when entering my classroom? They are furnished with literacy and content, something that they already had before our class. I cannot claim that many, if any, of those women have that at home. Equally, I cannot claim that they do not. But that was problematic and Elizabeth knew it.—English literacy. Are they forced into loving relationships with other languages at the chance of employment? I don't think that force can be involved in love . . . well, not in all kinds of love. Are they instead mimic-women who employ English lexicons to place themselves in a global environment? They are immersed in a culture of gendered segregation. That means that they deal with men who believe, however narcissistically, that there is some lack of skill in them. How then does English affect their engagement with such nefarious environs? Do my students, these women some of whom are married, pregnant, or engaged, create camaraderie amongst themselves and how do they then see their communities? What lines are drawn then between those from wealthier families and those from poorer if they are all separated out as women? What concerns should I have as a teacher and fellow woman about their safety: does their education increase their risk? I suppose that they could read unselfishly and to theorize solidarity in the classroom as peers. What could be the logical extension of that exercise in this place? It is such a drastically different battle than elsewhere. No war rages in the streets. Their mothers have fought different struggles than my American mothers. All of this teaming throughout the classroom. That potential that one or all of these women will see a violent or peaceful uprising in their lifetime. Will they remember me when the king is deposed? Will it be Abdullah? Salman? Will it matter? What would the point of remembering me be, but for my own wellbeing. Meanwhile Robert and the others are blissfully unaware of the intricacies of it all. Their focus on money blinds them to the undercurrents of discontent.

Elizabeth could not remember the exact moment when she thought of including Robert in her life. She had been drinking alone at the bar. That day she received her first academic rejection, one that stung truly, which made her resentful of scholarship and enlightenment: its limits and required ignorance. Elizabeth refused to accept that ignorance facilitated the furthering of education, a strong opinion which clouded her mind as she drank to forget the money she had spent on applying to that school.—The Ohio State, more like the Blohio State. She would not be permitted into this world, a sphere of well-financed writing and research, for many years. In being turned away, not even at the door, she took to the bar. She claimed to have remembered it; Robert would be hurt if she did not: how she suggested that they date. She moved on, looking to Robert, his ideals of something new, something without the limitation of structured study. For the first time, she turned her back on the academy, a position that Robert came to exploit with gusto. When Elizabeth remarked on the underbelly of dissatisfaction in Saudi and how it could all so easily crumble into a pile of dead princes and ransacked palaces, Robert asked her not to continue. He had nightmares about having to leave Saudi for the sake of safety.—We are dangerously close to Qatif as is, he claimed,—And it being worse would give me an ulcer. What Robert could not grasp was true distrust of government. He had never felt wronged by an institution or structure. He had lived his life in the comfort of ignorance and his own white privilege. Recognizing that privilege and how it shaped the lives of the others, those who did not experience advantages made him fearful of losing the life he had hardly worked for. The effort he would have to exert to overcome a collapse of his privilege would be beyond him. Robert was not up to the task of meaningfully complicating his position as a white straight male in the world.

Elizabeth tested the spring of one of the dull white toasters.— If we all move in tandem into another separate world, I into theirs, and they, arguably, into mine linguistically, do those commonalities of movement bring us closer? Can it be that in the foundations of our worlds, there still lie the building blocks which have been moved between one world and another? Moved between us by our mothers and their mothers before, however differently? And then there is the common experience of the complacent person in our midst: that person who has no desire, wish, or want to affect change in the world. I live with a man who sees no need for alteration. I doubt he would know what progress was if he saw it, let alone how to facilitate its growth. What lessons could I plan to expose those people who hinder progress? Would that not be dismissive or exclusionary? As an educator how can I school or teach emotion so that those who are moving forward do so and remain accepting of those who are just along for the ride, or those who do not want to ride at all?

Whatever hesitance Elizabeth had once felt towards her new partner diminished with time. She never told him of the academic rejection, just as he never told her of his then lover.— Listen, Julie, we need to talk. What happened to them was an increase in speed and silence. Each step they undertook together propelled them towards some idea rather than a concrete end. Robert's motivation became abstract in the presence of Elizabeth, as she moved him into his own head. Elizabeth felt the rush of the relationship as she constructed herself as an image to those outside of her. Her kindness, her wit, it all became separate, not a part of her own being. Instead, all that was substance within her own persona construction exercises, her mythos building and history construction.

Robert in turn advanced an idea of monetary worth in his own mind that grew without hesitance. In preventing Elizabeth from returning to the academy or allowing for a situation in which she could attempt to, he could use her intelligence to his advantage in adjusting to new jobs and places. He recognized Elizabeth's enthusiasm for research and had learned to create situations with which to capitalize upon those skills. Passively and slowly he hinted at a place, job, or experience and with time Elizabeth would have read enough about the topic to give Robert an informed and nuanced view of it. She had not realized it, but she had performed research on compound life in the Middle East some time before their move there. She had also learned about life in Canada, business in Bangkok, community organization in New Delhi. It occurred to her, with her finger thin and tanned on that toaster, that she had been misused so that Robert would not have to do the work that was required of him. Her chest grew hot with indignation. The opportunities she had had to teach English were mere byproducts of his selfish movements. She had guessed at this earlier in the day, but it seemed so much clearer now with the appliances and call to prayer. Robert would not be able to argue with her leaving because this had been the only thing with which he had outsmarted her. He used his ignorance as a leash. Her intellect was what he desired of her, and her body was a bonus.—That bald prick.

—Then what to do? Do I abandon my own class, one of the few chances I have had to shape intellectualism, for my own need to escape? The sympathetic ghost had left her. Now all of the instances of her being used by Robert to do his work arose in front of her: how to find employment, how best to format resumés, how to approach difficult situations, what edits to make on a document, how to format that document, primary research. So many of the facets of her being as an intellectual had done for Robert all of the things he could not. In reality, whenever he found employment it was Elizabeth that got a second job. She resolved conflicts and disputes at the office, pitched solutions to problems, provided valuable research, without realizing that she had done so or setting foot in that place of work. She had thought she was being kind to Robert. He was not a violent man, nor was he very malicious, but he had come to use Elizabeth's most sacred of possessions: her mind. Her own world had been secretly invaded and she had not realized it. What insights Robert had into any culture or language were because of her. His ability to parse difficult problems was not his at all. His own need for money and recognition propelled him to mistreat Elizabeth so slyly. He did not even care for her as of late. They would sit opposite each other and he felt fine to not speak with her except when he needed to or was required to for work. He could see in her some growing unease, but did not know how, if ever, she would express it. He had no idea to what extent she knew of his manipulation. He miscalculated and assumed that she had known all along and so accepted his ways. The one directional support that she provided him was foundational to their relationship. Whatever it was that had hurt her just before they began to date had allowed Robert to slide in easily and with haste. The space that he occupied, a vacuum of academic desire, he was ignorant of and it took time for him to terraform the expanse into something that he could mine for his own betterment. In Canada, he gradually had her teaching him more and more. On the flight to Bangkok, she tutored him on common greetings, thank-yous, and phrases. En route to Delhi he learned about Gandhi and Nehru. Before their marriage, he learned about his new tax status. Over Iraq he heard about American development in Saud's kingdom and the Eastern Province. Elizabeth had been his teacher and lover. He was amazed that he had been with her for so long and that she had agreed to marriage. But as the lovers became indifferent and the locales more exotic, Elizabeth's unease manifested itself in an awareness that Robert could do nothing to hinder and could only accept.

—There is no choice.

• • •

In a wakeful state of morning, Patrick looked to the phone he'd
been given at the office the previous day. In it were the numbers that had been attached to the various humans he needed to
be able to contact: formerly drunk Malcolm, not-yet-met Stacy,
not-yet-met Trent and so on. The screen showed a message from
his Canadian, the only Canadian that mattered to him. In less
than 25 words, Malcolm informed Patrick of three things. First,
the office was closed for the day due to a building-wide water
issue. Complaints had been that something sandy was in the
water on certain floors. This pointed to some flaw within the
infrastructure of the office complex itself, which must have its
water shut off in order to assess the problem: no telecommuting.
Second, the museum was open for his enjoyment. Malcolm had
arranged a date for today, so he would not attend with Patrick,
but everyone needed to visit the place, if only once. And finally,
this evening he would introduce Patrick to a woman. Patrick
did not know that this introduction would be some floors directly below him, a trick or temptation that Malcolm enjoyed
constructing for new arrivals to Doha who were staying at the
Sheraton. Patrick reread the message: No work, water stuff in
building. Go see art, everyone does, am only free tonight: let's
find u a woman!

The summation of his day would be simple. Food first, and
then he would have to visit the museum; otherwise he feared

not having much to say when he met with Malcolm. The morning stretched calmly over Doha. He wished he had had work, as that was a predictable progression of a day. He ordered coffee and toast to be brought to his room. He laid money out on a small table and looked through the bathroom. There was a comfortable shower and soft towels, all of which Patrick would wait another few days to use. The small soaps remained in their wrappings as he sniffed them. To that end, nothing within the bathroom offended him. He could not decide if he enjoyed the space or not. He found the fluorescent lighting too bright for his liking: it exposed too much of him for his own good. As he looked into the mirror, he was upset at how many of his own pores could be observed. He switched the light off and felt the surfaces of the bathroom instead of scrutinizing more deeply his own skin. The smoothness of it all had a cooling effect on him. He then moved the toilet seat down and sat waiting for his coffee and toast. He remembered that the previous day he had heard the prayers on his radio. He moved to turn on the machine, but at this time no calls could be heard. Some other program in Arabic was in that box. He left the Arab in the radio to chatter as he heard a knock of his door and he went to greet whomever brought his breakfast.

Softly, he handed over his money and took his coffee and toast in to his room. He set both on the desk that held his books and let both cool. This lasted at least twenty minutes, wherein he alternated between standing still and pacing about the room. He refused to drink hot coffee and eat hot toast. He waited until his breakfast was cool enough and then consumed them both as quickly as he could, not taking any breaks to drink all of the coffee and eat all of the toast. Then he sat on the edge of his bed. Within his body he could feel the digestible materials moving. He waited for the coffee to have a more pronounced reaction within him, as well as for the bread to fill a spot in his stomach. Then, suddenly, he was full and awake. A fog that he did not even sense was immediately lifted from him and he believed his mind to be quicker, and so better able to handle this day.

He opened his suitcase and looked through his clothes carefully. Patrick did not have a wide range of aesthetic knowledge or pretense, but he would look at his clothing before wearing it. He needed to observe his materials as he only washed his clothes rarely and would wear articles more than once. This was not out of some practice of ecological awareness, rather it was a deep laziness. He selected a shirt and pants. Laying them on the bed, he inspected them entirely, making sure there were no stains or marks. These clothes were clean, but this was habit. When he found a small spot on the pants he decided that it was fuzz from a sock and removed it. The shirt and pants passed and he dressed.—Ready.

Patrick hated art. In such aesthetic fields, he was at a loss for the ability to use his integers to his own advantage. Thematics and motif did not elude him, but they frustrated him in their indefiniteness. And so, he enjoyed visiting an occasional museum to engage in the frustrated catharsis of someone who enjoys being dismissive in front of large groups of people. He would not loudly decry any single work, but he would instead sigh roughly or scoff,—Pfff, hmmm, uummmmm. As a child, he learned how to roll his eyes in such a manner that exhibited stress throughout his entire body. Soon Patrick set out to walk to the museum, looking for his fun. He retraced his path through the park and along the line of the bay. As he passed the bench he pointed at it. The roadways rushed by him.—Objects in motion. People were moving to buildings that had water and Patrick sauntered, expecting to find something new to quietly disregard. Along the walk men and women jogged past the slowly-walking Patrick. The various boats harbored in the bay lay dormant. The morning was pleasant and composed along the water. It seemed to Patrick that no one here expected much at this time shortly before the heat came to rest on the streets and waters.

He peered into one boat and noticed three men in t-shirts sitting on the deck.—A strange fate to work on the deck of a ship with such cargo. The product available from these boats was a short, circular ride within the bay. The men took to the water in the afternoon and evening, and welcomed families and groups to look about the bay. Patrick smiled at the men in the boat and shouted a loud good morning to them, stirring them. Such mischief Patrick enjoyed. Soon the men would have taken greater notice of the day, but Patrick laughed when he saw them move about within the hull.—How are you? Patrick called in louder. The men waved him away as they rose to meet the day. All three of them had made a great deal the previous night and had talked happily into the night eating and drinking tea. They looked at Patrick's condescension with humor: the man had a bit of roundness to him that made him seem comical. Patrick had enough of the jocular interaction: he had no interest in knowing anything about these men, aside from the fact that they had been seen sleeping in the hull of a boat the night before.

And onward he moved. When he had reached the other side of the water, he noticed again the upward rising, twisting building to the right of the museum ahead of him. That building made calls at various times of the day. Otherwise Patrick had no idea what it was or who inhabited it. It was standing amongst the developing haze of sand and thickening morning sun. It was not an offensive building. It pleased him that the city had a wide variety of architecture. He hoped that the spiral building had some meaningful purpose.—I hope that it is not a museum or concert hall or anything.

Somewhere also on this side of the bay, the *suq* he had visited lay waiting for patrons. Shops would be opening. Men and women touring Doha would be ordering their breakfasts.

Young Saudi men would be walking slowly through the path-
ways. *Suq Waqif* had a genuine quality to it. Even with the
diverse set of visitors, the market was a welcome and warm
place. It did not feel like a place tourists visited, which made
it more so touristy. The cobblestones and alleyways were kind
to those who entered. Patrick thought of having lunch there
after his visit to the museum. It was late morning (11:45AM)
and Patrick realized he had had a late breakfast. He sensed that
soon there would be more prayers as he had not heard any yet.
His slow walk allowed him to take in the hot, watery air, which
distracted him from his eating and sleeping schedules. The jut-
ting edges of the museum stood in contrast to the flowing bay
water that moved past and against it. It was its own island. The
place had a sense of solitude. It, alone, inhabited this spot. It
faced the rest of the city with a kind of pride and Patrick found
himself hurrying to the entrance.

8

The moments that followed Xiaoqing's placement upon Scott's lap shaped James for many years. Much later, James would listen to the *Love Supreme* and shout alone, to himself, Coltrane's own words,

—ELATION

—ELEGANCE

—EXALTATION

—All from God. There was in him an appreciation for the actions that Jim had taken on that day so many years earlier. A spirituality came into James' breast, not a playful loving of God, but a recognition of the life that he had learned so much from: how he had resented and feared the world, which then informed his detached point of view, which subsequently drove him to recognize his own fallibility and ignorance,—One thought can produce millions of vibrations, oh how right you were, Mr. Coltrane. The Christianity that found James in his later life was solitary and well read. He did not like to visit the churches of his forefathers. Seldom did he share his articulate holiness: he kept it from his partners. He still enjoyed dancing and the night. Yet, he looked with a different lens at the people and places around him. He was not reborn except within his mind. He did not develop any antagonisms, racisms, sexisms, or other forms of judgment with his relationship with God, but a happiness that was for himself and for his notebooks. He worked with his spirit in ink.

Jim asked that day if they'd like to see something funny,—You've got to see what happens. Jim only occasionally visited with a masseuse, but that would change as tiny Tina wore him down. His fatalism stood out and clearly he found no merit in long term relationships: he had abandoned a lively social scene in Canada for the money of Saudi. Jim felt that there was a kinship between himself and James, not only because of name, but also in having left the youth and voracity of university to come to this. An aching self-confidence had convinced a younger Jim to go abroad. When he returned home, he felt so above those around him who had not had the privilege of international movement. He got off on the conversations with women in bars, the looks in the eyes of men who could not speak to his experiences. And so, he left and never looked back at Canada. Decades later, Jim would die in a motorcycle accident in Thailand. His body would not be recovered by his brother who was busy trying to reestablish himself as his daughter's father, but those are two different stories.

Jim ordered chicken wings without sauce and handed them over to some of the women that surrounded the table at Scott's request. They ate furiously and quickly.—Like animals, Jim observed: a sickening smile across his face as he spoke it. He laughed to himself. The comment had been made quietly but precisely. Jim's drunk eyes moved into a more serious mode and his character shifted. He seemed to realize the implications of the scene but would not appreciate it. He did not care about being an asshole. It could have been a kind act. The smell of the chicken turned James' stomach and he looked away from the eating women and Scott and Jim. James pushed back any reaction, bottling up his anger at Jim for the comment. He further suppressed his resentment towards Jim: at sharing his name and space, at finding commonality in their histories. No words were spoken at the table for several minutes, with the exception of Scott's whispers to Xiaoqing, who ate separately from the other women and drank nicer drinks.

James had never been in close quarters with prostitutes. He did not know how to act. The strange lighting of the place made his eyes hurt and the people spoke too quickly for him to listen when the anger faded and his ears stopped ringing. Gary took to it well. He had another beer and sat with a woman and tried over and over again to pronounce her name,—Sunda, Suda, Sundar, Sudarat, Sundarat! Sudarat Sudarat Sudarat! I'm sorry, can I call you something else? James had another beer and lit a cigarette. Scott and Xiaoqing mumbled to each other and then Jim and Scott laughed at something. The ceilings of the bar were very low and their voices carried sharply. This wasn't about fucking. This was about the act of being able to. Scott and Jim only wanted to demonstrate their power, whatever it was, over the people inside of this building. Jim and Scott had conceptualized a coalition between one another, and in inviting James and Gary to Digger's opened the group to further growth. That increase in physical size was controlled by them as brothers, compatriot Canadians, and teachers. They would have no need in including James, but Gary began a fascination with their style and how their lives were ordered and arranged. The power that both Jim and Scott had constructed, as contrived as it was, and would always be, was exerted with force upon Gary, who would accompany them several weekends to find women and pleasures.

This trio consumed with gusto, although a light-hearted affair it was not. Jim kept detailed notes on each of the women he slept with.—The details are expansive, including but not limited to geography, payment, and heritage, he later explained to Gary. He opened this notebook for all of his friends and shared and ruminated upon each woman with a stoicism that made him appear not only sexist, but smugly so to those around him.

Scott did not elaborate in much detail, not being so articulate as Jim, but constantly pushed the men he knew to have a variety of relationships. Gary, a good lap dog, was simply and dimly there, laughing and chortling along with the two.

James, who separated himself from these people, took no obvious offense to them at that time: he did not wish conflict upon himself during that year within the compound. When James traveled, he motivated himself with different factors: he visited the museum in Doha, the Burj Khalifa in Dubai. James' impetus for travel, for the rest of his days, became the moment when one first sees a noteworthy building or geographical formation: a tower, mountain, dam, statue, park, canyon etc. He thought fondly of that kind of silence when one's mind begins to make an impression of a place. Then he wondered what sentimentalities people developed towards location, how setting affected emotion and outlook. Digger's was forever in James' mind as a negative. It took many years for him to admit to himself that he disliked everything about the bar, but when he did, he did not feel a weight lifted from him, rather he felt as though he had been absolved or that his feet had been washed.

The six people sat at the table. James waited and watched and these men had their last beer and flesh before driving to Saudi. He was not sure what to make of it all. He took a picture of Scott and Xiaoqing. He drank one last beer and got light headed. Gary seemed more lean jawed when he sat next to that Thai woman, and in his relaxation hesitated to leave. Someone further down the bar had a British accent. James went to the bathroom. In a resigned way, a token characteristic of his twenties, he pissed and sighed heavily.

Unsilent, Whirling, Angry

The call entered her ears again and then a dull silence. Elizabeth did not want to buy a toaster so she moved on to a higher shelf, eye-height with blenders, which she would also leave with the Panda. The blenders, purple, red, gun-metal, white, silver, black (of three varieties) and grey sought to be exchanged for Elizabeth's money. She lifted the pitcher from the second of the three black blenders.—How can I inspire loving movement between worlds? Is there some kind of lesson that teaches our need to be immersed in various other planes of existence? Also, how can I evacuate unwelcome persons from a world that I happily occupy? Elizabeth and Robert moved without discretion, or so she had thought, from city to country and onward. She knew that he was a collector by how he would look at the stamps on his passport. She noticed that within 24 hours of their first meeting: he was Canadian and had used his passport as an ID at the bar. The next morning, he revealed this about himself over an egg-white omelet and two strawberry smoothies. She could not have been more pleased with the fresh berries: rather than never speak to him again, she consented to his staying. Robert had no idea that his staying was dependent on natural sugars, in fact Elizabeth was hardly aware of this either. She had wanted badly an excuse to understand something different. She engaged in these moments in a middle class need for convenience and ease. Robert was a simple, undemanding alternative to re-applying elsewhere and how he looked at his passport told her that she would see stamps within her own. His only stamp was Ireland. His father had taken him to visit their ancestral lands. He looked at that stamp with pride and fondness. Elizabeth's shortage of stamps bothered her until they first moved West to the East. In Thailand they were able to afford travel to other countries. Unknowingly, Elizabeth had opened more than one of her worlds to Robert and he settled in nicely.

Elizabeth gave up on the appliances, moving away from them toward the bakery.—No toast without bread and the blenders are uninspiring. She turned about-face away from the appliances and moved along towards the foodstuff past brightly colored displays and advertisements. Upon reaching the rows of commercial bakery goods, she again stopped her cart. Looking down at its emptiness she pushed it next to a display of flatbreads and rolls that had been baked that day. She fondled the list that lay upon the child safety seat. In scanning it once more, she folded the paper neatly and placed it in her purse. Many years later, after altering her academic circumstances and placing herself once more at ease, she would frame that piece of paper and hang it symbolically in her office. Her students would gape at the torn and frayed list of groceries, but none would have the courage to ask what eccentricities underlay its presence between the books and papers. Picking up a package of bread and squeezing it, she let out a brief exclamation.—Ah! She checked to see if anyone stared at her. But then she remembered that she must not let her confidence be superseded by the judgment of strangers.—If Robert has waltzed into one of my worlds and has taken root there, then if I leave him that world alters drastically. In a sense, that world that we secretly shared for so long is now part his. In leaving and moving away, I can grant him whatever is left of that plane in my absence and go on to create anew for myself. Then I can begin to experiment with teaching emotion and ration: is that a contradiction? I am clouded by his presence, in fact, I always have been. What scarcity of academic pursuit he has afforded me in these past years . . . No matter. The reality lies before me: I am still young and able. I have enough money in my pocket to leave. What of her possessions? She became silent and her pupils dilated as she thought about how Robert would be getting off work very soon: the prayer was ending. She did not have time to return home and retrieve her favorite books. She opened her purse with a heavy breath: she had her passport. She flipped through the stamps. She then took out her wallet. She had a credit card. She did not have a change of clothes. International flight without luggage from the Middle East would be tricky.

—Doubt, she shook her head.

She grabbed the cart and quickly put several bags of rolls into it. Seeing objects within the thing slowed her breathing some. Her words became jumbled,—The books, but what for the clothes . . . Packing for Robert, surprise, OH . . . As cluttered as her thoughts became, she was not powerless. She knew that she had awakened that day to her forgotten, or perhaps ill-used, agency. She pushed the cart to another display of bread. Her conclusions had become more drastic and dramatic than she had foreseen. What puppy-love naïvety had allowed her to tumble this far along Robert's path?—Calm. She did not want to seem out of place. Now that the prayer had ended, the store had been reopened and more families, men, and women entered to satisfy their shopping needs. All around her the murmuring of other people increased in speed and pitch. She thought of how disrespectful she must have seemed to have talked to herself throughout the prayer. She felt lowly of herself, and she thought that the scaffolds of her decisions were collapsing around her. She thought that she would have to return to the compound and to sitting across from Robert: it was inevitable. In her ebb and flow she moved between her newly found willfulness and her old reliable submission.

Then the anger took ahold of her. Elizabeth realized in that moment that violence was not limited to physical action. She realized her potential to violently quell the powers that Robert exerted over her.—The construction of new worlds may wait until I walk again on another country's soil. Her brief doubt transformed itself into such anger that she did not care if Robert saw her packing or asked her what she was doing. Balance was out of the question for the following minutes. Elizabeth laughed to herself as she imagined Robert getting more upset than he possibly ever could. The darkness of his fictional anger was fueled by her resentments. She moved around the breads and returned the rolls to their shelves. She now needed more time to parse through what she would say to Rob. Should she sit him down? Would it be better to yell at him? To not say anything? Write a letter? A short note? Call him on the phone and demand that he wait outside? Have someone else deliver the news of her decision? She could, of course, act as though nothing was happening: he might not notice. Tapping her fingers on the handle of the cart she waited for herself to catch up with these modalities. She could engineer some theatrics into the event, make Robert remember his first wife. On the other hand, she could save everyone the drama and focus her energies on her next moves in life. But there was a long flight to deal with, plenty of time there to ruminate on all of it. The tension slowly left her. She was more aware of her body now and she moved from the breads through the store to the teas and coffees. She did want to bring some tea with her: Lipton, the same as in America, but with Arab scripts written on the boxes and packaging. Scooting along the tea aisle it occurred to her that whatever she did, it would surprise Robert. The man, although he had been clever enough to manipulate her into his schemes for these past years, did not have the discernment necessary to make valid judgments of the future; he left that to Elizabeth. And so, regardless of what path she took to abandon him and begin the arduous process of divorce, he would find it astonishing. She placed three boxes of tea into the cart. She loved tea. In their travels, she had developed such a taste for tea that she abandoned coffee and its higher and more pronounced levels of caffeine. In her purse she heard a vibration, her phone wiggled its way into her attention. Text message from Robert: Big deal at office. Won't be home until past 10PM. She looked at her watch. It was 3:52PM on that Sunday. Robert often made jokes about the shifted work week. He was never sensitive to religion or spirituality. Within ten years he would be back in Canada and be born again, reformatting his sins in accordance with his revised worldview. Elizabeth had time. She could make it to the local airport in Dammam or even across the bridge to Manama, whichever flew sooner, leave a note for Robert and be off the next day. For the first time that day, she smiled. Her anger eased, but did not entirely disappear. Elizabeth needed to learn how to control that emotion: she would want to school others in the proper use of anger.

• • •

He entered the building and noticed the size of its atrium. It
rose high above, allowing natural light to reflect off of the colors within: even-tempered earth tones. Within, he assumed,
were valuable and historical artifacts created in the Arab world.
His distaste for the creative began to manifest itself in a selfish
glee that he felt in his chest.—Enter into the expressive. The
thorough and deeply rooted. To be amongst those things which
create identity on a wider scale than one's own words or actions.
It is an implied language that emanates from these objects. But
that is needless. What sense is there to hold on to these old
things, the things that represent the dead? Does the museum
function as anything more than a tomb?

People shuffled around him. He looked upward to where
the artifacts were held and moved slowly up the museum's
grand stair. The art that he was to see made no difference. To
Patrick, unless they had some easily calculated value, the objects had no significance. Patrick observed the stair, the light
filtering in from above seeming to anoint the hall. The significance of the absence of the outer heat made Patrick stop moving. The structure intimidated Patrick slightly. He thought that
this island habitat had some unique quality to it, it being intentionally aware of its own odd angles and corners.

He remembered visiting London with his mother: she loved
the English, although she never told Patrick why. She would

take Patrick to museums, galleries, anything that had some kind of display. All of this, despite Patrick's ever growing disinterest, which his mother observed to be youthful ignorance. Patrick, in light of certain political tensions, had a distaste for the English, but was shocked to notice that their museums inspired him, which he reacted to with a forced scowl. In some sense the way a museum welcomes in outside light, as a method of illumination, perfectly described how the British manipulated their own environments, and those of others, for specific ends. Standing at the bottom of the stair, he wondered just where all of these objects had come from and how it was that they had arrived here. The museum was an island, a man-made one at that, but it did not appear isolated. He felt that although there was a sheen of insincerity about the construction, it was as though a force of nature had demanded this structure's creation. As if nature, in its gendered processes, had decided that humans shall generate caves of their own accomplishments, and thereby deny nature's actual involvement in that progress. Patrick shook his head. He hadn't cared this much about art in a long time.

The frailty of those around him, the many white women and Arab men moving about silently, and in deep concentration, stood out as reminiscent of how he could not possibly connect with an object of art. They were all feigning understanding, he assumed. Patrick's lust for numbers was third only to his desires to masturbate frequently and eat large portions of savory foods in the evening. In school, his affair, and later rocky marriage to numbers, began slowly. He did not, at first, seek to go into deeper data analysis and statistical work, but finding that it suited him better than did pure algebra, he learned his way into his current job data mining for a Qatari. Perhaps, it was that these people were data mining with these objects, seeking some kind of abstracted human pattern that Patrick would never grasp. But to Patrick, that was not within his own set of modalities. He firmly believed that such indistinct notions as those that arise from an appreciation of art detracted from the real world of progress represented by mathematics and the sciences. He had no room for a balance within his mind. He linked art and religion quickly, not paying any attention to those of us who are, like him, atheists. And so, he stood at the bottom of the elegant staircase and waited for his thoughts to finish.

Once, while Patrick studied for his exit exams at university, he became insatiably jealous of a street performer who'd been brought on campus to relieve students during their finals. He failed to grasp what the man, or perhaps woman, had intended to do, —What the point was in her (his?) slow, calculated movements and silent language. As he watched her/him with guilt and semi-sexual pleasure, he determined that he needed to visit a museum in order to sort out that absence of artistic pleasures from his life. He simply found it too jarring to make value judgments about something so abstract. So, he left the performance and moved himself, in a somewhat hesitant fashion, to a nearby gallery that was featuring art from a professor on campus. It was terrible. He could not move past his own distaste of the values that the art presented. There was no uniformity or predictability. It looked to be all jumbled and confusing. He spent a long time considering the various objects, until the gallery closed. He could not parse the artist's motivations. There had to be some underlying procedure that could be concretely explained to him. As a gallery assistant approached him to ask him to be mindful that the place was closing, he looked at her with vehemence and asked how it worked. She laughed at him, thinking that he was joking, but he left flustered and without any conclusion other than to reject, for his own reality, the validity of most physical works of art.

The younger Patrick had never particularly cared for any artistic objects, aside from the occasional poem that his grandfather would read to him as a child, but this indifference morphed itself into distaste in the aftermath of his own guilt. The professor, who by her own admission was a Dadaist, a name which gave Patrick unpleasant chills, had given the gallery many pieces that displayed a sense of anarchy and nihilistic hedonism. Standing in front of this work that day, the younger Irishman could only shake his head. His ignorance of the forms' intersections with meanings had gotten to the point where he had decided to hate it. After he left, he walked the streets for some time trying to come to terms with the nature of his own studies. Over the next week, he failed two exams, as he had spent his time concerned with rejecting what he did not understand, rather than attempting to strengthen what he did.

Once the tests were finished, he called his mother, and instead of responding to her curiosity about his courses, he told her, or admitted rather, that he did not like art. He could not grasp it and so it must not be worth any of his time. Patrick's mother, who had become used to his sudden bursts, told him that was just fine, and again asked about his studies,—How are they then? He had no idea what to tell her. It was in this moment that he realized that instead of dismissing art as he ought to, he was obsessing over it, allowing it to dominate his time and energies. He hung up on his mother and set out to remove this fixation from his life. That evening, drunk in a pub near campus he had never known before, he met Laura. She was sitting alone and as he stumbled past her, he remarked that art was lame: she read into it charmingly, taking his use of the Americanism to be more cultured than it really had been: she would teach him about music and dance and art and he would repeat the artists that she mentioned and enjoyed only because it was information from her.

The two of them only spoke that evening, and Patrick had been aware enough to sense that a woman would lead him away from his own issues with the abstract forms he disliked: accordingly, he arrived at a compulsion to tackle a separate inconceivable and unquantifiable notion: romance. Again, he would fail to comprehend.

And so, Patrick stood in the Museum of Islamic Art.

The years that had passed matured the man, who in the bright and beautiful entry hall, decided to have another go at evaluating the place of art in a society of service people, number crunchers, and the few who can afford art in their homes. To his left, his feet moved him and he bought a pad of paper and a pen from the shop. He found a spot in the foyer to sit and began.—I rely on something, a series of abstractions, to form my notions of this world. But, it is the abstractions that I do not understand that bother me most. If only they sold beer in this museum. I'd take more to this if I could touch it, manipulate it. Throw a piece on the ground and determine its elasticity or brittleness. Where, just where, did it all come from? Who was the person who put forth that we need to pay people to generate things only for viewing? Who thereafter set about removing objects from in-home-use, putting them into cases so that I may appreciate their beauty? The thing about beauty. Beauty could be better explained if it weren't for artists. What shall I look for? What is the sense of looking? I know that I cannot comprehend all of this. I haven't even made it out of the foyer and up the stair. Damned if I could find the way to rate these things, to sense pattern. They say there are all different kinds of people in the world. That must be the line they use to comfort the dummies. I'm surprised that it would be so simple. I hate that sense of the world being open. It makes movement irrelevant. If we boxed up the different parts of the world into little, kind parcels, I could appreciate art. Sex relieves the loins, alcohol the urge to pollute the mind: closed events in a tangible, albeit abstract, space. Mother would obsess about Empire. She loved to be conquered. I assume that's why I do not know my father's name. I do like that art is somewhat overcome by the museum. Bundled up into temperature controlled areas, where the light is regulated and the people monitored. Akin to a zoo. What bothers me, however, must be the openness, which presents itself to the viewer, almost virginal. Judge for yourself! Enjoy your first time! How does it make you feel? But I oughtn't be dictatorial. Or nay! I should be. These kings do well for themselves with their motorcades and architects. I'd commission magnificent works just to hold it over others. Yes, indeed! Fine Patrick called for it, and so it was. I'd only allow for the pieces to be displayed in moist rooms, where it was too warm and too bright. I'd hire angry attendants to yell! Touch it all, dammit!

Patrick caught his breath. He'd been muttering to himself, he did not realize how loudly, and a woman across the way was staring. If only she could share in his delusion. He rose, making for the stairs deliberately. He had not written anything upon his notepad.—My fortune could be dedicated to buying objects with history and emotion at auction, under a false name. Those doodads, whatever they were, would then be publicly destroyed. The plague of Sotheby's. He ascended to the top of the flight. Glancing at the rooms, he calmed. The slight change in his relation to sea level cooled his mind, but still sweat gathered on his hands and so on his paper and pen. He awaited the decision of his feet. People shuffled by him. For a moment, he stared upward, curious about what the ceiling had to say.

With his mother in London, he'd spit at the street signs: aiming for the names. He felt better about the act, the more famous the road. This so greatly flustered his mother that she twice hailed a taxi, twice bought tickets to Dublin, and twice immediately left the city. She'd lecture him each time. —You haven't any clue of history and spitting is improper. These people made all of the things you love, spitting in front of them or at them proves nothing but your own crass nature. You know, one of them made you. Patrick was not meant for car bombs or action, and anyways that time in history was mostly past, but ideologies he'd flirt with. And so blossomed his rebellion against his mother. He remained silent through each of her reactions, not realizing that his own teenage actions were more jarring. Whatever she said, wherever they were, he respected her right to chastise him: for his spitting, cursing, sudden rage, obstinate hungers, etc., etc., etc. Spitting in London was as far as he'd go to provoke her while traveling. Her brow, furrowing in the gray sunlight, would gage how much further he must go. Yet, his disobedience limited itself by his vices. After each London meltdown, his mother refused to feed him. Patrick the younger's body necessitated a certain amount of calories per day, this his mother knew well. As such, she'd prevent him from indulging his love of food: over the years his metabolism slowed, but only so much that he gained only limited weight around his waist.

Because of the second breakdown, he developed a silent resentment for his mother, which he now expanded upon. Unemployed after the tiger was killed, no doubt by Germans who were soon to go after the Greeks, he was pushed to the East by his mother who was determined to enjoy her golden years. She cursed the Arabs, but secretly, deep within her being, she implored Patrick to move swiftly on any position that earned oil money. Her words called him incompetent to need such a position. —That damned doctorate, but her eyes screamed otherwise. She'd give him the house if he did so, so much he grasped. Had he not taken that taxi at the Doha airport, she would have sold the house, and cheaply too. Patrick's attachment to space was obvious. While jobless, he would quietly enter the house and sit in his old room to brood. His mother knew of this, but pretended not to, so as to silently use this fact about him to her own ends.

So, Patrick had moved to Qatar, packed with his limited clothes and his mother's account information: he could transfer his monthly salary half to her, one third to his own Irish account and keep one sixth for spending. Despite being a secretary, his mother's ability to manipulate numbers was astounding. Somehow, she was able to calculate fast enough so as to always be ahead of him in planning. That is how he came to know about this job, how much he paid in taxes, including mother-taxes.

He accepted, mostly, their dichotomy. The advantage to living as far away from her as he now did was that her visits would not exist. She would, in her own deliberate way, visit him at his apartment, unannounced and smiling. This never left Patrick time to clean, so he soon learned to eat out when he could afford it and to hide his laundry as often as possible, lest her judgments be heard. Freedom came at a price he was, at this time in his life, willing to pay. There would be, of course, the chance that something would happen to one of them, which would likely result in a test of their co-dependency. They only needed the idea of one another to be motivated to plan their lives. To that end, Patrick wished no lasting ill upon his mother and vice versa. Their familial animosities had limits.

Patrick's view lowered and he entered the glass doors to his left at the top of the stair. Within, the objects in their glass cases were backlit with placards in English and Arabic. He did not bother reading any of them. His ears heard his own mumbles now many years old.—What is it with her? Made of an Englishman? I must get through her things. Each room will be turned up. Love letters. Receipts for services rendered. Anything at all will do. Suppose he still isn't my father, even with his genetic material. Solider? Businessman? Was made on a trip, like this, to London? Is my hatred for these English rooted in my conception? As if I care for these sights and noises. Dammit, mother. Your persistence. What is anything I do to you? She spares me some kind of pain by withholding who he is. I suppose she will inform me of that when she dies, or maybe when he dies, if they still communicate. Still, people stare at her for having a bastard son like me. Suppose she is not the best Catholic. Rarely attends confession. Does not take the Eucharist with deep, meditative hopes of heaven. Could there be some way of coaxing the information out of her? Surely, no. Her stamina is in deprivation. I know where it is she keeps her secrets: in no physical form other than her own brain matter. Now that I am old enough she can be more sophisticated in her bickering with me. I suppose I ought to study hard and learn to combat her. Yet, she is already a veteran at it all. I shall have to be careful how I move forward. She bests me in that she is more controlling of her own emotion than I. Well it all starts calmly anyways. If I could stomach religion, I would use the priest against her, but she knows me better than that. She can sense my discomfort in the Church. Still I cannot get past her actions. Her wit is sharp certainly. What is this taxi man doing? Patrick did search their house and her possessions. He found no letters. He had greatly miscalculated her. She knew he would look and therefore set about to punish him for his wayward curiosity. He found her blue dildo and lube.

He moved slowly amongst the objects in the room. None appeared to capture his attention. Each was background. His feet stumbled at a door frame. The jewels and golds did not speak to him or enliven his distaste. What was the goal in Patrick navigating through this place? He stopped. Shortly after their second failed trip to London, which had largely failed because Patrick wondered if he could duplicate the first blow up, his mother had a mild heart attack and was laid up in the local hospital. When Patrick arrived after school, a priest was chatting with his kind parent, laughing about close calls and how they are good for bringing one closer to the Lord. Patrick the younger was at an impasse. The terrible, manufactured light of the hospital magnified the stress of his subsequent decision. He had to choose between confronting his mother further, in this instance with the risk of physically harming her, or succumbing to his childlike desire to be hers: inspired instantly by seeing her with so many machines surrounding her bed. In him emerged a kind of empathy, a maturity that challenged his desire to counter his mother. The two adults stared at him, waiting for him to speak. He entered the room with a calculated sense of sadness. His face showed each of the two people facing him that he was affected by this glum event. He sat next to his mother and took her hand, thinking, contemplating whether or not to reconcile his feelings toward her or not.

He, the logical, brilliant younger Patrick, determined that he could choose neither. As a result, he became more withholding, not aggressive and not passionate. He found so many faults with each of the other possible Patricks that he spent the next few years attempting to avoid all of them. The casual spirit that would fail him so subtly in graduate school arose from this decision. A further result was that Patrick learned to hold in most of his outbursts of emotion. Instead of seeming cold, he set out to prove he could be just cool, or detached, but not aloof.

This coolness then transformed over the years, as Patrick gained slightly more confidence. Unbeknownst to him, the look in his eyes which had developed out of that slightest bit of twenty-year-old-confidence confronted those around him with a jarring, menacing specimen of human nature. His look, although not violent or passionate, had a brooding quality to it that coupled well with his occasional anger or vapid joy. Instead of looking wise with his indifference, it seemed to those around him that his emotions lay just under the surface, waiting for exposure. He only knew of the sudden surges of emotionality, but nothing of this manner with which his face affronted so many, as most people were too afraid to question why he looked the way he did.

Staring blankly into the glass of a display, which held a golden bracelet once worn by a prince, Patrick, for the first time, maybe for the thousandth time, noticed this look. Those eyes immobilized his feet and he waited. He assessed the situation calmly, but gathered from previous experience with such personal surprises that he needed to form a judgment of his own face quickly. Was he that mean-looking? His eye twitched and the form of his face took on an underdeveloped kind of expression that alluded to its potential for rare, but significant, articulations of feeling. His focus moved onto his mouth, tightly lipped, seeming to seal itself from communication. This was not withholding that he observed, but an unintended result of years of self-discipline. He was not aware that there would be results beyond those that he had calculated. With force, he began to discern why Laura was so able to ascertain his mood without speaking to him. Equally, he was sure his mother had been able to gauge his feelings and thus more easily manipulate his decisions.

The unintended effect of his change in personality upset him. He stood rooted to the spot in front of the bracelet trying to fathom how he could alter this very superficial aspect of his being. Would he need to intentionally smile more often? Could there be some way to control his eyes? Was it even worth his while to make himself appear kinder? He thought that perhaps he could use the meanness of his look to give the impression of being above other people. Grimacing was not the worst formation of a face in an art museum at least: here it seemed more serious, convincing those around him that he understood these objects. Of course, once he left this place, a sudden refuge for him, albeit an unexpected one, he would be terribly self-conscious of his mannerisms. He would scrutinize his body language and the tone of his voice in new ways, all to see if they matched in some way the foulness of his visage. Could there be other features of his physical being that communicated his deep, and ignored, dissatisfaction with his life and the world? He had convinced himself that he was capable at hiding this from others.

The dimness of the room around him, as well as the many glass cases, offered no assistance at classifying his present contemplations. In yet another way, he had failed to properly interpret the world that surrounded him. In this crisis, he was not sure if there would be other facets of his self that he would learn to have been flawed. Thus far, his calculations were too casual and his countenance was far too menacing. He would need to pay attention to how he consumed solids and liquids. He remembered how quickly he had eaten his toast and drank his coffee. There could be room for changes in his life. This, of all times, would be best. He had not changed his name, as he romanticized, but now he could alter small parts of himself, hoping that there would be a larger change. At this, he remembered to second guess himself, and to call into question his own abilities to see through these changes. He did not even know what these changes would substantiate, but he had set himself to performing them. He took a deep breath and left the room, once more coming upon the grand staircase.

9

Finally, the four men climbed back in the van and headed for the border. The sun had set on Manama. All of the buildings projected florescent lighting outward upon the cleaned roads. Each street grew larger until once more the van rode upon the highway, where the traffic was easier. The radio played via Jim's phone, as if where the four men were headed was not a place that restricted rock 'n' roll in any way. James stared out at the passing trees and sands, and thought of his trip thus far: St. Louis 6AM, Washington 10AM, Kuwait Next Day, Manama Late Afternoon and Evening, Border Evening. The summary of his movements blurred within him. The further the group moved away from the city proper, the quieter Scott and Jim became. Gary thumped his hands along happily to the music that exited the speakers. The speed of the van obscured the view of the Middle Eastern stars that James had dreamed of.

As they approached and crossed over the long bridge that connected them to the land, James had to piss, badly. He held it until he was uncomfortable, and noticed the buildings of the border crossing between Bahrain and Saudi. Cars were backed up, waiting impatiently to cross back into the richness of Saud's land. Occasional honks and cries melded into the cacophony that then entered Scott's window. James grew fidgety in the plush backseat. Once the van halted, behind Mercedes, Toyotas, and so forth sitting under the street lights waiting to return to family, wife, child, and the like, James stuck his thin head in-between the front seats.—I have to pee. Cars waited 20 or 30 deep to cross over to Saudi. People cut them off and honked and yelled out windows. Arabs of all ages and western men drove towards work and home life loudly.

—Go outside the car on a wall, Scott said and he did. He had no choice. He left the van and walked between the many cars: the motion of his legs eased his need. James tried his best to be as discrete as he could, only to discern the comedy that many of the people who saw him found in the act: he was surprised that the conservative image of these folks did not conform with their reaction to his bladder. He had unzipped his pants subtly, but now grew confident and walked back to the vehicle relieved. Scott and Jim laughed and Gary's silence told James that Gary was intimidated by boldness. The van was spacious and when he closed the door and they began to drive once more he had space to avoid the looks of Gary and Jim who were blurred with booze and worries at this border. The sun had set while they were in Digger's and the city glowed behind them with a kind of forlorn radiance in the night.

The traffic at the border was still terrible. Jim decided to join in. He stuck his fingers out at an old man who had cut their path just as they arrived at the checkpoint for inspection. Gary watched the event from a better angle than James had: slow motion, Jim's overweight arms wobbling slightly and quivering as he rolled the window down. From this his middle finger arose, and Jim looked on as this happened, being sure that it happened properly, and laughed in a deep way. Then the arm raised and redirected itself towards the old man, who in his age and wisdom shifted his view towards the van of teachers in unison with the finger having been pointed in his direction. The entirety of this caused Gary's mouth to drop open and become void of words: he would not be able to speak in times of stress for his complete and total life: he spent every living moment hoping for peace, or at least the peace of those around him. In response to this, Gary had a Proustian moment of recollection: his father, the man who beat him, but also loved him, had been nearly killed in front of the very young Gary: Gary thought of his first interaction with a cop (#crimingwhilewhite).

At that age of 17, Gary possessed a full head of bright blonde hair, a car, and an in depth knowledge of Los Angeles. The mid-1980s were accepting of Gary in terms of aesthetic and attitude. His weed came to him promptly and his relationship with his father had improved very much. On this hot day, Gary awoke and walked in the Saturday heat to a nearby gas station, where the cashier was ignorant enough to sell him a six pack of future-Superbowl-advertisement-dominating-lagers. Gary's thinness grinned wide and he left to return to his father's house. He navigated the air-conditioning of his home, the kind of appliance that he would love for his lifetime, and sat upon the dead grass of his father's backyard opened a beer and rolled a small blunt.

Life was simple in those days. No one bothered Gary any longer: his father did not fight him, his mother was gone to Seattle, his brothers were in the Northeast. The crispness of the beer lingered on his tongue, and in the back of his mouth he tasted the corn that was used to create the drink he drank, in his stomach he felt the thrill of breaking California law. Gary did not like drunkenness, nor did he have an affection for law-breaking, but the sun reflected off of his forehead on that day, and he baked in peace. Thoughts of high school girls, how they would look during his last year of school and so on floated through him. From there, his mind drifted onto the classes he loved: reading books, doing simple geometry, and histories. Studies were simple for Gary. His schooling was supported by teachers who were reasonably paid and who received adequate materials and training. Gary did not face adversity in the suburb his father lived in, excluding of course his father and mother. The pop top snap of his second beer aroused his focus on the reality of his teenagehood. The pressure released itself from the can in a mist that landed on his hands and fingers.

Enter Gary's white privilege.

On the side of his house he heard a shuffling and as Gary was easy to fluster he stamped what was left of his weed. Out to his right, a man in uniform walked behind his house and addressed him as YOUNG MAN. The cop asked for his ID and Gary could only look at the beer and the trampled-upon-green. How dead the grass was stood out in Gary's eyes.—ID. He shifted his body and prepared his identification.—Sorry, man. Just got done with a job. Found some of the old man's beers and couldn't resist. He looked down again and held out his license. The officer looked at Gary and took the ID from his hand. The cop did not call in anything, nor did he say anything. Gary's pulse was never mellow, and accelerated during this event.

The cop's sunglasses were tilted downward and he crouched to look at Gary on an even level. —YOUNG MAN, he handed back the ID,—You know that this is not how it works in this state. Don't try me again. Someone in this neighborhood called worried about you drinking back here. I'll take these, he picked up the beers,—And you'll have learned. Had Gary been anyone else, or so he felt, he would have gotten a ticket or worse. The same cop who let him off, Officer Koon, had been friends with his father for many years.—Your father talked to me some time back about you, Gary. He's stopped hitting you so don't mess that up. You know the line is thin. The cop strutted off and Gary stood up: there was someone within the house, his father whom he had not noticed. Gary left the backyard, the opposite way as the cop, and did not stop walking for many hours. That night, when he returned home, his father and he did not speak of the incident. He would occasionally see the cop around and would wave to him kindly. Gary had learned that there were powers that he did not understand, but even so could attempt to manipulate.

Enter Jim's white privilege.

The old man at the receiving end of Jim's middle finger got out of his car at the checking area and hailed three officers to him. He pointed the four out as they pulled to a stop for inspection. Gary frowned dramatically, more so at his memories than his present situation. There was a moment, as he approached maturity, when he realized all that he had seen, and unraveled the associations he had with police, his father, and his self. Gary unpacked the circumstances of that moment and coupled them with his own history, a habit he had had for many years, and again frowned markedly. Gary's view of the night of arrival included so many cars and men that he confused himself with the futures of the four people in the van. James, to Gary, looked to be a man he could not connect with, even though he would want to. Jim and Scott had a brashness that Gary envied. California threw Gary out and did not want to welcome him back. His travels, his crossing of borders swum in his head. A small noise came from him, one that no one else could hear, that expressed this stress. It was at that moment too much for Gary. The guards came to them, and wanted to know why they had disrespected the man so. Everyone in the van observed the movement of arms and the quick Arabic with reservation. A sensibility descended upon the men, which sobered them significantly. No English was spoken within that vehicle for nearly thirty seconds. Jim, realizing his fault and the stony shift across Gary's small face, took the three men of authority aside and began to explain what had happened.

The Movements of Others

Elizabeth's departure from Arabia relied on several different realities coming together very quickly. She would, in planning her flight, head first to Washington Dulles. There she could get a hotel: she had more than $10,000 (USA) in her stateside account: plan her next move. She needed first to check what time of year it was with regard to graduate school applications. She needed a cheap apartment within walking distance of a testing facility that could furnish for her the GRE. She also needed a library to edit the relevant documents and to perform research within. None of this would take place in D.C., or Virginia, or Maryland, but in one of those places she would find her bearings, and let her own examination dictate the next move. As a start, the DMV offered free cultural attractions for her downtime and necessary distracted times. She planned on no more than 10 days in the area. That time would allow her the 48 hours she sought to counteract jet lag, the furious initial research, which would amount to 36-48 hours depending on diet and attitude, a 24 hour recovery period, another 72 hours dedicated research and planning, and time left over in case her schedule need be bent or flexed in any small ways. While all of this formed her main list of priorities, she also needed to find a lawyer, notify her family that she had returned to the States, visit a bookstore (with her Kindle so that she could get proper physical copies of books she wanted, not that the Jarir lacked, but that she had trouble navigating the place), attend to any communications from the students she left behind, if anything was communicated from them.—Fuck. Elizabeth had forgotten her students. Her idealisms, the humans she looked to most for the notion that the world was not so bad after all: they had been through so much, lived such different lives with such contrasting histories. Even those who had *wasta*, if even a woman in Saudi can have *wasta*, knew a struggle so outside her own that she needed them in order to affirm the privileges that she had, however many or few.

Elizabeth thought of the new world she was creating for herself. She spoke:

—Should I remain for them? To what extent can my own "selflessness" aid these women? If I am able to in some way move with these women into another world, perhaps a shared world, then would we not all benefit? I don't mean to want this, but I would feel validated should one of them write something that was banned by this government. They are in their twenties: should they not be afforded some rebellion?

Elizabeth stopped herself. She looked around the store at the coffees and teas. She looked at all of the packaging with all of the colors, some natural and some artificial—The commonalities that we most often shared are materialistic. But still the classroom has been a place for growth and openness. Am I then leading by example? Could I foster that doubt in these people if I merely leave without a word of notice? What trouble would they find if I were to write them all letters explaining my movements and justifying my decisions? I could make clear my worldview to them all in an email. Would they be pulled out of school? What would happen to the department if one of its teachers went out like that? What would that mean for my colleagues, the other women from the US and Britain? There is a preference towards convenience and simplicity, that keeping quiet is easiest. But then moving so suddenly across the world is not simple, nor is leaving one's partner. Just so, for some of my students education is not the easy route. They make sacrifices in order to attend. Some of their fathers are so hesitant that it causes real drama within the home . . . Mothers begging them not to go, other sisters shaming them, brothers not speaking to them. I can only hope that some of that is overstated and embellished. If I explained my absence, and they in turn identified with it because of the difficulty of the situation, perhaps then I could exert more of a radical influence, leave a more active impression, than if I stayed. But who I am talking to: am I so noble as to think I would sacrifice my own movement for the sake of others? Even without justification I need what is happening. She had the technology to keep up with the class. Her unreliable, yet somehow functional, laptop and phone, which was unlocked, a strange concept for American phone companies, would suffice at reaching out to the young women once she landed and checked in somewhere across the Atlantic. She had not been back to the United States in many months. She wondered to herself if their grocery stores and shops had changed. She also thought about the richness of bacon and liquor stores.

The infrastructure would take time to re-acclimate to: such rugged individuality and supposed variety. She needed to save her money as best she could. Perhaps staying in Washington was not the best recourse. She could find someone to stay with, but worried that her friends and family back home would see this as a breakdown as opposed to a coming-to-one's-senses. It would be a fine line for her to draw through her own narrative, one that would distinguish her as an agent of her own fate instead of labeling her as a victim. She needed to be composed and decisive. For that reason, she needed to communicate with possible schools as soon as she landed: to have a path, a calculated trajectory. She did not wish to enter free-fall, or at least if she did she did not want anyone to know. Frustrated as she had been, angry even, she would simply need to model the behaviors that perpetuated calm. Elizabeth's passion, willingness even, at debating people, at times passively while at others loudly, needed to be shaped into relaxed deliberateness. Instead of moving with sound and fury towards her ends, she needed to take pre-planned steps, to show wisdom. This would justify her time spent in the strange *Hauptstadt*. She needed practice, and strangers would function well.—To what extent can I change these attributes of myself so quickly? She had lost sight once more of her students. She came to no real conclusion about how she would frame all of this for them, or even if she would at all.

At that time, she had a group of 18 young women. Three of them were recently married, another four had marriage in their near future, and a further two had been in matrimony long enough to have children. At the beginning of the semester, one of the mothers seemed sullen and refused to participate in activities or discussion. She did her work quietly and began to fake smiles once the rest of the class caught on to her moods. Fatima did not want to share with the class what bothered her, and so she continued on, excelling at her written work while allowing for her spoken progress to suffer. She did not have outbursts, or act out, it was only that she was quiet and frowned. Some weeks into the class, another student admitted to stealing her father's car and driving it around the desert late at night. She had been fed up with his distaste for her studies and he would make jokes at her about being well read, but not being able to drive. The entire class laughed along with her at this story. Elizabeth was not sure it was true, but Fatima spoke,—Did you actually do it? The class was happy to have the narrative continued and layered with more detail. Of course she had stolen the car—My father will never know so don't tell it around, said Nadeeda. Nadeeda's openness continued over the coming weeks and the class felt more at ease with one another. Those who came from wealthier families and tribes did not look down on those from outside their clans, or at least not openly. Nadeeda was from a middle class tribe. Her father was very old, her mother had been his third wife. What money the family had was given over to the sons, Nadeeda's older brothers, who did not care for study and could not advance in the jobs they had because they spoke no English and were not able to perform necessary maths. But so, her family continued on and Nadeeda began to feel more at home within the walls of the schools she attended. Now at university, she studied medicine and hoped to be able to move abroad: to create her own standing and establish her own networks. Because her father did not believe that this was possible, so much so that he chided her for trying, Nadeeda turned to her classmates for reassurance.

Elizabeth facilitated this classroom environment, and allowed it to grow into a community where the women talked amongst themselves about whatever they wanted, but always in colonizing English. She challenged them to find the vocabulary that would fit their needs. Nadeeda led this with care. More and more, the other women began to share what they felt. The concept of sharing was not radical, but doing so in English had at least some thrill to it. Fatima watched as the class became more and more aware of one another. As the semester wore on, nearing its middle point, and closer to the time that Elizabeth stood in the HyperPanda, Fatima decided to share. One and a half weeks before Elizabeth crossed the threshold of the grocer, Fatima raised her hand. The discussion was about travel, or maybe etiquette on subways, Elizabeth could not remember. Fatima spoke,—I am sorry. The rest of the class looked at her, puzzled at her apology, hedging for what came next,—My husband took another wife and only sees her. He does not look at me anymore, or our child. The class remained silent. Slowly, the faces of her classmates shaped themselves into the kind, I-have-no-idea-what-to-say forms of people who feel empathy.

Elizabeth was at a loss. She did not expect this. Fatima, who had not spoken that sentence before in her life, looked nearly happy. Elizabeth moved to her and sat in a desk, level with her and the class.—Would you like to talk about it? Elizabeth thought that this moment could be transformative for the class as a whole, but she had ignored, or at least not been aware of Fatima's transformation—No. I only wanted to say it. Thank you. Some of the women laughed. Fatima continued her work and began to speak more in class.

Nadeeda looked on at Fatima that day with a quiet solidarity. Fatima was from an affluent tribe, and had married into another branch with similar privilege. Typically, Fatima would not speak with a person like Nadeeda, let alone share her pain with her. In the act, Fatima did not feel diminished. In all of her discontent, Nadeeda learned to look past the class of a person, past those obvious markers of wealth and well-being and to understand a common element of life on the Earth as a human: suffering. Elizabeth could not decide what to do about her class.—May it be true that my own marginalization can allow for their possible subversion? She wanted to know how to move forward, but she needed to make herself move past present spatial orientation. After Elizabeth left, her students would stop discussing the men in their lives and begin to discuss one another. They had shared some of the wrongs they had felt, but not how they felt. Whispers reached out between them, not about men or their ways, but about each other, their lives and their worlds. Elizabeth would not, could not, hear these voices grasping at ideas of solidarity and coalition.

Elizabeth was little aware of her own effect on other humans at that point in her 30s. That form of wisdom, being able to see in the eyes of another person when you have made them feel, good or bad, would have to wait. She had not yet trained her eyes to see her influence on others, to water slightly at the sight of her having said the right thing to inspire or support another human. She guessed at it, and she had been adept at guessing thus far in her life, but, in her 40s, she would feel it in her bones. Then she could come to a conclusion about what she did for her students that semester in Dammam. Then she could feel at ease with the decision she made, be at peace with the movements she had made and not made, and the discussions she had fostered and neglected.

Patrick left the main building: 1:42PM. To his left he saw another part of the complex, yet this structure was not part of the island. He knew there must be an opening. He had not taken any notes, and was still reeling from seeing himself reflected amongst those golden things. He stood for a moment and looked down the palm-lined drive that led to the main entrance. He could not give up. He needed more time in the museum to assess himself, and with some luck find solace in dismissing something. Accordingly, he moved towards the second building. Murakami's opening was that day. Therein he would find many works from that Japanese artist, and even though he had not the slightest clue about Superflat, he would look at most of it. The air was not as sandy as he had thought it would be. Still, the salt from the water remained in what he breathed. He moved with greater determination now, forcing his legs to take more assertive strides as he approached Murakami's Ego.

When he crossed the threshold of the building he smelled that smell exhibitions have: a sterile, living kind of temporary. He exhaled deeply, not allowing himself to be too angry at his own misconceptions of his looks. He walked slowly through the art, which was arranged in a deliberate, room to room manner, instead of employing the entirety of the huge space. The over-the-top nature of many of the colors, how saturated

they were, and how they affected the eye when layered, all impressed Patrick and distracted him away from his brooding.

He navigated the works with indifference, no reaction, sur-
prising himself with his own relaxed demeanor. That was so until he entered the biggest room of the exhibition, a giant space
filled with a circus tent, various other large objects, many people, a Kanye West song, and a series of huge paintings: The
Arhat Paintings. These objects produced in Patrick a sensation
of dread and happiness: a contradictory state. He was not sure
if he continued frowning or began smiling.

Along the two walls on which the Arhat stretched, Patrick
moved back and forth. He looked at many different areas of the
whole work, noticing small details as he went: peculiar wrinkles on some of the characters, certain textures behind others,
deeply interactive shades of red, animals with no biological reality, saddened blues, water stretching across centuries. What
hung on the wall was a work that pushed from his mind anything but its own details. There was, within that space, such a
large amount of people that he ignored in order to move more
fluidly with the art, in a way so that some perceived him as a
critic: he had no idea how seriously he was taking the work. It
was a kind of rumination that he possessed in this room that
he had not felt before. He walked along the piece, even rudely
stepping in front of others who were also beholding Murakami's
work. He did not care: for this time his mind did not race to severe conclusions as it usually did. He could not grasp why this
huge piece had any consequence for him. The serious and artful
happiness with which others looked at the Arhat was beyond
Patrick. He could not interpret his own reaction as his mind
was empty and there was no reflection of himself to consider.—
Grotesque, but balanced all these are, his first words, his mind
returning.—OH, but what shades these are. There is no point in
reading or rereading these scenes. Is it that I am watching this
without distaste? What are Murakami's vices? Does he mastur-

bate in the same way as I do: in that way do our hands share commonality? Where do we head after appreciating something for the first time? I cannot appreciate this. I should not. I find no quantifiable sense here, except of course the tension I feel standing in front of it. There there there. . . Misshapen with intent these are. Expose what's underneath. Are all of my art references, music and all, from listening to Laura: yes. She would talk at me about all of that, the people she enjoyed. Not my tastes, but taken from her for bibliographic purpose. There is more to my aesthetic sense than I had imagined. Perhaps, it is time I started to acknowledge it all: take the forms as they are, not as pure negatives. Have I been ignoring this sensibility I have, style that I have come to appreciate, all for the sake of my own sternness: for that meanness staring back from a glass box: yes. Another failure of mine: to fully reject something. Once again, I am at an impasse. Do I like this? What about the other things that come to my mind. I keep my likes and dislikes within; so does that stunt their growth? I have mistaken myself. What would Laura and my mother think to see me enjoy a painting or a composition? This is happening quickly isn't it? I should learn to shut myself up. But my life must be better than I perceive it to be if this is what consumes my time. Or am I belittling my own issues. These animals are so perplexing. I would like to know from where, within the brain, these shapes and ideas emerge. History must be a nightmare for this guy. There is a texture to it, something that speaks to push off people from getting too close. This set up is remarkable in how it draws all of these people in: brings them close, lets them think they know: very much how white people work. Make the intelligence segmented, box it, put it in public for display. Well done. The end. The variance of color allows for the ambiguity of it all. And that is the crap. The buzz in the air. I couldn't not not there here go. I reject it. No. Not for the likes of me. Even with the factory-like quality of it. Surely made with some machines in mind. Can a group of human hands assemble the likes of this? I have my doubts. If it is made not by the man himself then I fear it is not his. Yet, the names of those who made it I shall never know. Those poor humans. Even if I should like this, accept its ambiguity as beauty, its shapes and hues as value, they would never receive credit for their work. If I were to parse this, to catalog it, they would not make any comment. Only that one man. The one people are told to care about. And so they do. Genuinely, they look at his art and appreciate his mind, also his intentions. But really, he only thought of it. To him the spoils. I wonder how many books are dictated. I wonder how many paintings ghost painted. I wonder how many songs written by a nameless person in a studio. I would like to see a count of all of the works of art composed, written, constructed, shaped, painted, filmed, scored, choreographed, etched, molded, burned, sketched, colored, arranged, envisioned or otherwise by one human and then subsequently given to another for creation or credit. Then I would like a list of all humans who receive credit for another human's work, even if superficial. There should be a sticker on each piece of art that has this complication. I would like this if he had made it himself with only his hands. Or maybe I like the power he exercises in its creation. To no end can it be simple to generate such a work: it is huge. But still, it needs a sticker. I believe I like that convoluted aspect of art. Art remembered because of those who requested it, not who made it. Aw, fuck it all.

He stood, his eyes closed while he waited for himself. He would not like art. He could not ever. Although at times he may be challenged to do so, there was something that caused him to resist. Some part of the discourse that he could not engage. He found his way out to the salty Doha air. 3:45PM.

10

Gary was at a loss. The entrants had been stranded at the airport, taken to a whore bar and now this.—Why this? He had not researched anything about Saudi. For all he knew, they were about to be thrown in jail and forgotten about until CNN or LiveLeak discovered them. Each of the men were lost in Gary's mind.—Holy shit. This was all about a salary for him and now this. At that point, he didn't care. James thought that the worst would be having to fly back to the States, if it even got that far, with all of the yelling and gesturing of the old man and the guards. Scott was exhausted.

(*Paranoia entered the van. James, Scott, and Gary remain in the van while Jim exits and speaks with the frustrated old man and the border officials. Two scenes happen in unison, loudly. Backing music: Bela Lugosi's Dead by Bauhaus.*)

Gary: Holy shit.

Jim: It wasn't meant to offend.

Scott: We'll be fine.

Old Man: What do you mean, wasn't?

Sign Above Inspection Area (*calmly*): Welcome.

Scott: Gary, he's taking care of it.

Guard: You must apologize to this man.

Gary: Holy shit.

Old Man: How did I merit such rudeness?

Jim: How is he rude? He cut us off.

James: I wonder what time we teach tomorrow?

Answer: 7:30AM, buses leave the compound an hour before-hand. Good luck sleeping.

Scott: We'll get Turkish in Hufuf. OH, yes.

Jim (*sighing*): Alright whatever.

Old Man: Whatever? That is your response?

(*Jim's white privilege taps on the shoulders of each police officer and smiles at them showing ugly, rotting teeth.*)

Scott (to a vacant James): Canada's great.

Old Man: Amreekee . . .

Cars: blubblubblubblubblubblubblubblubblubblubblub-blubblubblubblub

Officers: Sir, you must know what you have done is out of line. Please, we do not want trouble.

James (*blank stare*):

Gary's Cell Phone: Powering down!

Van: ppppffffppppffffppppffffppppffffppppffffppppffffppppffff-ppppffffppppffff

Old Man (*Shakes head at Jim.*): hrumpf

Officer: OK?

Jim: See? Fine fine fine fine fine. SORRY.

Gary: Fuck.

Scott: Ever been to Nova Scotia?

James: No. I told you I've never been outside of the USA before.

Gary: Damn. And no. But Vancouver, yes.

Old Man: Am I cleared to go? I have had enough of this.

(*Jim, Old Man, Officers stand in silence for thirty seven seconds.*)

Scott: Noooooova Scotia's great.

James: um

Gary: ffffffffff

James: How long is this bridge?

Gary: Whoa.

Bridge: Long.

(*Jim, Old Man, Officers all hold hands and then resolve the conflict by clapping sixteen times and then shaking hands angrily. Paranoia exits dejectedly. Jim's White Privilege, who feels validated by the scene, disappears into the back of the van.*)

Jim: (*Returns to the van.*) Let's go. Holy shit.

Again, Jim got into the van. The commotion had distracted many people and the cars behind honked loudly and made the same fingers that had gotten Jim in no actual trouble.

The officers had reached some sort of conclusion and the old Arab drove off still fuming. Then the shortest of the three cops asked the men to step out of the vehicle while he performed a search. Gary shook himself absently out of the van and stood next to James. Both men beheld the scene around them. Still people rubbernecked them. The guard fulfilled his own need to touch their things and looked to Scott to take the two first-timers to have their documentation handled. The guard pointed his stubby finger at a building nearby.

James and Gary entered and waited in line. James could smell rum on Scott, who was busy discussing the process with a taller guard. Passports were handed over, and with some picture taking, James and Gary awaited the approval of their entrance into al-Mamlakah al-Arabiyah as-Sa'udiyah: an absolute monarchy. King Abdullah was somewhere at that moment ignorant of the two Americans that were permitted entry into his country. The staff of the border office made note of all of the previously completed paperwork from Gary and James. Each had been tested for several diseases and viruses, had their medical records submitted, background checks performed and so on. The process itself took weeks to complete, and as they stood at the border it was still not finished. The bureaucratic detail of the affair was enormous, enough to arouse any sensible pencil pusher to well past half-mast.

The building was dirty. Clearly none of the men who worked at this border station had taken it upon themselves to clean any of its many surfaces. Tiles were caked with sand and dirt. The walls were stained with the artificiality of air-conditioned air mixing with salt-air. The counters were worn at the points where people waited. The chairs, which were only occupied by officials, seemed old. The general sense of the premises presented to James was soiled.

He gazed over at Gary, who had developed a blankness in his eyes and tapped his right pointer finger on his left wrist. Inside his guts, James felt two sensations. First, he felt the need to evacuate his bowels. Second, he required calories. The adventure of the day had not for several hours included enough food for him apparently. Scott waited patiently on the paperwork. James decided to put bathroom functions temporarily on hold, hoping to stave off any further lavatorial advice. The coldness of the building settled on James, causing his sensitivities to spread goose pimples across his right arm. James thought it strange that no one was speaking. No casualness at this point, only procedure.

The hazy and muddled past few hours rang in James' ears as he reflected on how this had been the strangest day of his life thus far. To be standing on an island in the Gulf, about to enter the kingdom, James' first kingdom, and having met the people he had. His meandering brain was distracted momentarily by the procedure. The guard shouted,—Teachers! with a smile. Neither James, nor Gary, nor Scott, nor Jim had any passion for teaching. Jim obsessed over a kind of pseudo-academia, a study of light journalism. Gary had once dreamed of being a teacher, but found those dreams ruined by his difficulty with how he looked at female students. Scott, it must be said once more, was not well spoken and should not have been a teacher. This left James, who stumbled into teaching.

The pedagogical ignorance of the men did not prevent them from earning a wage that they could not have found elsewhere in the world. Earning more than nearly all of the people they would encounter on a daily basis (including but not limited to: gas station attendants, laundry men, day laborers, taxi drivers, cooks, handymen, mechanics, tailors, hole diggers, hammer users, and pizza makers) each would become comfortable with money. James would develop a spending habit that his continued teaching in the States would not be able to support. He bought headphones, books, iPhones, and so much else. He did not know anyone who did so straight out of school in the States, given he did not know very many rich people, but he also could not spend Christmas or Thanksgiving with his family. There was distance between them, and also those were teaching days.

With some furious stamping, Gary and James were accepted into the kingdom. The three rejoined Jim in the van. By this point, the gawking had stopped and Jim texted Xiaoqing calmly. The border guard did not find the two bottles of rum that Scott had hidden and the event, middle fingers included, was considered a general success by Scott, who was still unfit to drive. They entered Saudi and crossed King Fahd's bridge.

Elizabeth Leaves the Store

Elizabeth left the HyperPanda. Her excursion had been a distraction. She had her bag with two boxes of tea and nothing else. No one looked at her any differently; no one had noticed her talking to herself. She thought of the friendly ghost as she left the store, thinking that she did not need any imagined support where she was headed. That ghost waved to her as she left, intent on supporting someone else who would move through the aisles of the Panda, helping to sort out their life: what else were friendly ghosts for, after all?

The mall had become more populated after the prayers. Students and families entered. Some made their way for early dinners, others loitered. Elizabeth had, at first, disliked the mall culture in Saudi. She preferred to visit the older, or seemingly older, *suqs* and markets. She thought that malls were sterile and disingenuous. It occurred to her that *suqs* and malls were the exact same thing, just in different forms. When she thought of this, how those older markets were romanticized only because of nostalgia for an unattainable kind of history, she began to appreciate the humanness of the mall. There were children and teenagers. Newly married couples strolled to find things for the home. Old people moved about and watched the crowds. Elizabeth thought ahead to the future, perhaps to that day when malls would be irrelevant and the internet would be the most important marketplace. She thought about how slick companies would buy and refurbish old malls to capitalize on that same nostalgia that drew people to farmers' stands and flea markets. Some travel company would write of the place: beautiful mall just a short ride outside of Cleveland, with a food court and all of the trimmings. The food court, instead of having the cheap, greasy fair that she could smell from so far away, would have tables and expensive greasy foods, modeled closely on the old fast foods, but improved upon. The destination would inspire children to ask,—Grandma, did you really shop at a place like this?—Yes, young one. We all used to buy our clothes and things from places like these. Some towns even had two malls, at which the child would gasp.—Those were the days! Yes, they were!

Elizabeth wanted to get something for herself that would remind her of her time in Saudi. She did not want to share her journals and pictures with people, not yet at least, and wanted to have something that recalled the ups and downs she had felt. She looked all around. The people she saw knew what they wanted. They deliberated and discussed what to get and from where. So much of what she could see around her was the same as she could find in the States or in Europe. Sunglasses, clothes, pens and stationery, toys and clothes for children, books, those that were not banned, soaps, perfumes, jewelry. The money that Elizabeth had taken from the kitchen was substantial. She could save it, exchange it, and use it as cash in Washington.

In the middle of a concourse, at a small kiosk, a man sold prayer beads. Red, black, pale green, blue. They were delicate, and supposedly hand-strung. Elizabeth was reminded of an outing that had been hosted by some Saudis for the Americans at her compound. They went South, away from the coast to a series of caves. By middle morning, when the group reached the entrance and got out of the bus, the sun beat down upon the world. The day was particularly hot, so hot that many hesitated to get off of the bus. Their guide told them to grin and bear it, for the caves would make the heat disappear. The group did not seem convinced, but walked into the thumping sunshine. Elizabeth had forgotten her sunglasses and Robert's would not fit her. She squinted as she made her way down the sandy path. On each side above her rose pale rock, increasing quickly and dramatically in height. The mounds and crevasses of the system developed before her: all along her horizon she noticed the edges and pitfalls. The path the group took had a downward incline and the walls led to the entrance of the cave they would explore (the system itself was huge and had many dozens of paths and entrances). The experience was similar to descending gradually into a canyon. Elizabeth walked apart from the rest of the group, slightly behind them. They looked so small next to the tall walls of rock. The shade enveloped them. They crossed into the caves and Elizabeth remained, for the moment, slightly outside. She could feel the cool radiating out of the entryway. Ahead she heard the echoes of the guide.—People have lived in this area for tens of thousands of years. These caves gave them a break from the sunshine; they provided life in the desert. Here it is cool in the day and warm at night. You can see the evidence of the people all around you. Elizabeth crossed in. All over the walls there was graffiti. Some of it was new, Arab and English script that she could make out around her. But there were also worn etchings, fading paint, scratch marks. The shadows in the cave were many, and in front of her she could see some places where light was let in. These rays acted as their guides and the Saudi man who led them here let the Americans move about freely.

It was so quiet within the caves that at first the group hardly spoke to one another and if they did so only in a breathy whisper. Elizabeth felt the rock wall to her right. It was cool and smooth. The ground beneath her was less dusty and more solid than it had been outside. She had hesitated to go on the trip as she did not like confined spaces. Personally, she hated the symbolism of caves, of emerging into the sun. Her idea of what she was to see had been completely wrong. There was beautiful light in the cave. Its walls were tall: in some places upwards of 50ft. It was not a small space; instead a series of paths that were in places wide and in others thin. She could see living in a place like that. In some places, she could see and smell the soot of fires, of teenagers who had rebelled by partying or exploring the caves at night. She knew that the ashes from the fire and the writing on the wall had to be related. This would be a landmark of coming of age, of scale, a natural wonder seen, navigated, and cared for by generations. As the people moved through the caves, Elizabeth had become even more separated from the crowd. She found herself alone in one vein of the cave and for the first time felt the fear that she had assumed would take ahold of her immediately upon entering. She did not know if she could shout to find the others.—Isn't shouting dangerous in caves? She looked at the rock around her in its different shades of browns, yellows, and reds. How the light moved through the cave illuminated some parts and left others empty of light. She could see her way back, it was a straight path to what she remembered to be a larger vein: she did not need to scream or be flustered. She could see a bend ahead of her to the right.

She made the decision to proceed just to peek around the corner and then turn around. Her steps were silent, padded by the soft rock beneath her feet. She bent and leaned forward and looked to her right. In a medium sized chamber, where Elizabeth stood was the only entrance, there was an old man bowing. In his hands he held and moved his prayer beads and he prayed and bowed and kneeled. Elizabeth took another step and watched him. His eyes were closed and his long beard was white. She wondered if he was facing the direction of Mecca.—

He must be, she whispered. He continued to pray. She did not want to interrupt him or continue her peeping, but he seemed so serene and content. Behind her she heard footfalls and steps. The crowd of Americans had found her and was being directed into the chamber by their chaperone. She looked back at them. They were still silent, but their whispering and hushed talking had gained confidence. They took pictures and were less in awe than they had been. Many walked past her into the space and some stopped to take pictures of the praying old man. He too had heard the walking and had finished his praying. He moved away from the people and past Elizabeth, who looked not at him but at his prayer beads: deep red and black with matching red and black tassels. The beads themselves had been worn by use. They appeared to have once been oblong and round, but were now oddly flattened by wear. They looked so personal, as if they had been made for his hands.

Elizabeth approached the kiosk and began going through what was offered. She had no need to pray, but wanted to remember that old man. She was glad she did not have a picture of him; instead she had a mental image that was only hers. There were many for her to choose from. They needed to be subtle and beautiful; they had to be something that an old man would carry around with him, which his grandchildren would associate with his touch. Elizabeth's head felt clearer after leaving HyperPanda. In searching for the right beads, she got excited for the first time about her move. Transitions in life were moments for celebration. Whatever complications there would be, however difficult what lay ahead seemed, it was a moment for her to rejoice about her being alive. There would be doubt along the way. So would there be dread and unhappiness, but she would also feel joy and elation. The moments of smiling and frowning were related, brothers and sisters of psychology and emotion and she welcomed them to her. She was excited to feel those shifting angles. To be along the curves and pitches, to

plot the motion of her life. She wanted to look for signs of success and failure, to learn with renewed confidence about herself
and her life. She bought her beads; they were so dark red that
unless one held them up to light they looked black. She also
bought a new notebook, pens, and pencils, along with a small
metal sharpener and rubber eraser, from a stationery store. She
wanted to recreate her ideas and life in graphite: there is no
lead in pencils. The roughly 28 million people of Saudi, the
countable, but only estimated, women and men of that land
would not read her words. She intended to work through her
own history on paper. Her words would become worlds though.
Her first task would be a note to her students. This would have
to be in email form, but she needed to explain herself to them
first and foremost. She did not need to write a long note to
Robert: I'm leaving, will email when I land in DC. Her friends
and family could wait until she was ready to move to a perma-
nent place. She looked over what she had: new writing things,
tea, and prayer beads. Much of what she had in Saudi she
would leave behind. She only wanted her clothes and books,
not any of the knickknacks and trinkets she had collected over
time. Just as she prepared to depart with her relationship, so
too did she prepare herself to cast off many material objects.
She looked forward to this. She had thought of it as a surren-
dering, as a sacrifice, but she knew it was not. In reality she
had given herself a chance to refresh. She did not need what
was in her apartment and she knew it. *ctrl + r*

11

The desert didn't seem to be much outside the windows of the van. In some places large oil rigs could be spotted by their lights. Sometimes rocks on the side of the road jutted out towards the highway. The moon did not illuminate the sand well: there was a dullness to the textures that James saw. The road was loud and cars and SUVs passed the slow moving van with ease. Dammam, the capital of crude, the metropolis of oil disappeared quickly behind them. None in the car could make out its buildings or structures from where they were. James knew there was wealth outside of and around him in that city: wealth he would never know. The night kept Dammam and its people secret from him; it did not share their riches with any in the van.

The drunkenness and nervousness of the men sunk into a quiet recollecting. The radio remained silent and Jim tapped his feet on the floor of the vehicle. It was mainly taps that were heard: the engine, Jim's foot, Scott's thumb on the steering wheel, pebbles or small rocks against the window. The percussive nature of these noises wore upon James; they reminded him of the paranoia he felt at the border: a tapping at his feeling of safety.

There were two kinds of paranoia that James observed at the border. The intentional delusions of power that the border guards and staff perpetuated was a kind of deliberate paranoia.

This was constructed to be a line of defense for the king's power: restrict what can and cannot be brought into the kingdom, who can and cannot enter and so forth. The beauty of it was that the king never had to meet any of the border people, nor did any of the princes. These men took the salary that was presented to them and chose to uphold that one man's ideal. Some of those men would even go to Bahrain themselves to have a drink or a weekend away from the gender segregation that Saudi was infamous for. And still, they would report to work and arrest people who brought in alcohol or any contraband. Drug dealing is punishable with death in Saudi: a group of men would be executed weeks later, and James would feel another challenge to his indifference.

None of these defenders of Saud were particularly violent. They did not assault the people they inspected. They would occasionally beat someone they had arrested, but as a policing force were fairly docile. They left the nastiness of such brutalities to others, those who had been trained to maim and torture. Simple employment begets simple employees? The overwhelming sentiment of all of them was to work for their wage, ensure that that work was simple and not taxing, and have a good home life. Some would turn their eyes and heads when certain people would bring in contraband. That was, after all, a part of the fun: possessing the control, being able to supplement the deliberate paranoia that existed around them.

A second form of paranoia arose in response to this inorganic paranoia: inadvertent paranoia. This represented the organic, how ironic, reaction that most people had to the contrived sense of power on display at borders. Those crossing, in their own minds, would create their own ideas of danger and jeopardy. Very different from the men who constructed their hazards, these situations were flamboyant and exaggerated. The human mind worked not only to control at the border, but also to get out of control. Men and women both felt this unease, a sense that all could come crumbling down at the whim of any one guard or staffer.

Several situations had gone through Gary's mind at that time. Unknown to James, who merely considered the phenomena, Gary had firsthand experience with the extent that this adverse psychology presented. Neither Scott nor Jim had felt much of this recently. They had reached a point of stasis and were not aroused by the tensions of such situations any longer. The simplicity of it is what struck King Abdullah on that evening. Far away, in a palace, he chuckled to himself,—How simple it is! There are so many layers of that power, and to think that Qaddafi lets it all tumble . . .

He had recently, on the advice of trusted advisers, set into place many subsidies, for gasoline, bread, and rice, so that his people would not revolt. There were some problems in Qatif, but there always would be. The king rested on his wealth that evening, content to consider how well his father and brothers had done at creating this kingdom. There was nothing to stop his reign, aside from his ill-health. He especially enjoyed having power over the Americans he saw each day. He knew their lust for oil. These people would do anything for what he had, and he let them. War, intrigue: it was a simple distraction, a form of entertainment to him. There was some seriousness that he faced: the need to hold authority over his people. He was an absolute monarch, yet he felt more kinship with the heads of democracies than he did with fellow dictators. Yes, Abdullah laughed heartily that evening, as you can imagine.

—HAHAHAHAHAHAHAHAHAHAHAHAHAHAHAHAHAHA-HAHAHAHA.

In the van, James shook these thoughts from his head. He sat behind Scott. He could only see the distant fire of an oil rig, burning to coax the wonders from the depths. James thought of how Americans had once owned 50% of ARAMCO. Now, they had been bought out. There was something in that that scared him. Some potential his compatriots have to divide and conquer: oil in Arabia, peace in Europe, instability in far-east Asia. Not all pursuits were successful, but win some lose some. James thought of what his mother had said to him.

—There are people in this world, James, that only want. They do not know why they want, seldom do they know what they want, but they lust after something. It is simple. You can see it in a human's eyes, whether or not they have developed it. The want is in everyone, but mature people learn to control it. You may want food or companionship, but what these people desire is different, more abstract. They feel it within them to need ideals and extremes, like children with developed literacies and knowledge. You cannot fight someone who has the want. There is no reasoning. They feel within their limbs, inside of their veins, an individuality that cannot be spoken to. To their eyes, there is only the attainable. Most do not articulate the want, nor do they express it with words. They move through their lives silently understanding that they must have more. You see, James, these are the people who will stop you as you progress through life and make you think. You have got to fight the want, to be sure that you do not succumb to its thrills. In the honesty that these people feel that they must have more, there is no hope for them being convinced otherwise. There are presidents, kings, queens, and so many others on this planet, living as if it is natural for them to have so much wealth, so many houses, such priceless heirlooms . . . The only thing that this country did right was to refuse to serve a king. The rest has been a disaster. I still love it: our communities and schools, the kids' smiling and the older folks reminiscing. I have a lot of nostalgia in me, but I just get so angry that there is some need in these people to live at the top. The peak is only an abstraction: it is not real; those people die just as everyone else, and yet they have convinced everyone that we need them.

James' innards began to ache. He had been holding it in and would not be able to stand it soon. He stuck his head in between Scott and Jim's seats.—Are we stopping soon? The silence, broken for need to shit, dissolved and Gary agreed that stopping would be good for his legs. Scott replied,—We are just past Dammam. We can stop soon.

• • •

He had not consumed food since his late, light breakfast. He looked to his notepad and frowned at not having taken notes. If he could not write simple, true sentences about what he had just seen it must not be worth his time, or so he imagined as he made his way to the road passing the art museum. Geography now took hold of his interests. He pushed away the thoughts he'd had of his own visage, and indeed thoughts of Murakami's Arhat paintings. He assumed that somewhere around him he would find that market he had visited and there he would be able to find another meal just as good. Walking away from the structures he had just navigated, he looked to his right over the water, away from the direction of the market. There he spotted his hotel. The Sheraton rose in the afternoon sunshine and greeted him.

Again on his left, he saw the upward spiraling tower. He had missed the call by nearly an hour. The Maghrib would not be for another hour and a half. Patrick had no knowledge of this, but had noticed the gap in the afternoon previous. The scattered nature his thoughts had assumed that afternoon was beginning to tire him. He would need food and rest. He began to consider why the call enchanted him so, but found the sun to hamper this direction of movement. He was losing his patience. Walking along the water he feared that he would not be able to find a taxi. People ran past, families walked towards boats, boats loudly played music in Hindi, and couples ambled. Patrick Maguire balled his fists. Sweat collected on his forehead. He could not understand how all of the people were not still at work, as it was before 5PM, but he himself was not working. He looked across the bay to the tallish buildings that arose in his line of sight and held his breath.

He stopped walking. 4PM. He had made some progress along the water, but needed to collect himself. In order to prevent himself from shouting at these people, people he had never seen or known of until this point in his life, he started counting as quickly as he could,— One, two, three, four, five, six, seven, eight, nine, ten, eleven, twelve, thirteen, fourteen . . . He did not cease at this, even with his now erratic breathing, not to mention his sweat.—Thirty-three, thirty-four, thirty-five . . . his feet carried him close to the edge of the walkway overlooking the water. —Fifty-eight, fifty-nine . . . His tone was quiet enough that those passing could not hear him. Yet, they could easily sense his discomfort, even anger. His fists shook and his face turned red. —Seventy-eight . . . The counting became slower, but continued, —Eighty-eight, eighty-nine, ninety . . . The difficulty of it all pounded in his chest. His head ached. He knew no end of it. —One hundred and six, and seven, and . . . He closed his eyes to the water and the buildings. He felt his legs grow restless as if wanting to run. —One hundred fifteen, one hundred and sixteen . . . His shaking fists opened. He regained control of his breath, taking deeper breaths. —One hundred thirty . . . The tension in his face relaxed and once again he opened his eyes to look across the bay.

The water meant so much to Patrick already and he could not guess why. For him, although he still felt unease towards boats, the simplicity of the water was appealing. He thought in a moment that he would leave Doha and only miss this body of liquid. Patrick's counting ceased. He needed food: his fits were most often in times of hunger. He turned about-face, looking for a way to cross the boulevard. As he made his way across, he looked to see where people were: there would be the market. He judged from the flow of people walking towards the water, in the opposite direction as he, that he was heading on the correct course. He came by a small avenue, where cars were not allowed, assuming that this would be another end of the market. He looked back towards the Corniche and hoped he would find nourishment soon.

The amount of people around him had increased very much. All around they meandered, buying trinkets, sitting to drink coffee. He found his way into the covered section of the *suq*, and weaved his way past the many small hutches selling clothes and tourist wares. Still others sold spices and teas, groceries. The tightness of the space did not bother him, rather it was the sense that this place was outside, but allowed no sunlight. The darkness caused him to move more quickly, but the nature of its layout confused him. He could not have a breakdown in this tight of a space: he could not handle the embarrassment. He continued to control his breath. It seemed that these shops did not sell any food and Patrick was sensing his own misstep. He walked into a storefront and asked, too loudly for the small space cluttered with Arab-looking things.—How do I get out of here? The merchant laughed at him and shook his head. Perhaps Patrick had spoken too quickly. Patrick scooted through the many objects to get closer to the man; he must ask again. Behind the old man there were glass jars. Patrick pointed,—Candy? Yes, yes! and dates! Patrick did not care. He took out his wallet and put a bill in front of the man who shook his beard.—As much for this please. Dutifully, the man bagged up some candy and dates and handed them pleasantly to Patrick, who had a smile that revealed his teeth and oddly counteracted his usual grimace.

Even within the covered areas of the *suq* there were many people. Most of these people were Europeans or Saudis. Patrick had a fleeting wonder if he had just met a Qatari. With his sweets he reentered the flow of people along the shadowy corridors. He looked for a place to sit, but finding the spaces pragmatically filled, found only a small alleyway that exited towards the sun. He noticed that few people entered and exited through this particular way so he put his back against the wall and sank down, sitting peacefully on the ground: he had not sat in hours.

He opened his bag and smelled the honey and fruit. His hands got sticky from the dates. The first he put into his mouth whole, not realizing there would be a seed inside. He attempted to bite, bit the seed, and readjusted how he would eat. It would have to be more slowly, eating around the pit. With careful deliberation, he ate all of the dates and candies. He licked his fingers and set the empty bag next to him. He felt some remaining date in his teeth, but made no move to rise and leave. A calm arose in him after the food made him reflect: he had just eaten the only item he knew to be distinctly Arab. He could not think of a single Arab dish, only dates. He then realized that he was sitting on the ground. He scrambled to get up and, for the first time since arriving, laughed. He stood for a final moment in the shade. The darkness of the place no longer got at him. He understood the practical purpose of covering these tight spaces of commerce. He appreciated that work had been done to save him from the heat, although the weather in Doha on that afternoon was kind. Patrick comprehended a symbolism in it. In the sunshine, he found he was near the restaurants he had seen the day before. With that knowledge, he walked atop the cobblestones until he found the sandy boat and all of the taxis once more. A now familiar crew of Africans and Indians stood waiting for Patrick. He chose one and was off towards the Sheraton at 4:28PM. Text message from Malcolm: Irish Harp 8:30PM.

12

They stopped for gas at a white light station. The complex was large and at the junction of two highways outside of Dammam. The mosque, shops, and pumps stood strong in the dry air. James had not heard any recitation in his few hours in the Near East. The walls of the buildings looked as though they had never been cleaned. Cars and trucks were parked all over as people got sodas, snacks, and cheap gasoline. Scott set about filling the tank while Gary and Jim bought snacks in the quick shop. James headed towards the bathroom, which was next to the mosque. Inside, many men were washing their hands and feet: they appeared to have recently prayed or were preparing to. Moving past this washing area, the stench of shit and piss hurt James' nose. He was unaccustomed to this style of bathroom. The holes in the ground only went so deep, there was no flushing mechanism, and a hose or bidet instead of toilet paper. He was careful to shit in the hole and noticed at the sound of the turd's dropping how full the hole was with waste. Then, using the bidet, he cleaned himself. By the time he felt prepared to leave, his nose had become blind to the reek that surrounded him. He felt happy to be wearing shoes. Exiting to wash his hands, James noted how the men stared at him: he was again an outsider.

His sexuality would never be disclosed to any Arabs. James' mind often roamed to that necessity of his stay. He had to censor his online presence, and protect himself. He could never truly be himself with his students or most of his colleagues. Harvey had chided him at his choice to go to Saudi. His mother and father, who were accepting of him, worried without end that something terrible may happen to him. James laughed as he washed,—To be in such hidden danger in a place that smells so badly.

Jim and Gary had gotten paprika chips for the ride. Scott was insistent that they get Turkish in al-Ahsa, but Jim's comedown needed some immediate attention.—Once you pop, you cannot stop, Gary. As the haze of his time in Manama lifted, Jim began to feel queasy at the thought of prolonging things with Xiaoqing. Going behind Scott would be tricky, and he would have to move with care. Both Scott and Jim had taught together in Saudi the year before. The community of teachers was growing and there was a sense of home within the compound that had not been there for Scott's first year. Jim played a large role in encouraging his fellow teachers, men and women, to enjoy themselves within the walls of the estate. They held pool parties and movie nights. The compound itself, to which Scott, Jim, Gary, and James traveled, was laid on a square piece of land. To the north side, there were six apartment buildings along the outer wall. Each building housed eight apartments, one furnished apartment per teacher. Each apartment had a couch, table, kitchen set, refrigerator, sink, and television with kitchen and living room areas. Additionally, there were bedrooms and bathrooms. At a ninety degree angle from the eastern end of these apartments a new row of 12 apartments was being built: some teachers were to be temporarily housed in a hotel, as James received the last apartment. In the center of the plot of land was a recreational center, which was put to little use with most of its rooms empty aside from scraps of dry wall and lumber left over from construction. There was also a pool directly next to the northern side of the rec center and a soccer pitch west of it on along the western wall of the complex.

The previous year, Jim had developed a system of making homemade wine for the people in the compound. This was enthusiastically supported by Scott and many others at the compound, and it fueled their social events, which were planned around when each batch would be fit and ready for consumption. Gary would feel excluded by all of this during his stay at the hotel. As demanding as it was of his senses to be a social being, being removed from his fellow teachers would hurt his feelings. Only when he would own the experience, would he appreciate having his own space away from all of the people he worked with.

Internet was not provided to the teachers, they were required to buy their own or go without. Scott used this to his advantage with his ex-wife and daughter. Scott felt uncomfortable talking on the phone, and more so felt agitated when in video conference. He had convinced those back home that he had no access to the internet, and so could only reach them occasionally.

His daughter learned not to miss him. She stopped talking and writing about him in school. Jessica understood well that her mother was sensitive about Scott. And so, Jessica, aged seven, stopped asking about her father. She dreamt of him being somewhere important, of his having learned to do something that no one else could. She kept her idealisms to herself. She heard from her father on some holidays, and even saw him during summers. His absence made him more of a character to her than a father. She thought that he would be present at certain points in her life that she would never forget.

Scott, despite his failures, was not loveless. He transferred money into an account in Jessica's name monthly and felt that that sufficed. He did not learn for another decade that she did not want his money. Jessica was enormously hindered by Scott's truancy, as well as her mother's anger towards him. When she received access to the account that Scott had set up in her name, even with not having seen him for years, she wrote to him and explained why she did not need his money:

Father,

I have not seen you in some time. It makes me sad to think of you, still out there somewhere in the world, teaching even though you hate it, collecting countries because you do not know anything else and that brother of yours convinces you that it is worthwhile. I want to thank you for your thoughtfulness at preparing a college fund for me, but I am sad to say that I do not need it. I found a school last year that I really liked and have been working very hard to make my best effort at getting in. Not only did I get in, but they have given me scholarships and work-study. You should be proud. It is a privilege to go to school in the States, people work their youth away to go there from all over the world. You have no idea what the late nights have been like, studying and scrambling to do well. Mom doesn't drink coffee anymore, she's says it makes her jitter, but I have taken her place next to the French press. I wish you did understand what it has been like here, mom working all she can, school, my job at the indoor pool, more school. I'll be moving to the States in the Fall. I hope that you can come visit campus, but I won't get my hopes up. Anyways, I'll just write it, because I cannot ever seem to speak it to you when you call: Use your money elsewhere.

Jessica

James left the stink of the bathroom and looked to the skies above him. The stars shone brighter outside of Dammam. He thought of the kind of peril he would meet if he walked out into the darkness of that desert. He made mental note of all of the cars at the stop. SUVs were most common, aside from the trucks. Some of the cars he had seen at the border crossing were also getting gas.

Along the perimeter of the station, James could see sand, hints at the abandon beyond the lights. The gasoline was remarkably cheap, so inexpensive that James laughed when he saw the total. Scott motioned him closer, Gary and Jim were checking out.—James, I. . . don't have any more cash. Taken aback, James was not sure what to make of the situation. He waited for Scott's face to let on what should be done. James had exchanged some dollars into Riyals in St. Louis. He took these out and James paid the attendant for the gas. Scott had spent the last of his money on rum and beer and Tina at Digger's and it showed on his face.—Thanks.

When the four entered the van, the sullen nature of the ride had withdrawn. They were near enough to their destination that Scott and Jim grew excited to show the new teachers where they'd stay: Gary would bunk with Scott for the evening. Jim talked excitedly about the compound, but was especially thrilled to show Gary and James his favorite Turkish restaurant. They made wonderful hummus and mutable, but it was the kofta kebab that they needed to try. From the mosque, prayer was called. The pitches and modulations of it flowed from the Imam. He called into the evening air, praying for peace and mercy within the world. Neither Scott, nor Jim, nor Gary, nor James acknowledged this on the side of the highway at the white light gas station. The group drove off as the recitation rose, reverberating into the darkness of night.

16 Months Previous

Elizabeth rose from her bed with a throbbing, beating, pissed-angry headache. The blinds were drawn, but she could hear the street. In looking at her watch, she recognized that people had been out and about for hours by this point. She looked at her pillow: a delicate puddle of drool. It had been one of those nights where she convinced herself that if she were to drown in her own vomit that it would be OK. Death had not come for her, not then and she filled the percolator and prepared the instant coffee. On this day the cleaning lady would not come. She only came three days a week as Elizabeth felt uncomfortable about having such help. She enjoyed the bookstores and book sellers on the streets. Being overcharged by auto drivers did not bother her. She accomplished in any given day things that fulfilled her. The rushing hiss of the percolator slowed and the water boiled. She prepared a mug and mixed her coffee. Letting the liquid cool, she changed into what she thought was presentable, even with a racket in her head. It was the sort of ache that dumbed thought and sense, one that extended itself into fingertips and toes, which inspired tingling in forearms and shins. Dressed she got her mug and walked on the balcony. Their apartment was on the third floor. The small space that faced the street had a chair and a small table for her sitting and reading habits. She gazed down at the people on the street selling and buying, walking, and resting. Children laughed. The harshness of daylight focused the aching to the area behind her eyes, a tax of vision. The noise of the sellers reached her ears and she let out a brief sigh. To think of it later would be a blur. Her senses tried to make order, working more lucidly with each passing moment. Each increase in her awareness and ability to see the world was so slight she did not notice, so that after some time and some sips of coffee she felt better but did not remember how she got to be that way.

That was indicative of her wellness in general: Elizabeth seldom remembered the journey from bad to good, only knowing that the bad was bad and the good was better than the bad. The processes that took her from sadness to happiness, from hungry to satiated, unrealized to fulfilled confiscated from her the powers of detailed memory. As a child, she kept a journal to set these thoughts down, but found her words scattered and unintelligible. She threw the journal away and set to remember the images of her progress. The shape of the sheets on her bed when she was a teenager and out of breath, the grime on the barstools when she was in her early 20s and Rob stared, the tree that had fallen on her path in western Canada, the traffic in Bangkok. This moment, sitting on the small terrace looking at the street became another of those images. Later, she could not remember her exact thoughts. What had propelled her so strongly to remain on the path that stretched in front of her? No barriers could stand between her and the next step in her worldliness. In a month, she would look at her life as a patchwork. Not anything so functional as a quilt in the sense of warmth, instead something more decorative, but private, that she looked at to comfort herself. Some years here, some there. Each movement precipitated by monetary and material gain. Intellectually she felt validated by the adjustment to new cultures. Something happens to a person's ears when they hear a tongue that is not their own for long enough. Although that person may not learn the language, they do learn to recognize the flow and cadence. This operation was cherished by Elizabeth. She thought of all of the different sounds and combinations of sounds she had heard throughout the recent years, how they had confused, excited, and educated her. Remembering the exact sounds was impossible for her, the muscles required were too accustomed to English and she did not yet know of the IPA. It was part of the hazy vagueness of progress that she observed in her life. This fog, which she felt she navigated most often unaware of its presence in her life, fascinated her. Looking at the people below her, all of those humans symbolically underneath her, she set about imagining what forms their own fogs and progresses took.

The street itself, although active and busy with people and commerce, was a calm and happy place. It had not known violence in some time. There had been few people from outside of India that lived on this particular street. Robert and Elizabeth had moved in seemingly by accident, an apartment opening up with the shifting around the city of one of Robert's colleagues. Still the inhabitants of the street did not idealize their place or the places around them. There were poor people and the mistreated just as everywhere. Walking down that street or talking to one of the sellers, one could ask about the white lady that sat on her balcony and read and consumed drinks. None of her neighbors thought much of Elizabeth when they noticed her. On this day, when they looked up at her and took notice of her presence at her usual place, they noted the pained face, which grimaced in the sun. She appeared to be thinking deeply and would occasionally stare for a time in one direction or another. She did not seem to be able to reach a conclusion. If she had moved amongst them, they could have said hello to her or asked her how her day was. Some who saw her hoped that she would keep to herself that day: her sullen, thoughtful trance would interrupt business of the flow of walking traffic along the street and some of her neighbors did not have the patience or time

                                          Always the Wanderer

to deal with someone in such a state. From time to time she gripped the railing, or tapped her fingers on her small table. Once in a while she shook her head, looking as if she had approached, even courted, some conclusion about whatever she was thinking only to promptly reject those verdicts.

In this manner she sat and deliberated with herself for nearly an hour. She did not touch the coffee that she had prepared. She could not figure out the people she saw. She decided, temporarily, that she would not understand her fellow humans beyond a certain point and that how others advanced themselves and their intellects was past her limits of comprehension. She thought of billions of people all attempting to survive, trying to interact with their environments, to nourish themselves, learn, find partnership, seek peace. The goals of her fellow humans, although common with her own, were mysterious. She thought that historians had the job to sort through people's messes and place the chaos in some kind of order. Biographers had to do this on a personal level, interpreting the disarray of one person's life and history. Scientists did similar things for parts of the environment, or the environment itself, even for environments outside of our own Earth. Mathematicians sought to develop a language, or languages, to describe some of these things. Humans had the ability to make many languages, thought Elizabeth. Innovation has always been a bedfellow of human language. In each their own way, every human contributes to the mayhem of life, but also many attempt to describe the world as best they can. All Elizabeth wanted was some kind of conclusion. She thought of writers and researchers as stepping stones, people who allowed her to better herself and thereby clarify the world around her. Some writers only made this world more complicated with their problematizing and question asking. Truthfully, on that late morning, as much as Elizabeth may have wanted to find a conclusion she only sought them at that time in order to distract herself away from where she was headed and to attempt to cure, somehow, the hangover that had taken over her body.

The night before had been a kind of going-away, a farewell. Elizabeth and Robert had gathered their friends and acquaintances together for food and drinks. It had not been the dinner that had gotten Elizabeth so drunk so much as her sudden and unyielding need to finish the bottle of duty-free whiskey that had sat on their shelf for months. After returning home, after detailing that they'd soon be married and living in the desert, she dusted off the old bottle. She drank it straight and had no chaser. The grimace that formed on her face after each sip was remarkably similar to the frown that could be seen on her face the next morning during her hangover: foreshadowing. It was unusual of Elizabeth to drink like that. She did not care for drunkenness as many did, nor did she particularly enjoy whiskey. But still, the jokes about living in a dry country, which were followed by the sighs of realization that that would be Elizabeth's life so soon, had motivated her to have one too many. She poured Robert drinks as well, although he could not keep up with her. The discussion of Saudi had stopped as soon as they had left the restaurant. There was not much to say. Elizabeth had done the research and let Robert do the talking. Their friend group had mixed reactions. The first, and least common response, came from the country collectors, who like Robert desired to possess the stamps of as many lands as possible.—A GCC visa?! Well done. These people were envious of their having an access point to a GCC country. Some attempted to gain entry, the jobs were many and paid well, oil pay, but many were rejected, first from the jobs and secondly from the visa process. Robert and Elizabeth would make things easier with their marriage. Therein lied the second, reasonably common reaction at this dinner: surprise at the engagement.—You're what? Now that is something to celebrate! Elizabeth was known for her acerbic wit with regard to marriage (slavery: willed, wonderful, sexual slavery) and Robert had not proposed in a romantic way. The couple had reached the conclusion that if they were to take the path that led to the deserts of Arabia, that it would be a wise and pragmatic decision to be married before undertaking the process in earnest. The third, and most common response, was with regard to the safety of these two people.—Are you worried? What is it like for. . . —What are the living quarters going to be like?—How will you get around?—Does Saudi have public transport?—Weren't there radicalized Saudis? Robert soothed these fears. Elizabeth was impressed at the unease that some of these people felt, it was a mark of these expatriates to not be daunted by many things.

With her eyes, another woman at the table, whom Elizabeth did not know very well, questioned how Elizabeth's agency would withstand the intensity of gender segregation. The feel of the dinner had been calm and happy. The undertones of worry had been muted by Robert's calculated remarks about the company, compound, and job, but slowly as the night continued more questions arose in the minds of those around the table so that by the time everyone parted ways there was less actually known about what Robert and Elizabeth were about to do than just a few hours before. Elizabeth had hoped that it would be more casual than it had been. It was rushed together and hastily planned. There would be little opportunity to clarify any of what had been said. Even as Elizabeth sat on the balcony, Robert had gotten up to begin collecting things into boxes to ship the long way back to the States, to sit in a storage container. He did not want to bother Elizabeth, she looked deep in thought. The uncertainty that had developed for their friends had rubbed off on Elizabeth and she resigned herself to taking this new challenge on one day at a time. She needed to reconcile her dislike of marriage with the good that it would do for her and Robert to be united throughout the visa and moving process. As she and Robert drank the whiskey they did not speak much or listen to music. It was not somber. They opened the doors to the veranda and listened to the sounds of the city around them. They smelled the fumes of vehicles and the stenches of sewers and trash. They welcomed the night air in with them for glass after glass until Robert could not stand and Elizabeth's legs felt heavy with drink. This was one of the first times that they sat across from one another in complete silence. It was an enjoyable, reflective, and thoughtful way to binge drink and each felt better mentally prepared after that night to take on what would come to them. But like many things that start out so simple and pleasant, the silence between them began to mature and form itself into a negativity. For months this negativity hid from them under the disguise of agreeable contemplation. They thought they were being mature. Yet, that maturity was in reality denial. Robert knew that he had pushed their relationship too far in a direction it was not meant to go and Elizabeth understood that she could idle no longer. These silences, which became more common with each passing week and month, born unto Elizabeth the awareness that drove her to the HyperPanda and indeed away from Robert.

Elizabeth sat on the balcony in a heavy, watchful way. She sometimes held her breath or pinched her knee. She had superstitions about hangovers. Robert collected things off of shelves and small tables. They would need to arrange to have someone take their remaining nonperishable food and spices.—We could give these things to the cleaning lady, perhaps. Robert could not ever remember her name. The cool stone floor calmed Robert's aching body. The alternations between the tightening and easing of his stomach were relaxing and soon he would ask Elizabeth if she would like breakfast somewhere.

13

The rest of the drive was quick. Soon enough they began to see buildings. The structures had a dusty, run down quality to them. Roundabouts and palms mixed with businesses and homes. The infrastructure that James saw seemed forced. Jumbled together, it appeared that the outer areas of al-Ahsa were commissioned and designed by someone who had the money to build roads, schools, and hospitals, but cut corners at every possible junction. Approaching the city from the north on the 615, the van began to move past an increasing number of compounds and businesses. The amount of date palms, barely visible in the thickness of night, increased around them, and at last James felt that he had made it to Saudi Arabia. Aside from its worn-ness, the city around James looked to be lived in. He had been able to find very little about al-Ahsa and the surrounding areas in his research. The tightness of the roads made him excited, he shunned the wide American boulevards he had known.

The city was not bright, or well-lit in any way, although its restaurants, at least the ones they past, seemed shining and busy. The city did not seem particularly dark or brooding either. It possessed a similar griminess to that which he had seen at the border, and the white light station. While many of the places of business were visibly unclean, some looked brand new, as if they had been built and just opened that day. The contrast between the older and newer stores became readily apparent on a packed street. Some stores were bright neon, with flashing lights, while others had monotonous signage or piercing florescent lighting.

They had arrived in al-Ahsa on the other side of the city from the university. People shopped and drove about in the cooler night air. James had no sense of center and the geography of the place was not obvious. Gary was relieved to have made it; he slept a lot after they had crossed the border. The group hungered and were prepared to eat. Gary could not pay attention to the world outside of him. He did not eat on the plane, fear of air sickness.

The oasis that was and is al-Hufuf, al-Mubaraz, and al-Ahsa welcomed the group with pleasant, almost soft, night air. All across the town, students from each of their classes prepared to meet their teachers the next day for course work. Restless practice was completed and words practiced. In less than 12 hours, James would be smitten with his first group of students. He would grow wide-eyed and happy at the sight of his first structured attempt at aiding the learning of others.

In groves of palms, apartment buildings, compounds, and houses these young men spent their evenings preparing to go to school the next day. The oasis afforded all of these people some relief from the terrible heat of day. The black-tarred streets cooled for better walking. In the *suq*, men and women shopped for clothes and food stuffs. The *suq* was smaller than the markets of neighboring Dammam and Doha. There were no tourists. The functional quality of the bazaar remained largely unchanged. Laborers from all over the city ate and rested in restaurants. With the aching of their hands, they consumed their largest meals of the day.

This was not a desirable place for many of the city's expatriated inhabitants. Far away from the comforts of more "developed" cities, the residents of the oasis made what they could of their two malls, university, highways, parks, and many restaurants. The city itself was some miles north of the Empty Quarter, a region into which no one treads. Being so close to such void challenged James' imagination. If one were to drive south from al-Ahsa, as James later learned, on the Salwa highway, in the opposite direction of ad-Dammam and Manama towards Doha, one could see this vastness. The Salwa was a menacing road to undertake in the direction of Doha. If a car crashed, its driver and passengers would very likely die. At night, there were no lights on the road. The blackness laid itself heavily upon the route from al-Ahsa to Doha. Helicopters would not be able to see the freeway or crash, unless there was a fire. The distance to al-Ahsa or Doha would be too great to allow for an ambulance to reach those injured. The remoteness of the area meant that there was little cellular service.

For those traveling north on the Salwa highway, al-Ahsa and the communities around it were a symbolic as well as literal oasis. The perils of the Empty Quarter were dismissed as they perceived the city and its short buildings. Just so, inside the city Gary and James forgot the anxieties they developed in their journey. They did not know what their lodging or school would look like, but their geographical closeness to both eased the pressure that they both felt inside of their chests. The length of their travels was behind them, and they each in their own way sighed relief. Between these two and sleep there was only one meal.

The chatter of the van grew as they drew closer to their food. The idea of caloric intake animated the men, soberly, and they began to look at each other differently. Gary, who would remain captivated by Scott and Jim, began forming questions in his mind about the city for the two more experienced teachers:

How many people lived in the city? (Estimates differed, but likely near 1,000,000.)

What were its natural attributes? (A wealth of date palms, underground water supplies and springs, and natural cave formations.)

How long had people inhabited the area? (For thousands of years, given its coolness and shade, both from trees and caves, as well as the fresh potable water available in the area.)

What cultural experiences could one enjoy? (Many restaurants, as well as shisha bars, some pool halls, book stores, gyms, farms, *suqs*, etc.)

What local foods should he try? (Kabsa, a Saudi dish with a bed of specially prepared rice using black pepper, saffron, cardamom, cloves, bay leaf, black lime, and nutmeg to taste topped with chicken, fish, camel or some other meat.)

Could he too get a Saudi driver's license? (Yes, recognizing that he would need to get more bloodwork done and bribe a police official with roughly $50.)

How would he accommodate his grocery needs? (At any of the several well-stocked, and at times high end, stores, which had stand-alone locations, as well as locations in both malls.)

What banking options did he have? (A Riyadh Bank account had already been established in his name and he would find several branches and 24-hour ATMs throughout the city, one within a ten minute walk of his compound.)

Where would he eat lunch? (At the cafeteria, a nearby buffia, Hungry Bunny, McDonalds, TGIFridays, or any number of other fast (casual) establishments.)

James looked at his fellow passengers more calmly. He did not have so many questions yet, but wanted to feel the place, to see how his skin felt in the air and how the air tasted in his mouth. He thought about how the men had looked at him in the gas station bathroom, and it occurred to him.—What racial biases do Saudis have? This he treated as an observer, looking at himself. How his students and others treated him should not hurt his feelings, but he desired to make an informed judgment of them. He felt that he could hold onto that knowledge and possess it as his own: how Saudi men treated black American males. With whatever James and Gary would learn, they would only receive partial knowledge. They lived in a divided city. Any feminine perspective they would hear would be filtered through the American, British, and Canadian women who worked at the women's campus. They would not hear about the oppression that Saudi women, and the women that worked in Saudi, felt from the government.

Later, on, the day James returned home, he whispered sadly to his mother that he had not met any women or heard about their lives. It had worn on him to not be able to interact on a fundamental level with those members of his community. His decision to return to the States was calculated with his inability to immerse himself into the place he lived. He felt isolated and without. The months after his return, it was difficult for him to acclimate himself to seeing and speaking to women again. This had never been an issue before, but then he wondered if people could grasp how this had affected him. Looking back, he thought about how the other men he worked with reacted to this segregation. Some felt more at ease in their masculinity. Some lusted after women more heartily than they ever had. Others withdrew into themselves or spent time speaking with friends and family from their homes to maintain some balance.

James thought that there must be something he could learn from how uncomfortable it made him. There was in the school a boy's club-ish attitude. Many of the male teachers would go to eat at restaurants for single men only, which isolated female teachers, or female teachers would eat at family section only restaurants thereby excluding some single men. The system of separating the sexes was crude to James.

There would be no forward thinking or discussion of rights. He thought that perhaps some misogyny would be set in motion within him, and that he would move away from his indifference in the direction of a negative view of women. But that was ridiculous. Overthinking gave him a headache.—How can I not be complicit with the treatment of women in this country? He earned a wage teaching there. He did have his own concerns being closeted again, but he felt a lingering guilt that he could only remove with reading. He set about learning as much as he could about Saudi culture in the years after he left al-Ahsa. Now and then he missed the city and its streets. He enjoyed the dryness of its heat. After he worked through his thoughts, and had unpacked his own experience, he still needed time to express himself. The fight for Saudi Arab women's rights was not his, but he thought of and prayed for them in later years. He prayed without having spoken to a single Saudi woman. He held them in his thoughts without having heard one of their voices. He felt for them, unsure of how best to do so. They had changed him without having seen or heard or known him.

• • •

Patrick picked his clothes and changed into them as soon as he got to his room. Time passed as he paced the room, occasionally stopping to sit and stare out the window.

When Patrick entered the Irish Harp, he was early by ten minutes. He had given a woman at the entrance a piece of paper denoting that he was staying in the hotel. He approached the bar to find Malcolm sitting next to an open seat with a whiskey in front of it.—Hello. Who is joining us? Patrick worried he would not recognize anyone from the office.—You like whiskey, right? Malcolm pointed to the glass,—I ordered it for you. I miss it. Sometimes at bars I like to ask what they have. Or at a party I will enjoy pouring cocktails. It soothes me to be so close. Shall we eat? Long night ahead!

The pair ordered food and the bar filled, as it had on the evening of Patrick's arrival. Malcolm was intent on showing Patrick a good time, and in his construction of that experience was sure to see multiple drinks in the hand of the Irishman, and of course making sure he had eaten. The bartender approached Malcolm, but was quickly rebuked.—I can't drink, Malcolm smiled,—But I love to watch others get at it. The barkeep was confused at this, he had not heard everything that Malcolm had said, not to mention he was distracted by his own issues. Malcolm ate very loudly. He responded to his food with moans and grunts, smiling at the plate. Patrick found this enthusiasm

welcoming and felt more at ease about the evening. He did notice how Malcolm laid out two cigars for after the meal, and
each time his drink was finished, Malcolm would ask what he
wanted and flag down a bartender. Malcolm had such control
over the event. Patrick wished that there was another person
there to experience this forwardness, but given Malcolm's intensity, he understood why there wasn't. The plate that rested in
front of Patrick was soon empty. Amongst the dark woods during Patrick's previous visit he had not noticed the many knickknacks all around.

These objects were in glass cases, in frames along the walls,
or otherwise displayed to authenticate the Irish-ness of the bar,
to supersede the Filipino bartenders and the Indian men cooking in the kitchen. Some of the pieces were old and possessed a
kind of dinginess that would suggest their having been buried
and dug up again. The lights were soft and warm in the Harp,
which accented the old-worldly-ness implied by the bar's Irish-
ness. The food and drink were all reasonable, but there was
some distinctly mass-produced quality to it all, as if they had
shipped the Irish Stew from a Dublin factory to these Doha tables. All of this effectively masked the location of the bar. In
its design the Irish Harp moved its patrons towards a comfort
zone, which ignored the homesickness collectively felt by those
who ate, drank, served, cooked, and greeted.

—We are going to the Waterhole later on after dinner,
Patrick. His attention returned to his companion.—That is
where we will find you a nice woman. Malcolm's teeth and
tongue showed as he laughed,—The club is upstairs. You will
need to get an ID, but we can work it out easily. Have your
drinks here and get ready. It is loud up there, but hopefully
there will be some women we like. Should be a good evening
for it.

The reality of Patrick's situation became apparent when Malcolm clapped his hands together. In a childlike furor, Malcolm

rubbed his hands together. Patrick wondered what he would do if she demanded more money than he presently had in cash. Would they negotiate a price beforehand? In the bedroom or at the bar? Malcolm did not have time for such worries. His eyes were bright and awake with purpose and conviction. Malcolm's blood was alive with excitement.—God, forgive me for I will sin, he shouted at Patrick. Patrick worried that as the bar got louder, the two of them would have to shout to continue this conversation. He was not embarrassed per se; rather he did not find it appropriate in public to discuss such things. Yet, that was all prim and proper, why not let that all go: he was in a new place, none of the people knew who he was. To calm himself he said,—Fuck it.

The two continued to talk. Patrick asked about the women, how one acted with them. He wanted to be sure of his footing before taking a step. Malcolm could not stop laughing at all of it. His joy seemed to know no bounds. He exhaled deeply and leaned in, addressing Patrick:

—There is a certain kind of suppleness you want to look for: how taut the skin is, how soft. There is a great difference in making love to a woman who has had a child and to one who has not. It is a matter of taste, which I am sure you have developed. Thereafter, you must be wary of attitude. You will want someone who has a sense of openness to what you want. Frowning in the bedroom is bad for us all. However it is you like to act, you must be kind. I have noticed most ladies to be welcoming to certain fetishes, but there is a distinct line. Not that these people will judge you, or that you care, but prior warning is important to seeing certain things through, eh. Furthermore, when you are done send them on their way. If at any point you are not content, send them home. Do not forget that you are paying them. If you find one that is as soft and nice as you like, someone who seems open to what you are into, then talk to her. Upstairs, they will ask you if you want a massage.

That means open for business. At that point begin your negotiations. You want to haggle, but be respectful. If you go too low, they will walk away from you: there are plenty of white men around. OH, you know all of this. Your price is your own, but do not get ripped off, my man. That, again, is bad for us all. This is a community act. Because the notion of you fucking some woman remains negotiable, you must then act with the other customers in mind: don't pay too much, don't be an asshole and so on. Most of the women upstairs are Thai or Chinese. Don't ask their real names. Just relax and call them what they tell you to. It is important to share control of the situation. If it happens that we both like the same girl, it is at her discretion. Be a good sport.

14

Scott pulled over and they got out at the Turkish restaurant. A large blue sign said Kebabs and there was trash all over the road. Littered about cans of Bebsi, Coke, and Mirinda, in addition to paper waste and plastic refuse such as used bags for food or clothing. All of it was caked with dark sand and dirt and smeared with the mildew of the rare moisture that touched it. The street was active with people. In the night many people consumed their dinners and did their shopping or leisure walking. The bricks of the sidewalk in front of the restaurant had been laid out unevenly. James, in his exhaustion, tripped himself on some of these stones. Some were cracked and broken, others had been positioned where they ought not to have been. Several bricks were also missing and these holes were filled to a certain extent with the same mixture of soil and sand that smeared the trash in and along the road.

The road itself was loud as many cars drove past quickly. To either end of the road, there were roundabouts, each of which generated a substantial amount of traffic noise: tires, honking, drive shafts, engines, fist shaking. To add to that hubbub, the lights within the restaurants sign buzzed emphatically. At various distances, the clamor of men could be heard, en route to a restaurant or store. James thought he heard the droning hum of a gas-powered scooter behind him. To Gary's ears, it seemed to be more of a whining hum. From the door of the Kebab shop, the sizzling of the grills was made clear, as well as the squeaky rotating of a rotisserie, the hotness of the stove, the clangs of pots and pans, the plastic shhing of a meal being packaged (complete with the snapping closed sound of a Styrofoam to-go box), the tinkling of cheap silverware (used for serving only, not by customers), the scooping and slopping of hummus and mutable into containers, the scooching of chairs, the tapping on of table, and mumbles and shouts of various offers and orders.

There were no feminine sounds within the establishment. Women and girls were not allowed inside of that particular restaurant. And so there was a masculine, even misogynistic harshness to the clatter and clang. It was not felt by the men within who were deaf to the sounds of the own grunting and growling. Even the wife of the cook and owner did not set foot within except when the place was closed. Because the owner had no sons, and he failed to find any Saudis looking for work in the service industry, he had to appeal to his brothers and sisters in Turkey to send their sons to be servers and line cooks. Early on in its existence, most people underestimated the popularity that the food would demand. In those days, Mohammed was able to handle the entirety of the work, with his wife at home to enjoy her books, the only way she could cope with how she missed her friends and family in Istanbul. Now, at any point there would be several men waiting to dine in, and still others standing, waiting on food to-go because this was not a family-friendly restaurant.

They stepped into the establishment and a tall, broad shouldered Turk smiled at them, pointing to four open seats and a table in the middle of the dining area. Young men all around ate and talked. No one said hello to the Americans and Canadians, but also no one frowned. They ordered their food and after were silent in waiting. Scott had a look on his face that he would be in trouble for all of this. Jim looked like he needed sleep. Gary had finally realized what he was doing and was hungry and tired and nervous. James was happy to not be in motion. The cars, planes, and vans that had taken him the thousands of miles were paused and soon he would be able to sleep, at ease in a bed.

The upcoming sharing of food would be more pleasant for the four than the sharing of drinks had been. They had ordered two kofta kebabs, two chicken kebabs, hummus, mutable, salads, one Bebsi, two Mirinda Oranges, and one Mirinda Lime. Each was presented first with a small salad of iceberg and tomato, without dressing or fork. James ate his tomato with salt and pepper and left the lettuce to Gary, who wrapped his own glossy 'mato with it and consumed accordingly. Jim ate all from his plate, while Scott, with a frown, did not partake of either the fruit or edible leafy greens.

After this, they opened their sodas, Mirinda Lime for Jim, Orange Mirinda for Gary and Scott, Bebsi for James, and once again opened their mouths to speak. Scott knew that there would be some trouble for him: the Digger's trip was unplanned and unannounced: the group should have been in the compound two hours earlier. Nothing was made of this at the table. It was Scott's idea to get the drinks, so the other three felt it reasonable to have him face the director on his own, unless otherwise prompted. This, of course, went unsaid.

As they sipped, the carbonation of each drink dancing about in the mouths of men, the cook prepared their meals. The *halal* meats were prepared with care and tenderness. Jim was correct in his assessment of the cook's talents; there were not many kebabs as good as his. Further the flat breads were soft and doughy, yet crisp, in a delicate and deliciously balanced fashion: James would forever laugh at other bakers and bread makers. They were served their meal and each shared and ate well. The quality of it all ran together as beef and lamb juice mixed with chick pea residue upon their plates, and the clear running fluid from the chicken intermingled with them both.

James felt that this meal had been worth the flight and has-sle. His tongue often guided his perception of different people. He found himself distrusting those who had served him a bad meal, while feeling kinship to those who could cook well. He had a deep psychological connection with meals being served; a positivity grew inside him as his stomach filled. It was tem-porary, yes, but he felt relief from the heat and stress of travel as he sat there and ate the kofta, chicken, hummus, and muta-ble, all with the flaky, warm bread. He had some knowledge of Turkish food, but his inner epicurean awoke as the mush of chewed foods was broken up and digested within his body. At that moment, a passion developed for the taste and texture of a meal, how it could possibly make a bad evening good, or a good evening bad. This was, for James, a revelation. He had not simply eaten for nourishment and rarely did he find nuanced pleasure in what he ate. Soon, he could see the pounds added to his frame, a monument to the meals he had found in al-Ahsa. To eat so well, to replace most alcohol with food, meant to him a shift in his view of the meal. He looked at chomping, nosh-ing, and swallowing from another angle, less utilitarian, not so Marxian. There was merit in the preparation and serving of an overzealous or pedantic meal.

Never would James refer to himself as a foodie, such words did not possess the distinction of his love of food, a fire which began in his heart during that September night. In some years, he would quit smoking and take up exercise, so as to ensure his ability to eat any meal he chose to. He did not want to over eat, but rather spend money on foods that he did not know or already loved. He wished, the more he fell into his spiritual and solitary Christianity, to share these foods with his friends and lovers. He would immediately turn down a person who suggested a lackluster place to have lunch or dinner. His pre-tenses, so far removed from his callous indifference towards the social and societal needs of others, gave the impression for many years that his only love was food.

This aspect of culture and travel had not been any part of James' focus. He loved language and literature. He had no need to write yet, but sought to read. To visit a bookstore and purchase books that he could not find in St. Louis or Chicago. In this way, he was taken aback to notice that these Turks had presented him with such delightful and satisfying foods. When he returned to the States, he set about learning to prepare the meals that he could not acquire: Egyptian and Afghani fuls, Iranian kebabs (called Persian in Saudi), Kabsas, Saudi breakfasts, Yemeni lamb stew. His mother, Maya, smiled when James talked about food. When he was able to find his focus away from the negativity he saw in the world, which for some time he would not see as fixable, and talk about the simple pleasures of eating a meal in Arabia. As his mother, she pushed him to share with others how those meals were prepared, served, and eaten. She observed, in her own life, how food united people and allowed them to compose themselves. She would have James speak to guests in the house, send him questions via email, take him to restaurants in St. Louis, and try her own dishes. All of this she felt added to his positive psychology. She laughed when she thought of how he had to keep his weight down because he did not want to restrict himself at the dining table.

In that Turkish restaurant, those four men ingested much needed calories. Unlike James, Scott, Gary, and Jim did not enjoy their food aside from the cathartic senses they each had of fullness. The next day, they each had to teach classes. None of them had prepared their lessons or reviewed the materials that they would need. In fact, James and Gary did not have class rosters, or any other class materials. The semester had already begun without them: the intricacies of the visa application and approval process had caused James and Gary to miss the first weeks of school. The substitutes who taught their classes did not update either of the two teachers, who the next morning would be blind when they walked into their classrooms, having to borrow books from students to prepare a lesson on the spot.

James' students, who were by turn helpful and aloof, guided him in his first days as their teacher. The school and James caught up with one another soon, meaning that the classes were better and less hectic. He was able to find balance in his pedagogy with some effort. Scott did not care for his students and did no planning. Jim was more of a friend than a teacher. Gary found himself overwhelmed by the tasks of educating people in a language, especially given that at first he did not possess a single lexical item that he recognized as Arabic. The manic nature of this schooling was absent from the table when they ate their dinner. Jim and Scott had no substantial advice to give to Gary and James. Both would have to rely on students to guide them around campus and to the relevant texts.

The university itself had a sizable campus in al-Ahsa. The English offices were in a newer building on the northern end of campus. There each teacher had an office and access to a copier. Sometimes the water would not function properly or at all. Typically, James smoked on the roof. Classrooms were throughout the campus in various buildings belonging to the separate schools of the university. Palms were scattered outside. There were parking spaces and lots all over. It seemed that none of the students rode a bicycle to their classes and there were no racks should anyone ever choose to. In the heat of learning, men from further East, most often the subcontinent, maintained the grounds and cleaned the buildings.

On the way to campus the next morning, James would see some businesses, but focused more on the prison they passed. Heading from the compound to campus meant passing that prison, which was situated catty-corner to the northeast of the university.

James could not fathom that morning what inspired a city planner to place a university so close to a prison or vice versa, other than to remind the students to mind their studies. Would that prison be where James would be held if his sexuality was found out? A cold sweat beaded itself on his forehead as some nameless teacher pointed to the tall watch towers and barb-wired walls.

James was in no danger, he had a silence about himself during that year that sheltered and protected him, but in the back of his mind he simply entertained the idea of his own downfall. The thought of his arrest distracted him at times. The ride to the prison would be so short, they could even walk. He did not dare ask his students if they knew of the prison. One of his students, in an instant of intense sharing, told him that the *mutawa*, the religious police, had a station directly across from campus.—They are watching, you know. They want to see it all. James kept his eyes open and saw the station not only across from campus, but situated near the offices of the English teachers. King Abdullah's system of paranoia worked itself even harder upon James at the times when he remembered the police and prison.

It could not be tallied how much of his life James had spent worrying about violent figures of authority. The police, prison systems, militaries, and all the rest overpowered him at strange times: in a classroom or at a bus stop, making dinner or talking on the phone with a distant friend. Some deeply embedded danger reached him in those times of supposed peace. The older he grew, the more he learned to take deep breaths to counteract this reaction. Still it would be no help. The television, radio, or internet would remind him of institutional violence or brutality, a man shot 11 times or beaten nearly to death, and once again more evidence would support his being fearful, truly being terrorized.

But James did not know about the prison as he sat and relished the first proper meal he would have in Arabia. All was at ease for those seconds and minutes that he spent eating and imagining his new apartment and students. He fantasized about the things that he would so soon be able to make sense of. It was these moments of fantasy, when indeed he created a visual fantasia in his mind, that he felt most free from the anxieties that consumed him. He encouraged his brain cells to generate detailed scenarios, about the legs of a table in his new apartment, or the interest in an author in one of his students. Further, he indulged in these daydreams, hoping that one day he would find something just as he foreseen it. He thought it would be a great thrill to find a person or place that not only met his expectations of physical presence and makeup, but also character, texture, sound, smell, and psychology. How pleased he would be if he could extend just one of his delusions into the reality that faced him each day. James had no hope of actually accomplishing this, but for him it was a motivating factor to persist. He considered the possible modalities of a world so wide and yet so limited. He did not want to be considered a dreamer or a person who was within their own head, but could not help it. In that way his mind was as kind to him with his evocative and lifelike imagination as it was cruel to him with his dominating dread of imprisonment and violence.

• • •

Upstairs, outside the club:

Patrick sat waiting to get his picture taken. Malcolm was already inside the Waterhole.—What a terrible name. One can only hope a place is as bad or good as its name. The snap of the camera rang in his ears. Malcolm had fed him many drinks. He felt his limbs tingle, and his chest compressed about his ribs. His eyes were not sensitive to the light, but the air of the open atrium was stale in a deep hotel way, which bothered his nose and slowed his breathing. He looked on as his card was printed. He paid the money and glanced to the other men in the line.— No women waiting to get in here. Cast away from this place, for they know what it is. Can hear the music out here. Malcolm's in. Ordering a drink, but he isn't thirsty. Can he be a cuckold for a whore he hasn't been with? He wanted to remain away from the music, in light, but had no option. He still did not know enough about Malcolm to judge how he would react to that.—I could be too sleepy, too drunk, too intimidated, too scared . . . He walked through the entrance.

Inside, he saw the length of the place, which had a bar along the wall on his left side and a dance floor at the opposite end, with what seemed to be a lounge off to the right, from what he could see. The darkness of the place was cut by the colored lights that reflected off of the patrons. Most stood near the bar. Some men danced with women. Along the wall, there were women looking around, returning looks to curious men. With his ID came a drink, so Patrick stood in line to redeem it and scanned the area for Malcolm. That man's persistence would shape this evening. Once he ordered a beer, he moved along the bar, in the middle of the mass of humans, towards the dance floor. He could not move with ease, as the place was so busy with men. His impatience mounted as he tried in vain to find Malcolm, so he drank his beer rather abruptly. Finding that it was gone, and that it had already compounded the drinks he had consumed downstairs, he moved left again to order another.

At this midpoint, nearly halfway to the dance floor, he could make out the lounge to the right of where the men and women gyrated and quivered. He had to pay for his second beer and did so with some of the cash he had set aside for his companionship later. His forgetfulness did not bother him when he realized he would have to pay the women less after these drinks: he had not factored in his own or her consumption of alcohol before the act itself, a rare mistake in calculation. Within his confused dark, he made his way to the wall opposite the bar and continued along, making his way to the lounge. When he got to the edge of the dancing, he began to drink his second beer with gumption. Having emptied half of the liquid into his body, he scooted past the people moving together and entered the even darker lounge. It did not have the same colors as the bar area, or the heat and eagerness of the dance floor. This area seemed more shut off, and at its end, far from removed from the music and movement was another quieter bar. This lounge area possessed a large amount of tables and chairs. Occupying those, many men and women sat and drank and laughed. Some of the women took spots on the laps of men, signaling warmness. Patrick heard one of the women say loudly to counteract the music,—Are you ready for your massage? All of the men at her table laughed and shouted like children. He stopped in the horde of tables and finished his drink, so that when he reached the second bar he could order this third beer.

He advanced on the bar, nudging in between two people who were not talking and flagging down the barkeep. His words, although drunken and empty, repeated constantly,—New beer, beer, Malcolm, women, beer, more beer before Malcolm and women. . . The past two beers had amplified his drunk, and he worried about being able to make coherent sentences, as he had not spoken, except the words new, beer, Malcolm, women, more, before, and and since crossing the threshold of this hole. He muttered that word once more and waited to accelerate his drunkenness even more so. At this point, he heard the voice of Malcolm,—I don't drink 'em though. He glanced around to see where he might be. The bartender traded the beer for cash and Patrick drank deeply, while keeping his eyes open for the Canadian. He could not focus his eyes on any specific table of people, let alone and particular face or body. He became concerned that he would not find Malcolm, and would appear to have deserted him, or worse that Malcolm had grown tired of his company and left. Yet, these thoughts were too complex for his mind at that time. He let them drift away and continued his hazy search. Patrick only used his eyes at this point in the evening, saving his legs for the chance that he spotted the person he knew. With his third drink, his knees felt the tingle and weakness that he knew as a sign of danger, but always dismissed.

Finally, he believed he spotted Malcolm. He approached a man, about middle height and smiling,—Malcolm! But it was not him. The man moved away from Patrick and embarrassment set in. Believing that he could not find him, he began to stumble his way towards the dancers, and with any luck, out of the club itself. He finished his beer recklessly, and walked slowly. From behind him he heard his name.—Patrick Patrick Patrick. As the third beer rested in his stomach, he turned about to see Malcolm waving him down.—You walked past the table twice! I got you a beer, but you must not have heard me. Fuck me, you look drunk. Malcolm handed Patrick a warm beer that he had bought, another gift. Patrick realized the main purpose of this night and looked to Malcolm's table and saw him sitting with a woman.—Can I sit with you for a moment? Malcolm nodded happily. They sat at the table, all three, Malcom introducing his friend. Patrick did not make the effort to listen. He merely stared at the two and whispered a hello, sipping on this fourth drink. The sipping continued on like that for a few moments, all while Malcolm and his date laughed and talked loudly at one another. Patrick finished the drink and Malcolm stood.—Need another? She wants another drink. I'll buy. I love buying. Patrick agreed. He thought to perhaps make small talk with this woman, but would not. His mind could not produce language. His vision began to change: he could not see out of his peripheral, his depth perception altered and reduced. He sunk more deeply into the chair. Patrick blacked out.

A Future

On down the line Elizabeth moved, further and further away from the life of movement she had known. It had been less a life of travel, but more of occasional shifts engineered to be extraordinary or remarkable. Now she only wanted to head to the farmers' market or perhaps to the Amish store a ways away. She had done it. Her life was so simple, to teach some, write some, drink too much tea, have an occasional lover. Her house was one story. She had a small backyard with a garden and clothes line. Her front lawn was truly that: it was large, she had a table and four chairs, as well as a hammock that hung between two oaks to the left side of her house if you were facing it from the street. The house itself was old. It was properly one and one half stories, but the upper level was only used for extra storage. Her dog loved the place and her name was Novak. Elizabeth and Novak tromped through the garden together and said hello to the neighbor kids. Teaching at the bucolic university had brought fulfillment to Elizabeth's life. That should be clarified, academia, somehow, had brought on the quiet that now surrounded and pleased her. She only briefly had to struggle with the servitude that was adjuncting before she found a more reasonable full-time position in a small town.

The pastoral nostalgia of her new life was not absent of scandal. The school itself was in some turmoil. Students had been using the internet as a means to shame and deride one another.

A group of students had dropped out because of this. Others remained and turned certain classes, one of which was a writing course that Elizabeth offered, into pseudo-therapy sessions, which were not productive for their mental health or for the assigned topics in the syllabi. Elizabeth read some of these comments at her computer; one student had sent screen captures of their own personal abuse: she was sickened. It made her sad to see. But she remained grateful that she was where she was. The students would mature with time, and those who did not would stand out as such. Her contemplative, Socratic style of teaching intimidated many people and Elizabeth was not afraid to deride students or faculty for stupidity. With time, her classes filled only with those people who could handle the stress of preparing for discussion with such a person. Elizabeth's mood was not sporadic, but constantly calculated unless she was with Novak. On campus, she used her office and the library. Her routine was simple enough: office, tea, teach, lunch, teach, teach, tea, library, tea, home. This all depended of course on her teaching schedule, but she tried to stick to a Tuesday-Thursday schedule as often as would allow. She threw in office hours when she could, but when she left campus she left technology behind. She did not have a television or a computer or a tablet, nor did she want any of those things. Her home was for herself, Novak, her books, her bread, her garden, and her occasional guests. She did not evacuate her home life of technology because of needy students or creepy ex-husbands. It just seemed simpler to her. She could read and write more clearly. Someone asked her how she watched films, and she realized that she had been so out of the habit since living in a country without cinemas and graduate school that it did not occur to her often to sit and watch a movie.

An advisee of hers, a non-traditional student, approached her late in the semester.—I cannot grasp it. The material does not challenge me, rather it is the pacing. She looked at the framed list on Elizabeth's wall.—Do you feel that you are over-whelmed?—Well, when I decided to come back and do the de-gree, there was a suggestion of a conclusion and now it seems too far beyond me.—I don't think that you need to feel that way. Your writing is good and you have a grasp of the materials that demonstrates real high-level literacy. Her students blushed in a frustrated way.—As I said, it is not the material. I just do not know when I will be passed it: when will I be out of this town and onward or outward or whatever direction it is that we move.

The town itself, even with its size, had all Elizabeth needed or wanted. She would walk to a bar for a drink. There were some reasonable restaurants. There was a used bookstore that restocked regularly. Elizabeth enjoyed most that there were large swaths of land around that were reserved by the state as nature conservation areas. She would take Novak to the places, some 8,000 acres or larger, and roam the woods and dirt roads. She camped with Novak next to a river and had to hold her back at night when she heard the coyotes. The forests, fields, and swamp lands had a cleanliness to them that she had not seen in many years. Often when standing in a field or amongst a grove of trees, listening to the crunch of the brush and Novak's panting, she would wonder how far away she was from the nearest human,—One mile? Less? More? She set out to find the places that were furthest away from towns and people. If she camped somewhere and heard as much as one car drive past on a trail or road nearby she would cross it off her list. During the day, if she heard the gunshot of a hunter or saw the truck of an angler headed towards a body of nearby water, she did the same. These lands were public, but isolated. She brought books with her. When she did not camp, she brought picnic meals for herself. If she did pitch a tent for the night, she had a lantern and provisions. There was a way that the crickets chirped that especially pleased her. If there was a burn ban, she would spend her days out in the woods without being able to camp for lack of fire.

She learned to judge landscape in ways that made her hiking easier. Her knees had aged along with the rest of her body, but she was still able to do miles in a day if she planned correctly. She poured over maps. The nuances of topography and elevation became clear to her the more she worked with the documents and planned her outings. Novak, chipper and happy as always, would always accompany her and be on the watch for any malicious critters. Elizabeth looked at the maps and liked to imagine why the trails had developed in the ways that they did. She created scenarios of what had inspired movement in one direction through the woods and not another. Many times, she walked along the trails of a park or reserve and tried to learn what it was that made these paths advantageous. Some things were obvious: bodies of water, or crevasses. Other issues were more complicated, for example how to deal with slight changes in elevation or erosion. It suited her to be able to roam like this.

Once she and Novak had driven nearly 60 miles to a place they had not been to before. The map of the place was sparse, and the area seemed relatively flat, but with a complicated network of small ponds and swamps. A river moved through the property, flowing from west to east horizontally through the middle of the fields and woods. Small creeks, some connected to the river itself, flowed intermittently at various elevations between 750 and 800 feet above sea level. The main swamp area, the goal of the hike, was to the east and a little more than two miles away from where Elizabeth parked. The parking lot was at 800 feet above sea level, so Elizabeth presumed that the trip to the marshy land would be easier than the return trip, so she packed along enough water and snacks for both her and Novak. She did not intend to camp, but was excited about the idea of it as she got out and headed in.

The weather that day was mild. It was late spring, and at its peak the sun would only be so hot, perhaps 80 degrees Fahrenheit. The majority of the walk would be in open fields and she needed to wade the small river before she would reach the boggy area. It was warm enough that she felt she would dry quickly after wading the waterway. The fields were filled with wild grasses. Elizabeth crunched down on the growing greens. There was a quiet in the air around her: it had been a relaxed spring semester, filled with calm and peace on campus: the meanness of the internet subsided for the moment. The crispness of the air filled her nostrils and at that moment in the morning, the dew and the fog of the previous night had not yet dissipated. As she descended into the surviving mist, Novak sniffed about off-leash. To her left and ahead of her there were woods. She moved slowly and easily. She aimed not to rush the roughly five mile hike. The sun rose steadily in the east. She wanted to be in the bog land by late morning and to have her picnic there. The blueness of the sky clashed nicely with reds, browns, greens, and yellows on the grasses in the field that she navigated. Where there were woods the remaining shadows of the night clung to their lives hidden away from the brightness of day.

When Elizabeth reached the first patch of woodland, she aimed to head slightly north, so that she could move in between two creeks and head once more into an open, flat field. She could see the light of the field filtered through the trees, but she could not make out the sound of the creeks or notice any significant features of the waters. At the edge of the forest she stood with Novak. She had completed the descent down to roughly 750 feet above sea level, which would be the level of the remainder of the hike to the wetland. The woods themselves were not dense, but there was no clear path through the underbrush. It was laborious to move through it. The sticks and brambles stuck to Elizabeth's pants. Novak, who always was careful in wooded areas, treaded carefully ahead. Once spotted, they moved north along the creek until finding an opening they moved through to the next field. In the time that it had taken to get through the trees, the sun had risen enough to provide some heat in the air and evaporate any mists and dews that had been leftover from the previous night. A little less than a mile ahead, Elizabeth spotted another small creek, which she knew was connected to the river and would lead her to the point where she would cross water. She felt, when thinking like this, reminded of childhood dreams of those idealized westward expansionists, who if they were not killing natives were killing each other were being killed by the harsh natures they stumbled upon. She preferred her circumstances. In this second field, Elizabeth stopped briefly and considered reading. She had a small pocket book with her, an old and worn copy of Agha Shahid Ali's The Half-Inch Himalayas. She remembered that when she was introduced to the poems for the first time, Ali's home had recently been flooded. That place was so important to Ali's writing. It stood as such a significant landmark to him, how sad his family must have been to see the house go: Ali had been dead for years by that point. She did not read, but thought alone. When would she hold this field in her hand? Geography meant so much to her. She needed this, what she saw in front of her. The grassland was verdant and open. She ambled about, generally moving in the direction of her goal, but feeling and concentrating on the texture of the grasses in her hands. She bent to pick at some vegetation and earth: she needed to tend to her garden soon. The soil was cool and clumpy. The top of the soil was still slightly damp, whereas the grasses were now dry. Novak snuffled about, occasionally licking something here, or nipping at something there.

Once she reached the river, she would be halfway to the wetland. As she looked ahead she noticed the shimmer of the body of water and could, as she moved closer, hear the sounds of its movement. There was a small area in between two sets of woods that led her to the Middle Fabius. It had been dry recently and here the water did not rush by so much as it pushed slowly forward. It did not appear to be too deep, and Elizabeth was prepared to go at it. Because it ran low, she would not have to swim: a task like this could get dangerous after a heavy rain. Without pausing on the shore, Elizabeth and Novak moved in and across. Cold. It had been slightly deeper than expected, but the two made it across easily. Elizabeth had taken off her shoes and socks to hold them and Ali's poems above the water to keep the dry. On the opposite bank, they waited for her feet to dry. Except for where she stood, the river was mostly shaded by trees. Some had fallen into the river, victims of erosion or a bad storm, but still there were groves of tall trees on both sides in either direction. There was another parking lot. Here, the land passed a test: there were no humans or vehicles. The gravel lot and the road that led to it had not been driven on that day. Where she stood, she needed to move to the east so that she could continue her path. Only one large series of fields and a mile of walking remained between herself and her goal. Ahead they marched. The closer they drew towards the swamp, which was neighbored by a large pond, the more they noticed birds. Water fowl made their way about the area. Some headed to or from the area where Elizabeth desired to picnic. They raised with the flapping of their wings a cacophony that seemed to unsettle Novak. The closer they reached, they were a half a mile away, the more jittery and spooked the dog became. At first, Elizabeth did not notice that Novak was acting this way, until she growled, ever so slightly, in the direction of the wooded bog.

By this point, Elizabeth could easily make out the wetland and the nearby pond. The smell of stale, but natural, water filled the air which had become more moist and humid. The thickness of the air differed from the cleanliness she had earlier

noticed. When Novak growled, she inhaled deeply and suddenly, taken aback by the rare aggression that the dog was
showing: seldom did Novak make any noises that were un-
happy. Her tail had stopped wagging. Elizabeth observed nothing out of the ordinary, it was possible that Novak smelled
something foul, but her eyesight was slightly hindered by the
position of the sun in the East. She scrutinized her landscape
in more detail, using her hand to shield her eyes. Ahead was
the swamp, which was wooded and full of browns. To the left
of that was the pond. She could not see the entire pond, but
knew that it stretched north from where she saw it. Beyond
the swamp was another road, a dirt road, and judging by how
clearly she saw the tree line on the opposite side no one had
driven down it recently to generate any dust. She had been told
by a student that there was a field just beyond this road that was
filled with sunflowers. She had no interest in them. She found
sunflowers to be so obnoxious, but she knew that if there was
anywhere in this reserve where there would be people, it would
be in that area. She was confident that if she stuck close to the
swamp and pond that even if someone came she would not be
spotted. Elizabeth became aware that she did not want to see
anyone at the moment. She did not know what drove her to this,
but she wasn't prepared to be seen by any one person, in fact
she was afraid of the eyes of another. She realized that she and
Novak had not been moving. Novak had stopped her snarling,
but still stood at attention, eyeing the surrounding field with
caution. Elizabeth looked at her hands. They were balled into
tight fists, so hard that they showed white at the knuckles and
she had to flex her fingers in order to get proper feeling back.
She shook her head. She was ahead of schedule. What was it
that was bothering them? She undertook to ignore that she felt
so bothered by the idea of human eyes seeing her.

Elizabeth and Novak made their way more quickly now.
Elizabeth wanted to make haste in order to get past the funk.

Arriving at the swamp, the chatter of the birds had stopped. She could not see any other wildlife. The water was still and tepid and swept back amongst the trees. The pair sensed no movement around them, and in the shadows that were cast by the many trees of the swamp there were shapes and forms that confused their eyes. Elizabeth moved over to the pond to scout a spot to eat and feed Novak. She found a patch of short grass that she saw fit her needs and when she sat registered that both she and Novak were out of breath. She did not remember the hike there as having been too difficult, there were no drastic changes in elevation and very little stood in their way. She collected herself and watered the dog. The quiet had a sense that it had risen from the ground to envelop the surrounding landscape. Elizabeth found that she could not catch her breath. She closed her eyes. Strange how this had gone. But that was the nature of some of the hikes. Places she had never seen before could seem more unusual than they actually were and she was far enough away from the next town that there was no use in her succumbing to childish fears of nature. She kept her eyes shut tight and cooled her mind. She opened her eyes. She looked to where she had placed the canvas bowl for Novak to drink from. Novak wasn't there. She could not see the dog or hear her. This was not unusual. Novak sometimes explored. Elizabeth listened for her. Further down the pond she heard rustling. Assuming that Novak had found something to sniff or lick, Elizabeth went to check.

At first, she did not see Novak. The stalks of the plants near the water were parted in front of her. She spotted Novak's tail. She could not see what she was pawing at in the water. Elizabeth hoped it would be nothing. She readied the leash in case Novak would not be drawn away. She moved behind the dog and called her. Novak's head popped up, alert. She let out one firm bark.—Damn dog. It was the first spoken sentence Elizabeth had uttered since getting into her car that morning. She approached the dog to put the leash on to her and take her away. She could snack once they reached the car. Novak had two paws in the water. Her stance was firm even with her paws being on such soft pond bottom. Elizabeth grabbed at Novak collar and the dog scooted back suddenly, showing Elizabeth what she had had her front paws on: a broken grave stone. The text was illegible. The bottom of the stone was damaged so that it was clear that another part of this memorial was stuck in the ground somewhere. Elizabeth leaned down to feel if it was truly what she thought it was.—How tasteless to dump a headstone in a pond. She felt in the cool water the roughness of the granite. It was real. She could not make out any numbers or letters, the piece looked old. She couldn't make out its exact shape, but it looked rounded on the unbroken end. She reached out to brush aside some plants to see more clearly and then saw the rest. The pond was shallow. There were many stones in the pond, headstones that appeared to have been broken off and dumped. She counted: six, eight, ten, twelve and still there were more. Some amongst the plants and reeds, others further out in the water. Novak barked and startled Elizabeth. She put the leash on the dog and moved away from that pond. When they reached the middle of the field and could hear birds once more Elizabeth turned back to look at the pond.—Those nameless stones in that cold, brown water. When she returned to her car, Elizabeth immediately phoned the police—Sir, are you aware of the grave stones that have been dumped in the pond off of Seven Oaks Road. A woman laughed at her.—It's ok, dear, she laughed again. Elizabeth did not know what to make of it.—That's an artificial pond. When they set about creating the reserve, they needed a place for water fowl conservation, so they used that land as an artificial pond to ducks and such. Not that it works; no one ever sees any birds there. Flooded that whole place probably thirty years ago. No one protested the grave stones. There was a whole yard there. None of the people buried there had any living relatives so the state just decided to go ahead and flood it. Some of the stones got trampled in the process. You see, they had to bring in bulldozers and all that to engineer the thing. Scares someone at least once a year. I always wonder about the people there. The land was donated to the state some time back, and the people over in Memphis don't remember who the last people who lived there were. Judging by how worn those stones are, I'd say it's been a while since anyone's known. Funny thing, really. Now that no one remembers who those people are, they really are truly dead. No one to know their names or histories. It's a shame that some treat it so lightly, but that's the world we live in. I suppose we could get the high school to do a project or spend tax dollars on fetching those gravestones out of that pond, but to go through the state would take years. Usually there's a church or something near graveyards like that, a place that at least keeps a record of who was there, but the area was empty. Farmers couldn't ever seem to grow on the land so it's laid fallow since I can remember. I think the state claims that they grow different wild grasses there, but I haven't seen anyone from Jeff City there in nearly three years. Anyways, not to worry. You still there?

15

Scott walked to the van and Jim paid for his meal. They found the compound after one left turn, one right turn, and a final left away from the food. At the gate, a security guard maintained his night watch. When Scott pulled up and rolled his window down to talk to the man, he was in such a deep sleep that Scott was forced to honk. The man did not awaken until three honks sounded. The guard eyed Scott and Jim with a smile and opened the gate.

The compound was quiet and seemed devoid of population when they parked the van and unloaded the bags. Not a soul came to meet them on the curb in front of the northern apartments. The sound of Scott's tooting horn had not reached the ears of the teachers and administrators. James checked the hour, which he had not done since Manama, to find that it was past 11:30PM local time. They were now three hours late.

From between one of the buildings, a short Sri Lankan man came towards the group, wagging his finger at Scott and laughing, —You are late, Scott. This person, Naniyin, demonstrated his talent for hospitality by assisting Gary and James in taking their final bags and backpacks out of the van and shaking their hands firmly with introduction. His small grin opened up the compound for the new teachers. Naniyin paid no mind to Scott or Jim at this point and cared for James and Gary with the gentleness and care of a deeply religious person.

Naniyin had taken that job in Saudi many years earlier, before even the compound had been built. He had come to serve the Saudi owners of the property. For years, he served tea and coffee each day. He would also clean and serve them food at meals. He had not glimpsed his passport in many years, as the family held it from him, and he had not seen his family or his home in just as long. One day, as a kind of promotion, the patriarch of this family, whom James would only see once in his employment, took Naniyin aside and told him that soon he would work for Americans and Westerners. He was planning on bringing many white people to al-Ahsa to work for him and since he trusted Naniyin, would place him at the whim of the people.

Ever kind, Naniyin undertook the task. He witnessed the construction of the apartments, pool, pitch, and other buildings. He toured the facilities with the first Americans and Canadians to be hired. Before they moved in, he made sure that their beds were well made and their apartments deeply cleaned. For years then he worked each day coordinating various things for the busy teachers. He would take their clothes to the dry cleaners, fetch them pizzas and various forms of take-out, make minor repairs in their apartments, install new light bulbs, and much else. Never once was his pay increased for any of this. Seldom was he tipped by any of the men and women he completed tasks for. Most simply paid him the cost of the service or food.

Still, Naniyin looked at newcomers with a rare kindness. His genuine nature struck James, who was not prepared for the presence of such a person in his life. Naniyin sent most of the money he made each month home to his family. They in turn saved the bulk of his pay for his return, while using some of the riyals to ensure that their own houses were in order. With the few teachers that tipped Naniyin, he had to work against his own resistance to the concept. He had worked for so little for so long and was by and by so kind that he felt unease with it at first. Naniyin felt a deep luckiness that he was not a manual laborer in Saudi. He had seen so many ache and break under the intense Arab sun. As restricted as his life may have been, Naniyin felt that those who worked to build and expand within Saudi were significantly worse off, and they were. Even so, Naniyin deserved more than he would ever get.

Naniyin did more to work against James' detachment from his fellow humans than any other possibly could. Within ten minutes of their first meeting, James would awkwardly tip him. That first night, when Naniyin had left, James found a bottle of juice in his refrigerator left by Naniyin with a note that read: The water tastes bad. Drink this. As a relationship that was limited by language and history, both were kind to one another and sought each other out. Naniyin introduced James to several notable Indo-Pak restaurants in the area that were only known by those foreign workers that Naniyin knew. In return, on evenings when James felt the need for pizza, he would order pies to his and Naniyin's liking and share. Such a balance worked well to soften James to the world.

It was on the day that James left Saudi that his shell would receive yet another significant blow. While he mopped and cleaned his apartment, before he set right the kitchen and cleaned the bathroom, Naniyin entered and gave him a small envelope. Naniyin left to go handle the departure of a group of teachers, who were scheduled to leave the day six hours before James would.

James set about his final scrubs, intent upon removing the final traces of his having lived in that place. He set the small letter aside with his already packed luggage and completed his work. When he left with a small group, there was nothing remarkable. They said goodbye to the people that were around and headed once more towards Dammam and Manama, where James was set to fly from. They would not visit Digger's or find any tension at the border. Very simply, they crossed the bridge

and made for the airport. Once James had checked his bags
and sat awaiting his flight he looked inside his pack and found
what Naniyin had given him. He opened it and inside was a
single picture of Naniyin with a note on the back.—Thank you
for the friendship.

Before James could make way to his apartment and get settled, Scott took him briefly aside away from Gary, Jim, and
Naniyin. Scott handed him a bottle of off-brand Arab cola.—It
has rum in it. I fucked up not having money. Thanks. James
took the rum and stuck it in his backpack. That would be the
last interaction James and Scott would have. Scott was repri-
manded for how he handled himself that day. It was not shame
that made him have no desire to get on with James, rather he
felt a fear of finding some more trouble with him. Scott was
not cold towards James, but the two shared no similarities. In
fact, their only commonality was that they each knew they had
nothing in common. So James took the bottle from Scott and
guessed that it was a sacrifice for him to hand it over.

Naniyin took Gary and Scott to get situated and Jim said
his goodbye. James found himself standing alone outside. He
had to wait on Naniyin who had the keys and knew which belonged to him. The quiet all around was pleasant to James. He
could not remember the details of each part of his day and did
not think to write any of his memories down. He would rely
on his impressions of that day for many years to come. He did
not relate much of what he experienced home to his family except for in abstraction. He sent a mass email the next day in
the direction of America to the welcome and great relief of his
friends and family:

Dear All,
Made it to Ahsa. Details forthcoming.
Be well,
James

In the Saudi air, his head ached for need of sleep. He was thirsty after the sugariness of the Bebsi. There were no other teachers around to speak to. He did not meet any of his bosses or administrators for another few days. When Naniyin came to him and offered to take one of his bags he consented and walked towards his new, albeit temporary, home.

Waiting: Impatience

Elizabeth had called Abdelrahman. Now she waited for his arrival in that nervous, fidgety way that humans never grow out of when they are excited or scared. She sat in a coffee shop. He would take twenty minutes at least. Outside the Saudi sun beat down as usual. The Maghrib was approaching so Elizabeth ordered a coffee quickly and prepared to sit out another round of prayers while waiting for her ride. This and the Isha some time later would be the last prayers she would hear in the Kingdom. Often she recorded the prayers using her phone. She found the quality of the call to have such a dynamic and vital tendency. She picked up her coffee and sat at a table in the family section. This would be the last time she was shielded from the prying eyes of single men. There was a small bus that took her to the university to teach in the morning and took her home in the evenings. At times, there would be a crowd of young men from the male campus waiting to watch her board the bus, or some who would sit in their cars and stare through their tinted windows. Elizabeth was not as easily irked as some of her colleagues. She saw this as a result of how these men were conditioned and pitied them for being so immature. The coffee she bought was black and thick. She smelled the nicotine smoke of the people who sat on the opposite side of the wall next to her table. The Dammam Airport was near enough, but it would be best for her to go to Manama and stay the night.

She could find a flight the next day without question: it was not the time of the year when many people left the Peninsula for the States. The call started. The coffee accelerated her jitteriness and her leg began to shake under the table. She could not believe that it had taken her this long to make her choice. She should never have had to come to this mall. Even with her tea and prayer beads and notebook, it was not worth her time. She should be on the road to Manama already. She should be treating herself to Budweiser and a burger in the Best Western Juffair. What separated her from that was a long bridge, and of course the border patrol. Leaving on a family emergency is what she would tell the skeptical border man who hesitated to stamp her passport.—Hurry yourself, I have lost my closest sister, she would yell at the man.

The border was navigable, but only slowly. As a woman, there was an isolated border area that she had to enter. During each step, the border guards would stare at her and Abdelrahman and wonder what they were up to. All of this was along King Fahd's Causeway. The length of the bridge, or bridges rather, was extensive. She loved how the Causeway connected the land to an island. The nervousness that Elizabeth felt would not be relieved until she finally crossed into Bahrain. That final night, the bookend to all of this, would be spent in a large room overlooking an alleyway: she could read the backside of the Imperial Complex sign. She wished that she had chosen a place overlooking the water. The irregular pulse that made her uneasy subsided momentarily as she checked in. The maître d' smiled at her and told her about the room she'd take for the night on the fourth floor. She requested a wakeup call for 7AM, and she would leave for the airport promptly at 9AM. She checked in early to the flight; she had bought the ticket just the night before. Sitting in the airport for hours she read calmly. She had made every step some time before she needed to, with the exception of being picked up by Abdelrahman. She fidgeted all the way to D.C. During the night she could hardly sleep. She would be able to exchange her money in the morning at the airport. She had everything she needed: her clothes and the books she wanted to bring with her. She wrote a note to Robert. It was brief and understandable. He threw it away after a week of letting it sit on the table. The night she left, she sat awake in her bed wondering if she had received any emails from him, but she did not pay the money to the hotel to use the internet and find out. She did, however, order six beers and a cheeseburger be sent to her room. She tipped the man who brought it to her very well. She turned on the television, but found nothing. Instead she opened a beer and ate the burger humming to herself,—hmm hm hm hmm hm hm hmmm hm hm hm hm hmm hm hmmm hm hmmmhmmm. She did not hum around other people. She felt that she would be embarrassed by whatever melody she chose.

The next morning she did not put on her abaya or head scarf. When she received her wakeup call she ordered a taxi for 9AM. She drank the three beers she had left out from the night before as she showered and bathed. She packed, unpacked and repacked her bags. She had one check bag and a carry on: for her Kindle and laptop, personal items like the phone and passport. When she exchanged her Riyals, which she had used the night before to pay and tip the room service man, she had roughly $400 in spending money for when she landed in the USA.

Before any of this, before the foot tapping the in airport and the laying-awake-all-night-and-forgetting-to-drink-your-beers, she sat in the coffee shop and her leg shook. She tried to focus on the prayer, but it was of no use. The drama of recitation had worn off on her and she simply stared at the window into the hot parking lot. She did not want the coffee. She did not want to wait inside. She felt that if she was to leave this place, today of all days, she should feel the heat of the sun one last

                                          Always the Wanderer

time. She wanted to feel the fabric of her abaya stick to her skin. Sweat first developed on her arms, and then at her sides and hips, then under her arms and on her forehead. All of this sweat spreading took at most two minutes on a properly hot Saudi day, less if it was actually hot, more if it was cooler and so on. She considered waiting in the hot sun for Abdelrahman. Only ten minutes had pasted. He would be hung up somewhere, maybe dealing with his family or praying. She felt defiant of the air conditioner and left the building and found a place to stand outside. The hot air hit her as she left the mall. She moved and stood in the shade of the huge building. There were some people outside, workers from within smoking cigarettes on the break. Otherwise, she had the entire sidewalk to herself and she embraced the heat. She was surprised to feel the sweat develop on her shins first, this was a rare thing. She tracked the movement and spread of her body's reaction to the heat. It was not terribly hot, so the time amounted to about three minutes. Still, in the abaya as more time passed she felt hotter and hotter. The fabric was light, but she always insisted on budget buying her coverings so she did not have the lightest or most breathable fabrics. At the end of her three minutes she felt the heat of her hair under the black headscarf she wore. She thought briefly about focusing or again attempting to, on the prayers and about how beautiful they were, but her impatience could not be stopped. Her leg began to shake once more and she found herself hot, impatient, and anxious.

She got out her phone once more and called a colleague at the university—Hello, Martha?—Mmhmm, hey. What can I do for you? Martha was in her sixties. Her office was next to Elizabeth's and the occasionally shared lunches and sat together at meetings. Martha always read an old copy of *Herzog* and laughed. She also hummed Christmas carols.—Listen, Martha, I've got to get out. This is sudden, but I cannot make it to the university. Martha, who had been cooking coffee in the

Egyptian style in her own apartment now stood motionless and listening while the coffee burned and Elizabeth continued,—I am leaving and I want to know if you can pass a verbal message along to my class.—. . . The heat on Elizabeth's skin stood still and the recitations around her continued.—Sure, I can help with that. I do not mean to pry, but. . .—It is nothing more dramatic than it sounds, Martha. I am leaving Robert. Very simple. Martha had taken the coffee off of the stove and set it aside. She sat at the table in her off-white-tiled-kitchen.—What shall I say to them?—Just remind them that they can email me any time and tell them I am sorry for leaving so suddenly.—Do you want me to tell them why or?—. . . Elizabeth was unsure.— I'll miss the recitations. Martha tapped her fingers on the table trying to think of something to say.—Keep in touch.—Will do. Elizabeth hung up.—I guess I'm pulling a runner, or whatever they say. She looked at her surroundings.

Inside and across Dammam, indeed across the Peninsula businesses closed and people prayed. In some cities, in Doha and Dubai, businesses did not stop like they did within Saudi. The HyperPanda again shut the gates. Baristas and food workers smoked outside and in break areas. In the Jarir, a few people continued browsing books, perhaps planned their trips to Jordan or Turkey to find the books that had been banned in the Kingdom. In some schools, students took breaks from studying and reading to face Mecca. A unity of motion and direction surrounded Elizabeth. In neighborhood mosques people gathered in from the streets. In back rooms at the compound, security guards knelt in time with the calls. Also at the compound some of the women who had fallen asleep in the sun, tingling with pills awoke again with a start in the shade of their pool umbrellas. They were always annoyed by the calls, they found them eerie. Elizabeth did not really hear the call. There was nothing she could do but wait. She did not want to have to pack, or rush the note for Robert, but what had to be done would be done.

She was not a person to hesitate at the last moment. Her jitters were less related to how momentous all of this was and were more in line with her need to complete it all as soon as possible. She would not rest until she had an apartment, many thousands of miles away. Long nights, dragging days. She would remember details of this period of her life as being overexposed. The few grey hairs she had on her head would double, and eventually triple before she was settled. To her surprise, Abdelrahman pulled up in his car early.

He rose out of his stupor, only to realize that he had somehow solicited a woman. He did not remember what had happened in the Waterhole, or how he had returned to his own room with her. The motion inward and outward was not unpleasant to him, but to Patrick the mere act of his being with this person, when coupled with the monetary transaction that he now realized would follow his discharge, proved too much for his beer-filled stomach. He stepped aside from the bed, and curtly vomited on the floor around their feet. Simultaneously, she pitied him, and his lack of ability, and understood that should she leave she would have to solicit another man. Her handler would not furnish her with a ride "home" without profit. But the Irishman in his heaving of bile grew aggressive. He stomped to his bathroom and washed out his mouth and quickly returned pointing to the other side of the bed, where she subsequently bent herself and he threw a towel on the carpet to cover some of the smell of the vomit. He viewed her from behind and understood with his eyes that he need not be as emotional as his vomit had provoked him to be, but having set up a power structure, one involving sexual transaction regardless of drunken idiocy, he assumed his role of dominance.

Rarely had Patrick attained such a position and the thought of that power, once more tied with money provoked in him a serious movement of thought that attempted to either strengthen or diminish his erection. He half thought and half spoke,—And so it goes for the capitalist, but what society does not have prostitution? The symphony of flesh as conducted in the halls of our private spaces. But the drive of the economic and the polyphonic, requiring money as it does, extends into the sexual. The tiger cannot maul this. What becomes of a dead tiger, but that another replaces it. And it does not even need be a tiger, rather a Celtic Whoremonger or a Celtic Fiend. What folktale would mother relate this to? The Pooka? She'd not watch this polka. And in the course of denying that art what would a mother say to a son who needed the sex? Loneliness does not remain static in one's life, but travels with one until death or sex or possibly birth. What is this but a mimic, an attempt at a mimicry pointed at my biology's want to produce my own tangible numbers? Fucking hell.

Now, as her hips began to swirl, Patrick noticed that he had lasted much longer than he had anticipated, and this coming as a surprise, seemed to him more of a negative result of his thoughts than his masculinity would allow. To further his longevity, he began to smell his feet and feel inside of his nostrils how that stench clung itself to his nose hairs. This reek did not provoke any further pleasure in him and it seemed that for the first time in his life Patrick Maguire would be having intercourse for more than the rough 5 minutes and 34 seconds he was accustomed to.

She, not expecting the vomit, inexperience, or general demeanor of the grunting and mumbling and thrusting Patrick, had hoped to only go a short time, and avoid his stare. She had a half success in this, insisting, despite the Irishman's, at time forceful, attempts to change position or kiss her. She knew that he was good for the money: he had showed her the cash in the elevator. Also, knew that he'd seek her out again. To her then, as their skins became wet with sweat and the various organic and inorganic liquids involved, she considered where she would go to solicit, should she wish to avoid Patrick. She did not yield many options and this prompted her only spoken moment in their entire physical discourse.—Do you always puke? Patrick's grunt in the negative sounded confident enough to her and she then decided that should another encounter of this kind happen, that she'd preface it with a ban on bile and payment at the beginning.

He had been too drunk, she thought. His force scared her, but she would have no trouble escaping a lumbering fool such as this. The flash of it all was typical: he must have arrived recently. She sensed that he had been lonely a long time before he had come to Doha. Alone in her head: At the Waterhole, that bastard Canadian had taken Betty aside and we could not get him away from her. Then he came to me and tried to negotiate for this man. I figured I could get easy money out of it by taking him up, making him pay me, but he had come to and is aware of the world again. I hope Betty is safe. I wish we did not have to use these diminutive English names. And then there is this dunce, he can't get himself off and won't let me find my rhythm. I wish he'd just get it done with.

Patrick stopped. He sat on the bed. The room smelled like sex and vomit. He would have to clean as soon as she left. He could not finish. She did not know what had stopped him, but at a coy smile of his began to put her clothes on. The scattered nature of this encounter bothered both of the people in that room that night in Doha. As Patrick stood from the bed and moved for the money, a flood of relief ran over her. He handed her cash and they locked eyes once more. They shared no sentimentality or positivity. She was glad to leave him to stink inside that room. She had second thoughts if he would have the courage to solicit her again.

Patrick opened the blinds and sat once more on the bed. He stared out over the water at the rest of the city. He did not know the direction of his movements now. He could not stand the smell of the place: he thought the smells may never leave. He looked at his watch: 1:52AM. He could not decide whether to feel guilt or indifference. He thought that the next day he would call his mother and have a talk with her about how things were going. She would not hear the story of this evening, but she would enjoy a description of the architecture and character of the place.

Doha brooded that evening. Still there were two weekend days for the crowds of Europeans and Americans to "explore." The taxi men would be busy night and day. The boatmen would have their most productive evenings of the week. The restaurants and bars all around still had patrons, even at this late hour. All around Patrick, money exchanged hands, was looked at and scrutinized. In other hotel rooms, and indeed in apartments, other exchanges occurred. Their situations went more smoothly: these people were not drowning in alcohol as Patrick had been. Tall buildings were lit for those eyes of all the people. Near the water, a bike share lay unused. The people and the flow of the city did not cease that evening. Few within the limits of the city prepared themselves for the prayers that would be happening in a matter of hours with rest. With all of this, the city grew, increased itself, used the humans to gather its own strength: cities do not care who dies when a building is constructed or when a road is paved on a too-hot day. Self-preservation was at the center of it all, coupled with a lust for power that could only be satiated by increased capital gains.

Patrick sat on the bed with his head in his hands, looking at it all, —. . .

16

Naniyin took James into his apartment. The tile and furnishings were simple, but new. Naniyin was happy to see James and showed him each room in turn: kitchen and living room with stove, refrigerator, television, table. Next: bathroom with shower which was attached to the bedroom which had a full-size bed, amour and desk. Everything was clean and just as it had been described in email. Naniyin gave James his key and explained that he could arrange the place however he liked. For the duration of his contract, James could do as he wished within the walls of his apartment. If he was not used to the teetotaling lifestyle, Jim would know how to set him up.

All around in many of the other apartments, individual teachers worked on concocting their own wines: sugar + water + active yeast inside of a size appropriate plastic bottle topped with a balloon through which two small holes had been poked with a pin or needle sat under the sinks of many and waited. James had no interest and laughed this away. The final bit of information that James would need.—Transport to campus at is 6:30AM. There would be no choice but for James to suffer through his jet lag. He could not afford to have another day of substitutes in his classroom. The clock approached midnight. The travel would not stop until the next weekend when he would be able to finally rest properly. Until then, he looked forward to coercing his body into function with caffeine and adrenaline. James was aware that when he was hungry he could not sleep, so for the next days he would deprive himself of calories in order to make it through the day, only eating before he slept.

The stress of that first week was simple. He had been immersed in a place he knew so little about that he only observed and listened. He did not want to make unwholesome judgments of what surrounded him, and so in that first week he spoke very little outside of teaching. His students were interested in what his impressions of Saudi were: apparently many teachers openly complained about Saudi culture to their students.—I don't hate it, I don't hate it, James muttered to his class with a friendly face. He wanted to feel more aware of his geographical placement before he found cause to complain or deride.

He watched a good amount of Saudi television that week in order to become accustomed to hearing Arabic spoken so quickly. He followed along with translations of cartoons that he knew, namely Arthur the Aardvark, whom he had watched so happily as a child. As Arthur matured and grew with Buster and DW and all the others, he employed such a fluent and fast-paced Arabic that the plot lines that James had once known so well became blurred and confusing.—What exactly were they doing at the trash dump? When did DW grow so emotional about that snowball? All of those cakes. . . Aside from trusted Arthur Read, James watched game shows and news broadcasts.

Each day, updates were broadcast from Libya and other collapsing states. James needed no translation for the violence he saw there. People were brutalized with such ease. Regardless of language, the images James saw of people dead in the streets or firing weapons at some foe were enough. He felt the sadness that any person would know at having seen those things. He was so tired and impressionable, but felt that he needed to hear the language being used with regard to the fighting. He wondered what tone Saudi broadcasters took toward freedom fighters and rebels. He asked himself,—Am I watching the Fox News of Saudi? The MSNBC? What slant are these people working with? What ridiculous bias?

Four times during that first week he video chatted with his mother and father. Two of those times he fell asleep during their conversations. They watched him so far removed from their home as he slept. The mixture of comfort and unease that his parents felt about this unsettled them as they never had been before. They were not used to a Williams family member moving so far away. They hoped that one day James would find himself within the physical closeness that they yearned for. He was their only son and they prided themselves upon him. Maya had known many accomplishments in her time. She worked well as an academic. She was well thought of, well read, and well admired. When her fellow faculty were not busy tokenizing her, they praised her for her elegant and wide-reaching work. Yet, in her heart she did not hold her accomplishments in the academy on the same level as she did those with her family. She had made her husband grow up. She pushed him to read, saying that she would not marry him until he had heard a certain number of voices. She also registered him to vote and refused to entertain his political apathy. The work that she had invested in that man was remarkable. When James came along, she felt ready for the new challenge. She had not predicted the disillusionment that her son felt. It saddened her to think that he saw no peace in the world, but she did not force him into any understanding. She wanted James to discover his own peace in his own way. She was unsure of his methods with moving to the Saudi Kingdom where so easily men and women were beheaded and stoned and segregated.

In the weeks before he moved, while he and his father worked so hard to complete and attain the visa he needed, she scoured libraries for books and articles. She did not find much for him. Some Saudi novels, but otherwise very little outside of mass media junk. Maya had hoped to provide some kind of literacy to James that would prepare him for and assist him in his journey. Yet, this time her son was truly alone. Later in life, he would provide her with books written by authors who had been banned in the Kingdom and with theorists who had noticed the dictatorial tendencies that the American lust for oil had allowed for. This she took as a sign of his newly rekindled interest in the well-being of humanity. James was aware of the kindness of his mother's intentions.

For undergraduate work, he had specifically chosen not to apply to the school she taught at so that he could avoid the chance of having to take her classes. His entire life he had felt educated. This was not in the sense that he felt knowledgeable or well spoken, but that he could not avoid being taught the many lessons that his mother would teach. He listened not only to his mother, but also his father, who justified, supported, and loved her pedagogical home life.

—She intends to make you a better person. You see, she comprehends things that you do not. When she speaks to you like she knows more than you, it is because she does and she is trying to condition you to be open and accepting of the smarter people in your life. If you are open to learning and growing, she thinks that you will be removed from the temptations of violence and idiocy that bleed through human society. Your mother is only trying to make sure that you are wise in who you are and what you do. It is a gift, James. She gave me that same gift many years ago.

—When I met her, I was so deeply infatuated with her that I could think of nothing else. She had nothing of me and would not until I started thinking about all kinds of different things: community, nonviolence, literacy, voting, gender roles ... It was devastating to think that I would have to study to make her happy. OH man, she had me reading and watching films. I was doing it all only to talk to her and I did not even get why I kept at it. Your grandpa, old Frederick, he would make fun of me for running around after her. But he would talk to her too. One day, I caught your old grandpa reading a book that I know was Maya's, because I had seen her reading it a month before. You know, I had never seen that man read. It is hard to think that old man reads and listens to music and watches movies too, isn't it? I remember it. I was an unusually cool August day and he was reading *Go Tell It on the Mountain* and he had tears in his eyes. Tears!

—She's good, your mother. I know you are resisting, and James was, he was hardening to the world around him.—All I ask is that you think carefully about what your mother has got to say. She is standing up for you in a way that you do not even know right now. And she, well us both, will continue to support you wherever you go. It is not something that is a question: we are behind you. It is only that we would prefer for you to develop your worldview in a more nuanced way than we had to. I suppose it is that drive to make your child's life better than your own.

James' first week in Saudi, even though it seemed unremarkable to the naked eye, opened him to the kind of intellectual work he would want to do for the indefinite future. It was not simply the stifling nature of what made up Saudi government and law that concerned him. He wanted to know how the Saud family had so wrongly coupled Islam with their dictatorial laws. He was curious about how it was that they convinced this nation that they represented a religion that they so happily and clearly exploited. James was not a Muslim, but he would read the Holy Quran in its entirety at least four times in his life to reflect on how those dictators used religion as a weapon. Christians, he read and knew, had always done similarly somewhere, whether in the Vatican or in Washington or the Bible Belt.

The more James critically reflected on his life, as his mother had always suggested, the more readily he accepted his circumstances and the setting that he found himself in. He found, however, that he could not depoliticize how his view of organized religion or public morals. He guessed that there was something more to the corruption that goes along with power, but he did not want to know what ticked within the psychologies of those men and women who sought power and influence. James thought, late in life, that there must have been something wrong with the evolution of those who were presidents, senators, and kings, as they so readily fucked everything up for the rest of the people in the world. It just could not be that their biologies were stable with the foolishness elemental in their decision making. It was no funk that James experienced. His underlying skepticism towards authorities developed steadily throughout his life and never ceased in its growing.

There is no metaphor that would be appropriate at this point in James' story that could categorize this development. Instead to taxonomize how James felt, consider that he moved from curiosity to indifference with some limited knowledge of the unjustness of his world. Then with evidence compounding against those who exploited the cheap temptations of power James was moved gradually to vehemence. At first, after his indifference he was informally dismissive of people he knew that sought influence. As he became more aware of their intentions and histories, he then actively disliked powerful people in government and business. At this point in his life, he established a distinction between community leaders, teachers, and authorities that help societies and those that used their power for no one but themselves. From that point, in his early thirties, he felt that something should be done to hinder the progression of those who actively strove after dominion. This phase lasted the longest in his life. He was not extreme, but thought that businesses and communities should distrust any person who had attended Harvard or had a senator or governor in the family: he did not include them in the forgiveness of his Christianity.

Only in his oldest ages, shortly before he died, did James advocate for anything more than distrust. As he grew older and more impatient, his sentences grew shorter and more imperative. He demanded people to read to his words, he did not know which exactly would be his last.

He could be found in those dying years telling children and teenagers, really anyone who would humor him, that the rich and powerful needed to be dismantled. He spoke of these people not as though they were human, instead he treated billionaires (by this point in the future, trillionaires or some other imaginary distinction of wealth) and politicians like machines. The people, specifically the youth, needed to have confidence in how they took these contraptions apart. It was not so simple as taking and distributing their money to all peoples. As money seemed to be a human right, as in no human could possibly live without the use of it, then each human was entitled to have a certain amount of it. Just as water and clean air were necessary for living, so had become money. Those who had power used the capital of others and those who had enormous amounts of money used theirs for power over others. In that sense, James grew to feel that each person was due more than just a certain amount. This was not welfare or a livable wage, or social security, but a certain amount of dollars, euros, riyals, pounds, or other monetary unit to be human. In order to do that, the rich and powerful would need to be deconstructed and reorganized into something that could be more useful than they would ever be. What that would be in the future, the old James did not know. Yet, he was confident that at some point people all over the world would see the fallacy that was inherent in having people who were "above." The construction of class and hoarding of capital and wealth was a sign of stupidity, and it was one of James' dying wishes that there would be a world evolved past such ignorance.

Such an idealism did not speak to the James that stood with Naniyin on that early September evening in 2011. The lessons and ideas that James had just learned from college were fresh within his mind, without which he would not have found employment so far away from his home. James stood on that tile as a young man, not yet 25, waiting for the world. He had thought that he had interpreted and understood "enough" by that point. He assumed that his world was as simple as for him to be able to dismiss it after one quarter century. He had no regrets for the life that he had lived until that point. Whatever embarrassments or humiliations he had felt were of no consequence to him as his eyes beheld the small man in front of him in the middle of the artificially lit living room. Just as when he would lay upon his death and dying bed, he found confidence in his previous movements and current trajectory. The physics of his intellectual movement would prove to be constantly one directional: each day of James' life would make him smarter, even if he had spent some months or years in indifferent ignorance.

The multitude of things that shaped him through all of his years told him that he had had no need to prove himself in the Saudi sands during his twenties. He did not need to establish himself as he did, but it was sincerely important that he had. He had come to appreciate a different group of humans. He knew how so many Arabs had been systematically othered over centuries, but that was only because he had been in their homes and taught their sons. He grasped that the Saudi government exploited its people and the world's lust for oil for its own profit, but only because he had seen its rigs and oil systems and read the propagandic newspapers.

The world changed and shifted around James with each day he grew older. Eventually, he would forget much of what he had seen and heard in the deserts of the Middle East. He would never find a partner that could handle his idiosyncrasy, but that did not equate to sadness. The more he aged, the happier he was, even if he distrusted some people so intensely. James' passions and willingness to engage in abstractions, which both grew as he edged nearer to death, were most readily articulated in his last ten years. James did not know many other people his age then. To this end, he would wrote his ideas and thoughts down into notebooks, and communicated many notions over the phone to relatives and well-wishers.

In this way, his ideas and visualizations would not disappear for some time in the future. Well past the century mark of his birth, the murmurs about James and how he had gotten old only to have an active cynicism towards those who polluted his world continued. James' life was simple and well lived. He loved food and died peacefully.

In his apartment, he looked at that table and television. Everything around him was nicer than he had expected, in fact nicer than he had ever experienced. The one bedroom apartment would be well used in the following months. James would cook as often as possible, refining his skills. In the spring semester, he would move the large flat screen into his bedroom and illegally stream movies while he sat in his bed. That bed would be the focus of his attention in that apartment. He would read banned books and canonized fiction. James wept in that bed and laughed at the films that he refused to share with his fellow teachers.

Naniyin showed him the commode and various accessories of the place. Naniyin had paid special attention to James' apartment because they were the same age. He warned James that he would need to sweep often to combat the sand and mop afterwards to ensure a deeper clean. Naniyin lived in the furthest east building along the northern wall. In that last building, there had been constructed a third floor, specifically for Naniyin. In the crawl space above two of the four second floor apartments, there was a small room with a bare mattress and a series of boxes. In those boxes, Naniyin had collected various objects that he thought his family and friends at home would enjoy. He lived a spartan existence at the compound. He had installed some hooks to hang his clothes upon. Never did he invite anyone to visit him in his own apartment. James did not even know where Naniyin lived and would never learn the conditions that surrounded Naniyin. There was no sense in sharing a thing like that with the young James. Naniyin recognized James as a person who needed time to grow into himself.

James and Naniyin moved around for some time in the apartment from corner to corner. James had been within the compound walls for less than 20 minutes. He knew that his time within the walls was limited. He could not possibly have the many years needed to assess and learn from the different surfaces and areas. For much of the year, James smoked in the bathroom with the window open and the fan on. Sometimes he opened the window in his bedroom and stared out at the sky. Often, he did this when he read books or felt out of himself.

James did not have words for how he felt that night. The past developed around him and he moved fluidly forward. There was no stopping of economies or educations. The Earth moved upon its axis without delay. The Sun provided invaluable energy to the planet and beings. All around animals lived and ate without regard to James and his thoughts. Soon, people would harvest dates from the palms around al-Ahsa. Those same dates became ripe and healthy with girth. Tectonic plates continued their shifting. Ocean currents were not to be stopped. The Moon persisted in its effects on the Earth. Farmers awaited their harvest or had already begun to reap the rewards of their work. Politicians contemplated their control and considered their borders, wishing they could move past their own limits. Writers sought ends that they could not imagine. Teachers planned their lessons. Children fell asleep in their beds under the watchful eyes of their parent(s). Machines clicked and moved along.

Ships carried freight. In many parts of the world, police shook their batons violently. In others, rebels loaded their weapons against the powerful. Corporations broadcast the reruns of their shows in the languages humanity understood. Designers considered shapes and tones. Prostitutes prepared themselves for their evenings. Drug addicts awaited their fix, while dealers prepared their packages. Hunters skinned their prey. Restless civil servants read in their sleeplessness. Factory workers felt their carpal tunnel. Couples made themselves ready for love. Journalists typed furiously before the morning. Some novels were Kafka-esque-esque. Students engaged in their wishful thinking. The Simpsons did it. Arthur learned his lessons. Chemists thought deeply about polymers. Pharmacists prepared compounds. Warmongers strategized. Scaremongers sculpted their propagandas. Adjuncts remained underpaid. Recent graduates hardly found work, if at all, while older professionals neglected to retire or be able to. The rich got richer. The poor remained poor. There was a fluidity in that moment that James stood with Naniyin, but nothing moved either of the men to speak. They futzed around the bedroom of the apartment. James could not make out any noises. He had still not met any of his colleagues in his hours on the ground beside Scott, Jim, Gary, and Naniyin. A deft numbness came upon James. He undid his tie and laid it upon the table. He looked at his slacks and his shirt. Both were wrinkled from having been worn for 24 hours. He needed to lay out his clothes for the morning. He could feel the bags underneath his eyes. He looked at his clouded environment. His cufflinks, which had been given to him by his grandfather, remained on his wrists. His feet cramped in his dress shoes. He felt how unkempt his hair had become. The many hours it had taken for him to walk into his new apartment stretched out his skin and sunk into the tingling in his shins. James' knuckles were rough and at last he set his bags down next to his bed. He looked at the bedding: it looked old and unclean. The thin blanket was raggy and did not match the sheets. There was a slept on quality to those sheets that would have unsettled James had he been any more awake. The room was adequate to him in his sleepiness. He could not wait for Naniyin to leave.—It seems fine, he muttered. Naniyin shook his head and beamed at James. The approval that James had given was well-received. Unless James ran away this would be his home for the next year like it or not. It did not matter, the layout or design. It was not of consequence if he was offended by the furniture. To James, it was enough.

Naniyin pointed at the window,—Do you want to see your view? James nodded slowly, he was tired and needed sleep. Naniyin opened the opaque window, revealing an empty, unlit lot. In the night air, James spotted some junk about the emptiness: there was nothing but a huge, empty lot and a mosque in the distance beyond a tall wall.—That out your window, James, is a graveyard. When you open this you will see Saudis bury their dead. You may even see a body descend into the ground. They have not marked the graves well, as you can see: there are only found objects used to mark the people. But do not worry. There are no ghosts in al-Ahsa or in Saudi. The dead are dead. It is those who are not dead you must worry about.

In a Taxi, In Movement, In Flux Towards a Conclusion

Elizabeth got into the car and asked to be taken to the compound. She was not sure if he would be available to take her to Manama on this whim. She had not even thought of him or his obligations. She sat in the back of his car frozen, not sure what to do.—I am early. Why are you waiting outside?—I wanted to feel the heat. She was being vague and in her head a racket of possibilities were laid out before her: Abdelrahman could drive her and would, could and would not, could not but would, could not and would not. She grew even more anxious. Who else could she call if she could not leave this evening before Robert came home? She could spend the night on the couch, but she had come to appreciate the drama of what she had planned. There was traffic in the city even though it was prayer time. The roundabouts were still packed with early evening traffic. A buzzing developed in Elizabeth's head. She would not resent Abdelrahman however this turned out. She was set on respecting what he chose to do. She could get where she needed to be without him. She thought about how he had been so friendly on the sidelines of her life.

—Abdelrahman, do you care for my problems? Sometimes, you drive me around and I find myself just droning on to you. I am sure you know more than I could imagine. At this point, I can only think: did you listen? I am supposed to fear Saudi men. Yet, you have always been calm. I have met your wife. Your daughter has been in my school, and still there is something I worry about in you. Although I possess this fear, and it is real to me, for some reason, I am in such a position that I feel some comfort in explaining to you my life. I did not even comprehend that you could speak such fine English until your daughter gloated that you all spoke it around the house. Yet, I am concerned that you may make some judgment of me that differs because your worldview is so far removed from my own. I see that I am merely one human, as you are as well, but we come from such differing histories that I am worried within the past years you have come to some idea of me that I would not approve of, or at least dislike. Do you think that you could possibly remember all of the troubles I have had, the feelings I have felt. You were the one who would drive me, and sometimes others, around to places in the town that were of value: the graffitied caves, the many gardens, the wonderful places in the *suqs*. You pointed out to me that some parts of the city experienced gentrification. You made note of the other schools, of the hospitals. You had even made that list of the best restaurants for women to eat at. But was it out of some pity? Did you recognize that I am some white woman who is dramatically out of her place, or was there something else underlying those actions? Something simpler? Sharing can be so fundamental, yet so strange. I look at my family and wonder if we could share again, if as members of a unit we could exchange ideas and thoughts and emotions. The ups and downs that we move through. How my mother cried when I called her from Saudi for the first time. I had to have Robert calm her on the phone, but tears came to my eyes when I understood her first impression of my situation. At the end of it, I have reached no conclusions. There has been nothing concrete for me to latch onto. The insight I had hoped for remains elusive. The readings and writings: The conversations with students: Where I go: What I eat: How I think: all of it floats by me in this small amount of Earth that I inhabit. I can change what sections of the Earth it is, but that only complicates defining it. I have hoped without reason that something would help to clarify the practices and procedures of those humans around me that provoke my curiosity. Perhaps, it is that I am wrong. Or, it is that my view is ever changing. That constantly some kind of evidence is presented to me that suggests some conclusion. I see, or observe, an event and from that point move to shape some educated opinion or knowledge. The more events I behold, the more my view of what surrounds me expands, but also the more capable I am of drawing wider conclusions. I became terribly frustrated when I realized how ignorant I was about the world. It infuriated me to come to terms with the idea that all of my knowledge still did not propel me into another atmosphere. It was at that point I fully understood that I was smart. I had to train myself to grasp my own ignorance. And you know, Abdelrahman, that moment could have happened anywhere. In this taxi. At the front of a classroom. In a bathroom at a McDonald's. Anywhere. And for my life, I cannot remember, I cannot recall, where that happened. Maybe, it happened in my sleep! Or, better, while I was mediating! Perhaps while in the throes of passionate love! It has made me stop sharing with many people. I no longer exchange ideas with old friends on the internet. I seldom point out things about Saudi culture to my friends and family back home. In a strange, disturbing way, I am at peace. But that conclusion unsettles me. I am leaving Rob.

—Have you ever considered what drives a conclusion? asked Abdelrahman.—I am afraid that the world wants us to think. But the thinking is difficult. It is strange. We move in and out and never really know. Blood on the hands is only a symbol. Whoever did anything to you cannot stop you yourself. Understand men, women and children question themselves. The rains that so rarely fall here spread your questions. It is those that believe who move forward. You may sit and think or stand and think and make decisions, but I believe that you were meant to make decisions more important than Robert or a school run by these men. You know, men still tell you what to do, even if you are in "charge" of the women in your classroom? Make your move, but do so quickly. They will not have mercy for you. Men are clever and decisive things, but their brutality has no end. You can move, but only if you wish to. You see, Elizabeth, I am a hard determinist. I learned that phrase from a man I drove around this very city. He was British and he had many words for things that I am and have been. We talked over coffee and he would tell me what I was. The most lasting impression he gave me of myself what that I, a brown, Muslim, male from the Eastern Province of the Kingdom of Saudi Arabia, am a hard determinist. This man, this white man, the kind of white that did not burn in the sun, said so with a wonderful kind of relish. He told me that I believe that my Lord, Allah, has set everything in motion. Further, He has fixed every single possibility for me and everyone around me. He knows all. He set it all in place and motion in this space. Now, Elizabeth, I speak to you about this because I have driven many white people around this city. And I have thought each time, does this white person know I am a hard determinist? Is it a thing that all of these white people are taught? You may wonder why I tell you about this. Because, you see, I want to know what drives you to your conclusions. I would like to have you tell me. That British man did not afford me such privilege, because he already knew. Something happened in me that he would never have expected. I changed. The progression has been subtle. And my life is surprisingly comfortable here and I do not wish to abandon it. But I know now that I have changed. I am still who I have always been, but the view I have on this world has shifted, even if ever so slightly. I have an education, I have a job. I drive people for fun now. At the time, I did it to help my family. I also studied. I drove around people from Britain and America to strengthen my English. I learned the nuances of chemical sciences. I read poetries and learned to sing. When this man told me I was a hard determinist, I had to stop myself. I had to halt my learning and assess what I was. His words threatened my developing idea of the world. We share a space that we constantly seek to define. You place yourself in various environments and attempt to learn from each. What I had intended to do with my studies was to box in my thoughts. I wanted to shape everything into compartments for storage. Then I could organize what I thought of the world. I had never thought, not for one second, that everything about me was determined, but I must admit it was. God had set it all forth, and I wonder if by having that Englishman talk to me in that way set me free. Certainly, I know that the world will not stop when I am gone. Just as when you leave Saudi, the streets will still be driven upon and the buffias still eaten in. Men and women will still walk segregated lines and you will not be here to see the dust storms or feel the heat. I wonder what focus the world will draw on or around Muslims and Christians when we are both old. Will they remember how fondly I have thought of you? Your kindness when my family members have been sick, or my acts to you in your own hardships? No idealism will save the feeling in this car. Your moment is your own and no person can change that. Sadly, they can influence that, and will try to do so with all of their might. Be wary of men, shy of women, and worry for children. For in the end, all I am is a hard determinist, driving a taxi for a white woman who has more rights that my wife can ever imagine: not here of course. I look to the world and grow restless in my own way, as you have. I have a feeling in my joints, near my knees and elbows, which makes me want badly to move. I walk around the block to ease the tension it creates. And then I wonder, was I ever free in the first place?

Elizabeth moved. She had already made up her mind to. She listened to Abdelrahman's words and in her own way had already arrived in her next position. The two of them arranged what would happen over the next few hours: Abdelrahman dropped Elizabeth off at the compound with the aim of returning to pick her up once again the following hour. In the meantime, Elizabeth was to pack and write a note, Abdelrahman felt that to properly leave a man there had to be a note which reassured Elizabeth about how she had chosen to proceed. She should act as though nothing was wrong and not speak to anyone, these were her rules. She did not speak to many of the other women outside of yoga, so this would be no problem.— Fuck them, she said to herself. She moved her fingers and toes as if preparing for physical activity. She needed to be agile. There needed, in reality, to be no rush: Robert was a passive fool, and would do nothing to stop her if he watched her leave himself. While Elizabeth prepared, Abdelrahman would return to his wife and explain what he was doing. He decided that it would be best to bring her along so as to make the border crossing easier. He felt that she would support Elizabeth's decisions, and would happily tag along. Abdelrahman's wife was especially fond of Elizabeth and would want to see her one last time. In preparing to leave, Asilah shook with nerves. She hugged Abdelrahman tightly. Neither knew what Robert would do or what would happen to them if he resented their having assisted Elizabeth in her flight. The risk they were taking was not a small one, but it was also inconsequential in ways they would never know. Neither knew the exact details of Elizabeth's relationship with Robert. Asilah prepared some snacks for the trip: dates and other fruits, as well as cashews. She wanted, above all else, for the three people driving across King Fahd's Causeway to be calm and steady. This last taxi ride, the final movement of Elizabeth's time outside the borders of the country of her birth, was chatty. Abdelrahman and Asilah wanted to know all about what she planned on doing in the States. Abdelrahman and Asilah exchanged email addresses with Elizabeth. They wanted updates. It's funny, Elizabeth thought during a lull in their conversations en route to Juffair, how quickly people become so important in one's life. It is strange how the details of a car and a seat within that car become embedded in memory, how the smell of the salt in the humid air could make all three of them laugh so hard and so emotionally. Elizabeth had chosen to involve Abdelrahman and Asilah for what reasons? Why were they being so accommodating to her? She remembered the textures of those hours for years to come: the cardboard sleeve of her coffee, the porous and somehow cool stone of the outer wall of the mall, the leather of Abdelrahman's seats, the outer fabric of her suitcase, the softness of Asilah's hand, the stickiness of the dates, the grainy saltiness of the cashews, the dingy feel of the counter at the border, the feel of her own skin as she held her own hands in her lap and left Saudi for the last time, the magazine feel of the printed tickets she soon paid for, the plastic of the door key to her hotel room, the cool sweat of the beer bottle, the metallic cold of the handle of the faucet, the feel of the water against the skin of her face. She had flashes for some years after when she encountered similar textures. There was a Proustian quality to how she experienced these things, but her flashbacks did not startle her or arouse her nostalgia. She had lived a life she now needed to work through and unpack. She was happy and ready to learn more about herself. There was no moment of revelation or exultation. She had regained her footing in her studies swiftly and with ease. What had been so unforeseen, had been a simple set of moves that she needed to perform. She had the privilege to live as she did and she used that standing to propel herself to where she wanted to be.

Arabia had taught Elizabeth many things, one of the most important was to learn to acknowledge that privilege. A strange, rugged individual way to view the world and herself it was, but she accepted it. Her worlds, as they spun in the gravities of her varied realities, which had been set in motion without her realizing it, were beautiful places to be.

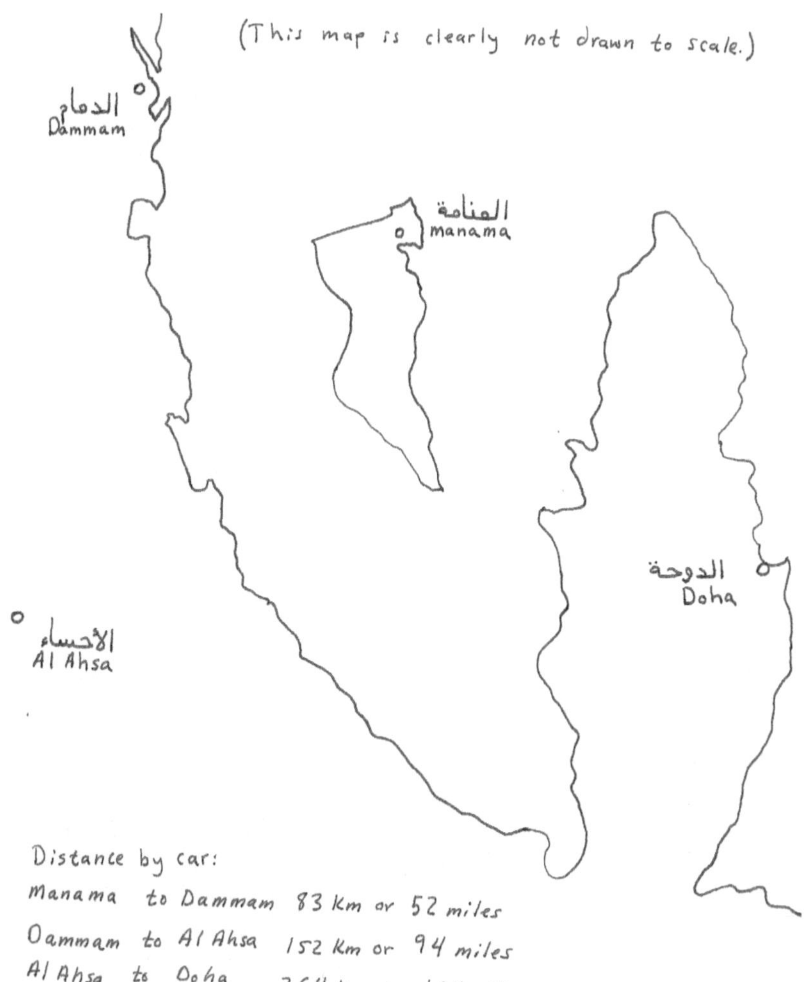
(This map is clearly not drawn to scale.)
الدمام
Dammam
المنامة
manama
الدوحة
Doha
الأحساء
Al Ahsa
Distance by car:
Manama to Dammam 83 Km or 52 miles
Dammam to Al Ahsa 152 Km or 94 miles
Al Ahsa to Doha 264 Km or 164 miles

About the Author

George Koors was born on October 3, 1988 in St. Louis, Missouri. *Always the Wanderer* is his first novel.